Also by Gary Paul Corcoran

The Trip Into Milky Way
The Last Love of Eleanor Sands
It's Always Christmastime In Cratchitville
The Tribe
Postmark: Paris ~ Destination: Unknown

Afghan's Lipstick Warriors: First Chronicle
Afghan's Lipstick Warriors: Darkness Falls
Afghan's Lipstick Warriors: The Deadly Sins

From The Michael Devlin Series

South On Pacific Coast Highway
Love In A Dying World

With Gary Paul Corcoran

The Slow Train to Rishikesh
Purgatory: Origins

The Twelfth Commandment

A Novel

by

Gary Paul Corcoran

Published by Stargazer Press
Charlestown, Rhode Island
http://garypaulcorcoran.com/

Printed in the United States of America
ISBN: 978-0-9971265-6-3

Visit us and blog with the author at
http://garypaulcorcoran.com/

Acknowledgements

To all the special forces folks who have asked me to help them write their tales over the years, with a special big thanks to Rob Williams, who lent me his expertise for this particular story. Thank all of you for your service and allowing me inside your world.

For the Kurdish people,
your great courage, heart and decency
deserve nothing less in return,
than the world's undying respect,
and at long last, your own statehood...

The Twelfth Commandment

Prologue

North of Moka-Kurdish Territory-Northern Iraq
Winter-2012

The narrow mountain valley wound its way up higher and higher between two nearly vertical peaks and ultimately arrived at a summit, that summit blanketed by a forest of Aleppo pines and the pines just then drooping under a fresh dusting of snow. It had been an especially harsh winter, with record snowpack, so that a man could easily have mistaken the valley floor for an alpine glacier. To stumble upon this place for the first time, and in those bleak conditions, you would not have thought it possible for a road to exist beneath all that snow and ice, but it did and followed the valley up and over the mountain into Turkish territory.

The jagged slopes on either side of the valley were checkered with more of that winter snow and Firat was positioned up there with a handful of his fellow YPG soldiers — two women soldiers among them — left with little choice but to make a last stand. A Turkish sniper had them pinned down from higher up on the opposite slope and more Turks were coming. It would soon be a bloodbath.

Hearing footsteps, I turned to find Mendoza approaching. Snow had gathered on the hood pulled up over his head.

"Listen, Sarge. We need to get our asses out of here. I just got word from headquarters down in Erbil. The Turks are coming and we're being told not to get in their way."

I looked back up among the snowbound rocks, trying to picture the scene, Firat and his handful of fighters huddled against the cold and facing certain death.

"Come on, Sarge," Mendoza said. "Time to move out. I know how you feel but this ain't our fight. Anyway, the son of a bitches shouldn't have crossed over into Turkish territory."

I looked back at Mendoza.

"And what would you have done if the Turks had taken one of our own?"

"Go after him, sir, of course. Leave no soldier behind…but I still say it's not our fight."

I looked up the valley. The drone of approaching trucks was faint but steadily growing louder.

"All right. Get back to the team. I'll be down there in a minute."

"But Sarge…"

"Just get back down there and await further orders, Mendoza."

"Okaaaaayy…I guess we'll be seeing you down below then."

Mendoza looked back several times as he moved away. The rest of the platoon was positioned a few hundred yards farther off in that direction, around a bend and out of sight. I waited until Mendoza was well out of range before calling Firat.

"Yes, my friend," he said, answering. "What do you know?"

"They're coming, Firat. You need to get out of there."

"I would, my friend. Trust me, I would, but every time we poke our heads up, that damned sniper tries to pick us off. He has already killed Zoran, the poor fool. There is really nothing left for us to do now but fight to the end."

I looked back up towards the summit. The trucks were not yet visible but their arrival appeared to be inevitable. If not for all the snow and ice, the Turks would have been there already.

"All right, Firat. I'm going to give you cover but we've got to make this fast. I've been ordered to pull back so we have about ten minutes before this thing turns into a major shitshow. For both of us."

"I would never ask you to risk your career over this battle, my friend. We will fight valiantly until the end and soon be with Allah."

"No, goddamn it…Look, I'm heading down the valley. I want that sniper to think I've left. Then I'll slip back in among the trees and give you cover from below. Do you know where he is exactly?"

"Yes, unless he has moved since his last shot. Do you see where that lone pine is clinging to a vertical rock face?"

I looked back at the opposite slope while moving away.

"Yeah, I see it."

"He is in a cleft of rocks just above and to the left of that pine."

"All right. Hang on."

I hurried on until I was out of the sniper's line of vision, then slipped in among the trees and focused the scope of my M4 in that direction. After a moment, I saw his barrel move.

"Yeah. I've got him. I'm on my way back up now. Just get ready to move out. As soon as you hear my first shot, you make a break for it."

"What about Zoran?"

"You have to leave him, Firat."

"It would be a blasphemy for us. You know that."

"I do, but the Turks won't know he's up there. Just let things cool down for a couple of days and come back to retrieve the body."

There was silence.

"Come on, Firat. The man's not going to rot in all this cold. Just get ready to move out before this really does turn into a shitshow."

There was a long pause.

"You are a good man, Blake."

"Yeah, well, there's some folks who'd give it another name but I'm not going to let the Turks slaughter you...Now get your asses ready. I'm on my way."

I ended the call and started back up through the trees in a sprint. The trucks were still a good click away but the sound of their motors kept echoing louder off the rock walls of the valley.

Once I had settled into position, I called Firat back.

"Are you there?" he said.

"Yeah. I've got him in my sights. Just get down here to the trees and we should be all right."

"I am waiting to hear your first shot."

"Okay. Be ready to move out."

I ended the call and trained my scope back up to where I had seen the sniper's rifle barrel. The snow was coming down in earnest now. I had been staring through the snow drifts for a number of seconds when the barrel moved again. I took a shot and the barrel quickly retreated. When it reappeared, I resumed firing and slowly but steadily unloaded an entire magazine.

While reloading, I heard a roar and turned my scope in that direction. The convoy had cleared the summit. Thank god the Turks were fighting a couple of feet of snow on the ground.

I slowly emptied another magazine at the sniper and paused to load a fresh mag. While I did, I heard the slap of a bullet in the trees off to my left. The son of a bitch had figured out I was down here. He just didn't know where yet.

I had taken aim at him again when my phone buzzed. It was Firat.

"Where are you?" I said, answering his call.

"In the trees. A hundred yards away from the sound of your fire. We are coming as fast as we can."

"Well, hurry up. That convoy's almost on us."

"We are doing our best but we have wounded...And Zoran."

"Jesus Christ, Firat."

4

"I could not leave him, Mr. Blake. That sniper knows he made the kill. They would have come to defile the body."

"All right, goddamn it. Just hurry up."

Mendoza keyed up his radio as I was ending the call.

"What the hell's going on, sir? Are you all right?"

"Yeah, yeah. Just get the convoy turned around and be ready to roll. And I mean ready. We'll be rendezvousing with you in less than five mikes."

"We, Sarge?"

"Just get the goddamned convoy turned around!"

"Fuck, okay."

I hung up and looked off through the trees. Come on, Firat.

At last I saw them in the distance, moving through the undergrowth as fast as the wounded would allow. There were seven total with one woman among the wounded, the woman Firat and his team had gone across the border to rescue.

The sniper was firing randomly into the woods but I let it go. Returning fire now would only serve to pinpoint our position.

I stood up as the Kurds drew near. Two of the men were helping the two wounded and Firat was carrying Zoran over his shoulder. I shook my head.

"I'm sorry," Firat said. "I could not leave him."

"All right, it's done. Let's just move out."

Before I could turn away, Ariman grabbed me by the back of my neck and stared into my eyes.

"Thank you," she said and kissed me hard on the lips.

She pulled back to stare again.

"Thank you."

I nodded.

"Come on. There's no time to waste."

I went out ahead. Firat, the wounded and the two men helping them fell in behind me. Ariman and the other man covered our rear.

We cleared the woods just as the top of a Turkish troop transport came into view, a quarter click away. I fell back and helped with getting everyone around the shoulder of a hill and safely out of sight. The platoon team members were standing astride our idling troop transport and two Humvees, intently watching us approach.

"What are we doing here, sir?" Mendoza said.

"Don't worry yourself about it. Just get these people in the back of the transport and tie the rear flap down tight...Now, Mendoza!"

"Fuck. We're going to catch some heavy flak for this shit, sir."

"You're not going to catch any flak. I am."

I looked at the rest of the platoon.

"This is all on me, men. The rest of you were just taking orders. That's the way I'm going to report it and that's what you're going to tell anyone who asks. Are we good with that?"

Without much enthusiasm, the men nodded.

"Okay, then let's go. Tucker, Grimes, Higgins and Cash, you stand guard at the back of the truck. Mendoza, you and the rest of the men, get your asses in a seat and your foot on a pedal. We'll be rolling out on my command."

In the time it took for everyone to get into place, the Turkish convoy had come into full view, two hundred yards up the road. A minute later, it was pulling to a stop in front of us. Their troop transport truck had led the way, plowing the road as they came.

A dozen or so OKK troops piled out from the back of it and parted as their officer, Colonel Arslan, appeared from farther back in the convoy. He walked up to me and saluted. I saluted back.

"What can I do for you, sir?" I said.

He let his eyes rove from our troop transport and the men guarding it to the two Humvees and back to me.

"It would seem that a rebel Kurdish patrol has suddenly vanished into thin air."

The colonel's eyes darted another look at the transport truck and back at me.

"I wouldn't know anything about that, sir."

"Ah. Then you wouldn't mind me taking a look in the back of your transport truck, yes?"

He waved at his men and four of them came forward. I raised my right hand and the men guarding the back of our truck raised their weapons.

"That is not going to happen, sir."

I thumbed my chin back up the valley.

"That's Turkish territory. Back over that summit. You can do whatever the hell you want on that side of the border, but you're on Iraqi soil now and I'm in charge here."

The colonel stared. The Turks had a way of making you feel like you were being gutted.

"So, if we're done here, we'll be on our way."

I motioned towards the drivers.

"Move it out slowly, men. Tucker and Higgins, go ahead and jump in. Grimes and Cash, you stay here with me."

As the convoy inched forward, the three of us backed our way down and gave cover.

"Your superior officers will be hearing about this!" the colonel called out.

I saluted.

"And I will remember you! I will remember you and this insult! You and I are not finished!!!"

The three of us kept a rear guard until we were well down the road.

"All right, boys. Go ahead and jump in."

Grimes stared while holding the door to one of the Humvees open for me.

"This is definitely going to be a major shitshow back at HQ, sir. If you don't mind me saying so."

"I already told you. This one's all on me."

"Oh hell, Sarge. We'll cover for you."

"I appreciate the sentiment, Grimes, but that's not going to happen. Now let's move out. We need to drop these folks off in Az Zibar before we head back to Erbil."

The Twelfth Commandment

One

Bosporus Strait-Istanbul
December-2015

You couldn't help but smile. Across the strait, a trawler was chugging into port at sunset, the three sailors topside mopping decks while being pestered by a plague of gulls. When one of the men swung wildly at the birds with his mop, I had to laugh.

Jesus, we were helpless at times.

High on the opposite hill, a final ray of sunlight glowed upon the golden dome of a mosque. Then the light winked out and the enchantment of twilight rushed upon the world, the blue waters darkening at the end of the day, the busy strait cut white everywhere by a crisscross of boats.

In this ancient place, ancient things were in the air. The footsteps of Alexander, off to conquer Persia, the cries of wild Scythian horsemen, off to maraud along the Black Sea. Caesar and Darius had stood here, sinners and saints, but no matter the man or his station, he would have witnessed this same eternal moment, a bustle of boats upon the sea at dusk and the salt of the earth hurrying home with their fleeting concerns.

I had been lost in these thoughts for a few brief moments when the call to prayers echoed across the city, and with it, the haunting images returned. The ill-fated man forced to kneel with his hands tied behind his back, the Muslim fanatic standing behind him, brandishing a dagger while admonishing all infidels in this world to repent. Then came the sting of the knife's edge at the poor fool's throat and his lurch face downward onto a rough concrete floor.

"Noooooooooo!"

The memory of his anguished cry seized my heart again and again. I could not help but feel his final, hapless moments in my own heart.

Oh god no, god no. This can't be happening. Please make this nightmare go away. I'm supposed to be home having dinner with my fiancé.

The mind was a strange thing, holding onto whatever frail reed of hope it could find until the very last minute. Then it would finally hit you. You fool. These ruthless men don't give a damn about your hopes. They're about to take your head off, and painfully so.

I wanted to think I would have been stoic about it all, but who knew? To feel the blade at your throat like a razor's edge?

Oh well. I was the fool to have watched that video in the first place and was resigned to having it haunt me for the rest of my days. Those sandaled zealots rushing to drag the man upright again and their bloodbath ensuing, the man's lifeless head held high in defiance less than a minute later

I pulled my coat up against the winter cold and turned away from the strait, cursing those men and everything they stood for. I had tried and tried to put the gruesome memory out of my mind but could not and was in this place now, intent on exacting revenge. Collectively or one by one, it did not matter to me, but those men would soon know the same horror that I could not seem to escape. By the time I was done with them, they would be begging me to take their heads off.

As I walked along, Tom's anguished cry echoed in my mind again.

"Noooooooooo!"

Good god, man. Couldn't you have met your fate bravely? Why did you have to grovel for all the world to see? Death was inescapable at that point.

I was no longer sure what I despised more, Tom and his lack of courage or the bastards who had taken his head off.

And David, you're a bastard for having arranged to meet me in Istanbul. You know I'm not welcome here. I'm not welcome anywhere in Turkey, let alone the poor part of this city.

Not that any of these impoverished back alley Muslims would dare to threaten a Westerner, but they would gladly look the other way if someone stuck a knife in my back and left me for dead. And not that I gave a damn what any of them thought, about me, or about anything. I just hated having to suffer their disapproving looks.

I had not gone another ten paces when the beheading was back in my thoughts. Save for a moment here and there, the images of it played on loop in my head. I cursed again under my breath, hating zealotry, in any form, but knowing full well I had become as zealous as the men I was pursuing, ready to kill every damned Muslim in this world, just for the very fact of them being Muslims.

I was just then passing a small, traditional clothing shop and about to turn the corner when a hand reached out from a darkened alcove. I had my knife at the man's throat before he touched my shoulder.

"Easy, boy," the voice said softly.

I exhaled and lowered the knife.

"Jesus Christ, David. You're going to get yourself killed."

He smiled acerbically. I smirked at him in his traditional coat and cap. With the dark beard and all, he looked perfectly Turkish.

"Caution," David said. "Always caution."

"Yeah, right. If you were being cautious, you wouldn't have arranged for us to meet in Istanbul. Let alone this shithole part of the city."

"Oh no. It's much easier to keep from being noticed this way."

"Yeah, right. Everyone I see wants to cut my throat."

He shrugged.

"You want to meet in the Levent? With a camera on every street corner?"

"No. I don't want to meet in the Levent. I didn't want to meet anywhere in Turkey! Why the fuck did you drag me here in the first place?"

"You're the one dying to go on this death mission."

"Yeah? And what does that have to do with us meeting in Turkey?"

"It was the only way I could get you into Syria without alarm bells going off."

"Yeah, right."

"You want my help or not?"

I stared.

"Then we're doing it my way. And that means steering clear of Baghdad. And Damascus. And Amman. And frankly every other place where they have their shorts in a knot right now. This ISIS business has everyone on edge, except for the Turks."

"Yeah, and you know why. They'd get into bed with Atilla the Hun if it gave them a chance to dust a few Kurds."

"Welcome to the real world, partner. Now if we're done moralizing, let's go. Your room's down this way."

He put a hand to my back and pointed me back up the alley.

The two of us went along with these poor Muslims viewing us even more suspiciously now. To them it looked like one of their own was consorting with a Westerner. You may as well have pissed on a copy of the Koran.

When we came to an intersecting alleyway, David paused, looked both ways and spirited me off in that direction.

"Here," he said a few hundred feet farther on.

I stood back as he unlocked a recessed door.

"Go on," he added with another look both ways.

I stepped into a small, dimly lit vestibule. David had another look up and down the alley before closing the door and relocking it.

"This way," he said, pointing me up a flight of stairs.

At the top, there were two doors. David unlocked the one on the right and held it open for me. The room was spartan, with a single bed, a dresser, a wooden chair and bare wooden floors. Another door opened into a bathroom. There were broken tiles in both the shower and on the bathroom floor.

I sat down on the bed.

"The company got you on a budget these days?"

David grabbed a laptop from the top of the dresser and joined me.

"Like I said. The better to stay hidden."

He studied me.

"You understand…I'm covering my own ass here. I shouldn't even be seen with you. Let alone lending you a hand."

I acknowledged his point with a sarcastic nod. To anyone above an O-5 rank, I was a pariah now. I had barely escaped that Kurdish blow up with an honorable discharge. No one wanted to hear my name.

David studied me before opening his laptop.

"The folks at CIA are 99 and 9/10% sure this is him."

He turned the screen so I could see the image of a man.

"Saleem al-Ramadi. His face was masked that day, hence any lingering doubts, but an Iraqi source said he recognized the voice. And intel had him in the general vicinity during that time frame, so…"

David shrugged. I stared at the man's eyes. The horror of a live beheading aside, with all the shrieking and struggling and gargling of blood, that was what I remembered most about the video. This man's eyes. They had appeared to be lifeless. Cold and lifeless, far more than they were brutal. It was as if every innate human kindness had been bled out of him by some prior trauma.

"That's him," I said. "Any leads on where he is now?"

David stared at me.

"We assume somewhere within that shrinking circle of ISIS controlled territory. Where every SOB in the intel community has already been trying to track him down, mind you."

"Anyone who can help me?"

David nodded slowly while staring at me.

"I've been working with a man named Faisal al-Khabur."

"Jesus Christ, David. That's the last thing I need right now. Being seen anywhere near another Kurd."

"I thought you were in love with those people."

"That's not the point. He'll just draw attention to me."

David scoffed.

"Like you don't already have a target on your back. Look, he's a good man. Plus he was born along the Syrian/Iraq border and knows the area well. You want somebody else, I'll have to get back to you in a couple of days."

"No. Forget it. How do I hook up with this guy?"

David pulled out a piece of paper from his coat pocket and handed it to me.

"His cell number. He's expecting to hear from you once you're on the ground. You two will have to work it out from there."

"Fine. When can we leave?"

"We. Like I'm going in with you."

"When?"

"Christ, Blake. I know it has to hurt but why don't you let it go? We've been bombing the crap out of these people for months now. They'll all be dead soon enough. Or on the run. What does it matter if you personally put a knife to that monster's throat?"

"When?"

"All right. Fine. Tomorrow morning. I have a special ops team flying into Mosul. We'll make it look like you're one of the boys and you'll have to break off on your own from there."

"You think you can get me into Mosul quietly."

"Quietly enough. Let's just say if I don't, I'll have CENTCOM up my ass. And the Iraqis will be up yours."

"All right. What time tomorrow?"

"0600."

"Where? Atatürk?"

David nodded.

"You're on a private transport down to Incirlik. And military from there to Mosul. The head of the special ops team, Rob, he's cool with the situation. Thinks you're running a special op for me. Can't say how the rest of the team will feel about a stranger in their midst."

"Fine. Transport?"

"I made sure that Faisal had an SUV."

"And one that blends in, I hope. Nothing new."

David gave me a look.

"And you say I just call this Faisal once I'm on the ground."

David nodded. I looked again at the photo of Saleem. Born into Iraqi poverty. Found his way to a madrassa school in Pakistan in his teens. Radicalized along the way, as usual, until he was as certain of his beliefs as any religious fanatic. It was said that every major religion went through its inquisition phase and Mohammed had come along roughly 700 years after Jesus. That suggested we had at least two hundred more years of this crap. It made me sick.

I noticed David's hand being held out again and looked over. It was some paperwork.

"Your IDs and orders."

I had a look at the IDs. I was Cole Jeffers now. Army captain. There was a matching CIA badge. While looking at the orders, David held out his hand again. It was a photo of Saleem al-Ramadi.

"I assumed you'd want this. Just be careful who you show it to. It's a death sentence in the wrong hands."

I took the photo and tucked it away in an arm pocket of my zip jacket, along with the IDs and orders. When I looked back,

David had produced a syringe. The mouth of it was big enough to spit out a grain of rice.

"A tracer? Forget it."

"It's for me, you stubborn jackass. You get yourself into trouble and I'll need to know where to find you. Or maybe you're just keen on having your own head cut off."

"Maybe I am."

"Oh quit with the drama and take your jacket off."

I did and pulled up my shirt sleeve. He found a fatty spot at the back of my upper right arm and paused with a look in my eyes. I pretended not to feel the syringe going in. There. You can take my head off and I won't say a thing.

David stole glances my way as he depressed the syringe and pulled it out from my arm. I stared at the floor while he grabbed his laptop again and checked for a signal.

"You're good," he said.

He patted me on the shoulder and stood up.

"0600. On the corner where I found you. This is your room for the night. A place around the corner serves great Döner kebab to go. Best not to hang around outside too much. Or drag anyone back here with you. But you already know that."

"I'll be fine."

David stopped at the door.

"Why don't you go home. The world doesn't need another grieving mother."

I stared at him.

"Fine. I'll leave it alone. See you in the morning."

David stared back for a long moment before going out the door.

☐

Two

A lone again, the nightmare returned. I pulled the knife out of my thigh pocket and ran a thumb across the razor sharp edge. The impulse was there to rake it across my neck, to somehow know the horror Tom had experienced in his final moments. It would start with blood gushing from your carotid artery, but then what? Would the very fact of an interrupted blood supply be enough to numb you to the rest of the pain? Or would you feel the agony of your tendons and trachea and esophagus being ripped open?

However long it took, the knife would eventually crunch through your C6 vertebrae and you'd be gone from this world, but then what? What came with death? A holy light? Celestial music? Would you be looking down upon your own severed head with something like detached pity?

I put the knife to the side of my neck and pressed ever so slightly. Another ounce of pressure and I would have my answer soon enough.

This obsession had come to me the first time while standing in the kitchen, my eyes drawn to a knife on the counter, the impulse to rake its sharpened edge across my own throat so powerful, I had to shove the knife back into a drawer. It was as if I no longer had a choice in the matter.

Coming back to the moment and that cheap room in Istanbul, I realized I still had the knife to my neck and let my hand fall away. Goddamn it. I should never have watched that video.

Looking up through the lone window, I noticed the stars high above, and with a pang, recalled Lydia's cold hearted goodbye. She had texted me the night before my departure to the Middle East with a brief message.

Can we talk? Around nine?

My gut instinct was, sure as hell, this is some kind of dear John number, but when we ultimately got on the phone together, she was as sweet as could be.

"How was your day? Have you gotten any of your Christmas shopping done?"

Buying into her sincerity, I had set aside my concerns and answered her questions as if we were chatting over a candlelight dinner.

Then came a pause in the conversation and Lydia's awkward segue.

"Well, I don't know quite how to say this but..."

Instantly, my ears burned, realizing that I had been suckered. And even though I already knew it was checkmate, that reasoning with her at that point was utterly useless, I had gone on with that futile exercise. Which naturally had degenerated into one of those better forgotten conversations.

"Look, Blake, I just think it would be best if we went our separate ways."

"What the hell brought this on, Lydia?"

"Oh, maybe that you're off to save the world again and I'm tired of waiting around for you?"

"I'm not off to save the world. I've got orders and I can't tell you what they are. You know that."

"I thought you had finally retired."

"Well, something came up. What can I say?"

Round and round it went, with me knowing I had lied, but not about to acknowledge the true nature of my mission.

Then Lydia had suddenly blurted out.

"We're not going to do this, okay?! I'm not going to do this! I'm not going to go on arguing with you!"

"We're not arguing."

"Okay, Blake. Look. You're a good man. I mean, there's so much desirable about you. You deserve the best but I just don't think that…"

"Oh fine. Fuck it. Fuck you. Goodbye and good luck."

I had slammed the phone down that night, left to dwell on her blow off for hours alone, and growing evermore furious, the more I did. If your mind was already made up, why drag me through your damned spectacle? She could have explained herself in an email. But no, she had to act sweet while twisting a knife in me.

I was enraged anew, remembering the way she had so often hit me with that *you're always getting mad and yelling* card. BS. No matter how much the woman frustrated me, I had always been civil in return. Raised eyebrows. A shake of the head. A bit of wry humor.

To her that was yelling. Christ. The baggage some people dragged around with them in this world.

And yet, despite it all, I looked at my phone, impulsively wanting to call her, wanting everything to be all right again.

As the seconds ticked by, bitterness overtook any inclination I had to grovel. Face it, Blake. Even with knowing that Tom had been killed, she went ahead and pulled that shit on you. And you're going to care? And let her know that you do?

I stood up, wanting to taste a woman's kindness right then. The end seemed all too near. This might well be my final chance.

Before heading out the door, I pulled off my canvas barn coat and tactical vest, removed the Glock 19 from my Kydex concealable waist holster and laid them on the bed. The tactical vest also held a Sig 229 and a shitload of ammunition, so I suddenly felt a bit naked but still had the Springfield Hellcat in my ankle holster. I took an extra 11 round magazine out of the vest, tucked it into one of the zip pockets on my jacket sleeve and pulled my jacket back on. Between the Springfield and the Stryder knife, I felt reasonably well armed.

I went back down to the alley and around to the street but continued past the restaurant David had recommended. At the next corner, I found a cab sitting idle and climbed in.

A few miles across town, the driver dropped me off in the red-light district. It was an industry that Turkey ran with the same efficiency that it ran its secret police. You didn't have to think hard to imagine all the pissed off Muslim clerics.

I had been in and out of three establishments before I found what I wanted. She could not have been more than eighteen, nineteen. Pale-skinned, but Turkish, not Russian trash. Beautiful, auburn haired and blushingly modest. She should have been in school. God only knew what tragedy had landed her in this place.

I got the madam's attention and nodded at the young woman.

"How long?" the madam asked me in heavily accented English.

"Two hours."

She raised her eyebrows.

"Two hours," I repeated.

"A thousand lira."

I counted out the cash. It was a bit less the two hundred dollars, American. I would have gladly paid twice as much.

The madam tucked my money away and nodded at the young woman. She stood up and came towards me with eyes down. The madam led us to the end of a long, dimly lit hallway and opened the last door on the right. The room furnishings weren't opulent, but clean. The bed had a decent comforter and two pillows.

The madam locked the door from the outside and went away. I looked at the young woman. She began to undress with her eyes on the floor, as if punishment was imminent. I went around to the other side of the bed, pulled the comforter back, removed my jacket and sat down to unlace my boots. While I was pulling off my shirt, I felt the woman slip under the covers behind me. I removed the ankle holster and positioned the gun where I could easily reach it, then pulled off my pants and briefs, hit the light and climbed into bed.

The young woman lay on her back and stared up at the ceiling, as if waiting for me to climb on top of her and get started. Instead, I got up on one elbow and drew her body close to mine. While my free hand gently explored her tender flesh, her eyes came up to look at me. I could almost feel her quivering.

"Such beautiful eyes," I said.

She blinked once but kept staring.

"Such beautiful everything."

She blinked again and kept staring.

I smiled sadly and kissed her ruby lips, enamored of her even more so because she had not responded in a gaudy fashion. There was no attempt to prove she was passionate. Her lips had responded in exactly the way I had kissed her.

I kept kissing all around her head and neck and shoulders and exploring her body until I knew she was wet, then gently exposed her clitoris. Her body jerked when I touched it. I was careful not to apply too much pressure, just brushing it gently with my middle finger, as a zephyr might tickle her naked skin.

Slowly, her kisses became more impassioned and her body convulsed. I felt her trying to pull away now and saw fear in her eyes when I drew back to look.

"My god," I said out loud. "You've never had an orgasm."

She stared, not understanding my words. I gestured to let her know, it's okay, it's okay. Just relax.

She did so, mostly, until the climax was exploding within her, at which point her body convulsed even more wildly and her eyes again filled with fear. I gestured again. Just relax and let it happen. I'm here to catch you.

She bucked and squirmed for nearly thirty seconds and then was staring up at me with a look that any man could have mistaken for love. When I gently kissed her lips again, she wrapped her arms around me as if she would never let go. I smiled and rubbed her nose with mine.

Though it was not necessary, I made her come again, so that she would know it was possible, then had my way with her, first on top, then with her on top of me, then from behind and she responded as a woman does who cannot please a man enough, hands at my hips, pulling me into her, reaching back and riding me high.

Afterwards, I lay there stroking her tawny frame and feeling her purr and wanting to rescue her. If only I knew for certain that I would make it back. The thought of leaving her in this place broke my heart.

We had made love again and were lying there quietly together when the madam knocked on the door.

"What's your name?" I asked the young woman before getting up.

She stared.

"Blake," I said, pointing at my chest.

I tapped lightly on her chest with my finger.

"You?"

"Emine," she said after a moment.

I nodded and rubbed her nose with mine.

When I started to pull away a moment later, Emine reached out desperately with one hand. I kissed her forehead and pulled the hand away before standing up. Her head was turned in the other direction when I left the room.

Famished now, I caught another cab out in front and had the driver drop me off at David's restaurant. Honoring his wishes, I bought one beer and something to go, then walked some distance past the door to my room before slipping out of sight. Such caution almost seemed laughable but you never knew.

While I stood there, a cat appeared and made several passes at my leg. You saw them everywhere in Istanbul, rich neighborhoods and poor. The people of Istanbul had a love affair with cats.

This one was a female tabby. I petted her and broke off a bit of my Döner kebab. She promptly began to feed, purring.

When a minute had passed with no sign of anyone on my tail, I petted the cat one last time and started back towards the flat.

Upstairs, I sat on the bed, ate out of the foil wrappers and drank the beer. My impulse was to undress but I collapsed onto the bed with my clothes still on and stared up at the ceiling, haunted by two things now. A man's gruesome death and my feelings of love for a beautiful young woman.

☐

Three

In the darkness before dawn, I awakened, took a shower, got dressed and went about checking and rechecking my gear. The go pack held a Dakota Tactical D54R-N Reverse Stretch 9mm pistol with two extra magazines, five flash grenades, extra magazines for my Glock, Sig and Springfield, binoculars with night vision, a power cell for charging my phone, an extra pair of Wrangler tactical pants, two extra CQR Men's combat shirts, long sleeve, camo, five extra briefs, five pairs of socks, a pair of gloves and finally, a first aid kit with some pain meds.

The tactical vest had a holster for the Sig 229, pockets for two flash grenades, an abundance of ammo pockets, a silencer for the Glock, my satellite phone, a water bottle, protein bars and jerky and a flask filled with Wild Turkey.

I kept the Stryder .75 AR Digicam knife in a slip pocket of my pants for easy reach. The zipped sleeve pockets of the jacket held a pen flashlight, two Sharpies and a folding terrain map of Syria and Iraq. The coat was made with water repellent canvas and had two hand-warmer pockets and knit storm cuffs to lock out cold drafts. It came with an insulated hood, armpit Gussets and bi-swing back for easier maneuverability. The insulation rating was good down -5 °F.

I packed and repacked everything twice before being satisfied. Last thing, I placed my new IDs in one of the zippered sleeve pockets and headed out the door. It was a few minutes before five, bitterly cold down in the alley with stars still sparkling overhead.

My tabby friend must have been playing sentry because she quickly appeared and made a pass at my leg. The little rascal. I petted her and headed back around to the street.

The eastern horizon was growing pale as I turned the corner. A minaret punctured the skyline above the dark hills. A morning star dotted the minaret.

I had started across the street towards an unopened coffee bar when the muezzin's call to prayers echoed above the city. I quickly retreated back into the shadows of the alley and waited. Not that I gave a damn about insulting a Muslim's religious beliefs, but nothing was going to open until this nonsense was finished.

After a minute of silence, the muezzin's iqama called out, beckoning the Muslim faithful to bow towards Mecca. I shook my head. What proof did these fools have that the words of a desert nomad from fifteen hundred years ago were anything but the ramblings of a sun baked madman?

While standing there and waiting, the ghastly images of Tom's beheading returned. I tried to quash them with the memory of Emine but not even our sweet lovemaking could dislodge the horror of his final struggle.

My heart raged anew, remembering those fanatics and their bloodbath. I could not seem to rid myself of my own bloodlust now and stood ready to kill them all. An eye for an eye was etched in my blood.

Some minutes later, I was startled from my thoughts by shop doors opening along the street and merchants rushing to set out their wares. When the doors to the coffee bar opened, I slipped out of the alley and started across the street, greeted with looks of suspicion everywhere I turned. I cursed David again. If it had to be Istanbul, couldn't you have made it a more civilized part of the city?

Inside the coffee bar, the proprietor's respectful nod cooled my emotions a bit. He took my order for an espresso and went to work. While I waited, other men came in and jostled for position around me. I looked at one face, found a condemning stare and did not bother looking again.

The thick espresso was delivered to me in a miniature cup. I stepped over to a service table, added a teaspoon of sugar, downed the contents and returned to wait on the opposite street corner.

The men passing by continued to make their contempt for me plain. Well, I'd just as soon see all of you dead too. Had it not tended to complicate matters, I might have gone on a killing spree.

David pulled up a few minutes later in a white Land Cruiser, saving me from my worst impulses. He had a look my way while pulling away from the curb.

"How are we doing?"

I didn't answer.

"Did you hear about the Jordanian situation?"

I shook my head.

"ISIS brutally killed one of their own in Syria yesterday so King Hussein's gone on a major bombing campaign…With the American's blessing, of course."

I nodded.

"I guess Hussein's pretty pissed off. You might not find much of ISIS left once you get there."

David glanced over at me.

"It's an eye for an eye with these folks, you know."

I nodded.

"Did you try the Döner kebab?" he asked.

I nodded again.

"Good?"

I shrugged and nodded.

"Do anything else last night?"

I didn't answer.

He turned the corner with a glance in the rearview mirror. I noticed him flash several more looks that way and looked over my shoulder. It appeared that we were being followed by a black Suburban.

"You're sure you didn't do anything else last night," David said with his eyes still on the rearview mirror.

"What would I do in that shithole? They're probably following you."

He nodded knowingly.

"I hope that piece of ass was worth it."

I did a double take his way. The son of a bitch. Having me followed.

"Just get me to the airport," I told him. "The last time I checked, Suburbans don't have wings."

David hit his signal at a red light and pulled into the left-hand turn lane. We were the first car in line. The Suburban did the same, but two cars back. We were both hemmed in by a line of cars on our right.

Before the light could change, two men in dark suits got out of the Suburban and came our way. David hit the gas and blew the red light. Tires screeched. Horns honked. I looked back. The two men had scrambled back to their Suburban but the driver was hemmed in by passing traffic on his left and idling cars in the other three directions.

"So far, so good," David said with his eyes on the rearview mirror.

I soon lost sight of the Suburban but David continued dashing in and out of traffic and blowing red lights until we were braking to a stop in front of a metal hangar at the far end of the airport runway. A sign above the front door read Conway Delivery Systems, Inc.

"You're welcome," he said with a deadpan look my way.

I nodded sarcastically.

"Maybe next time I'll put a tail on your ass."

"Just looking out for you, my friend."

"Yeah, well…since you asked, she was definitely worth it."

He shrugged.

"Can't say I blame you, and it's a bit late to be grousing about it now, but you're in a police state. And a police state that happens to have a major hard on for you and that shit you pulled up in northern Iraq three years ago. You shouldn't be taking dumb chances like that. The folks at MİT probably know which way you wipe your ass."

David smiled facetiously.

"Anyway, it only gets worse from here, partner. Next stop, a truly fucked up democracy, if you can even call it that. And once you cross the border into Syria, I don't even know what to call that place. The prophet's revenge? One of the most fucked up places on the face of the earth right now. A white guy's worst nightmare."

He held my gaze.

"You can still turn back, you know."

I nodded.

"Who am I meeting here?"

"Oh, Danny. Ex-CIA. A maverick freelancer but he still works for the company from time to time. He can drop into Incirlik without anybody much questioning him. He'll hang around long enough to make sure you hook up with Rob. And then just give Faisal a call once you're in Mosul. I'll check in with you periodically to make sure you're still alive so answer your phone."

"I'll try."

I shook David's hand.

"Thanks."

He nodded.

"Just remember. My ass in on the line here so let's make this short and sweet. In and out. I don't want this mission coming back to haunt me."

"I'll keep your name out of it."

"Yeah. You know you can turn back anytime."

"You already said that."

He nodded. I reached out and bumped his fist.

"I'll buy you a drink once I'm back."

"Yeah. Well let's hope that happens."

I climbed out and headed towards the hangar.

"Around back!" David called after me. "Danny rarely answers the front door!"

I waved without looking and circumvented the hangar to the right. The sprawling airport came into view, teeming with fuel and food trucks and luggage trams crisscrossing the tarmac. In the distance, a mechanics crew had the panels of a jet's avionics open for inspection, bundled up against the cold. Everyone was bundled up against the cold. A bit of snow and it could have been St. Paul in winter.

I rounded the side of the hangar with a Swiss Air 747 screaming into the sky. A Malaysian Airlines DC-10 was just then landing on the opposite runway. More jets were lined up in the sky behind it, five miles apart and ascending in height as you gazed in that direction.

If you ever wondered why Muslim fanatics hated Western culture, this was it. Everything about us was an affront to their cherished pastoral existence. And I could almost sympathize with their feelings. You just didn't go about taking people's heads off because you were pissed.

I came to the mouth of the hangar and found a man with his back to me, polishing the paint of a Cessna Denali. He was roughly six foot tall and had a head full of fluffy brown hair. There was an air of cheerfulness about his enterprise that could have been mistaken for whistling, though he wasn't.

Hearing my footsteps, he glanced over his shoulder and smiled. His eyes were equally cheerful but had grievously dark rings under them. Doonesbury came to mind.

I headed his way with a glance at the stripped down Bell helicopter on the other side of the hangar. Desert camo paint job, with a .50 cal and missile stanchions on either side. Someone was ready for battle.

"You must be Blake," Danny said.

"I believe it's Cole Jeffers now."

"Oh yeah. Well, I know David well enough to know we can dispense with that bullshit. At least for this stop.

He shook my hand.

"Danny Conway. You know, David said you were crazy but you don't look it."

"Looks can be deceiving."

His smiled broadened.

"They can. They can...Hey, a cup of coffee before we go? I've got a pot still warming back in the office."

I was in no mood for delays but figured I owed him the courtesy and nodded. Danny polished one last spot of his paint job and headed over to a work bench.

"So, how long have you known David?" he asked, dispensing with his cloth.

"Too long," I said.

Danny smiled and waved me towards his office. I followed him across the hangar with my pack.

"He mentioned that you two had been in special forces together."

"Yeah."

He looked over at me, still smiling.

"Back in the nineties," I added, seeing that he wasn't satisfied.

We had come to a door and Danny opened it for me. I started down a hallway with a makeshift set of wooden stairs on my left. Glancing up, I saw that they led to a loft of some kind.

The hallway dumped me into a cluttered office. Some people made no sense to me. From a spit polished Cessna to this mess.

"Make yourself at home," Danny said.

He settled on two coffee mugs amidst the clutter and blew into both of them before pouring the coffee. The glass pot looked as if it hadn't been scrubbed for twenty years.

"Cream and sugar?"

I nodded. It was going to take a lot of both to make that shit go down.

Danny handed me a cup from his side of a desk and plopped into a chair. I was not at all surprised to see his feet go up.

I got out the five thousand cash I owed him for the ride.

"Might as well get this out of the way."

"Oh yeah. Thanks."

Danny leaned forward, took the money and placed it in his top drawer with another sip of his coffee.

"So, you were saying about being in special forces together."

I stared, in no mood for chit chatting.

"David and I met up during an op," I said finally.

Danny smiled and kept staring.

In the Balkans," I added.

"Christ. Those were simpler times, weren't they? Who'd have thought we'd be looking back at that hellhole fondly?"

I nodded. He sipped his coffee again and cradled the mug in his hands.

"So you ran together for a while?"

"For a while…Then David took a desk job. Which is a place I've never fit."

"But you stayed in touch."

"We stayed in touch."

"Sorry. David told me you wouldn't want to say much."

I took a sip of my coffee.

"Probably best that way."

He nodded.

"Yeah, well, just so you know. Where you're headed? You can abandon all hope. That's what I tell everyone. You're walking into Dante's Inferno. Nothing but desolation and ruin. Madness and destruction. And that's before you get into Syria. The rings of hell descend rapidly once you cross over that border. People go in and don't come back out. Or at least not the same way they went in."

My gaze had fixed on Danny's neck as he spoke. Such a tender place. So easy to rake open with a blade. How swiftly those men had severed Tom's head. I saw it being held aloft, splotched with blood, the tormented eyes now dead and glazed over.

"You all right?" Danny said.

"Yeah, yeah," I said.

Maybe Lydia was right. I should see a shrink. It didn't matter who I crossed paths with these days. I kept fixating on their throats. I took another sip at the rot gut coffee while Danny studied me.

"Well, like I was saying, where you're going's hell, but as long as no one's asking me to go in, I figure it's none of my business. Just keep in mind. You might need some help on the other side."

I nodded my head again.

"I'll be fine."

He sipped at his coffee and looked out the front window. My gaze followed his, certain now that David had been talking, and pissed again to think that he had. Yeah, he was just looking out for me, and I knew there might well come a moment when I'd be glad to hear from David, but I still didn't like the feeling of being chaperoned.

Growing impatient, I tossed back the rest of my coffee and audibly set the mug down, hoping to signal Danny. Time to go. Instead, he kept staring out the window.

"Ever flown into Incirlik?" he asked.

When I failed to answer, Danny looked my way.

"Yeah," I said. "2006. A backdoor mission to hook up with the Kurds."

"The surge," Danny said.

"Yeah. The Americans had told the Turks we were just going in to meet with some Sunni elders. By that point, the Americans were ready to get into bed with anyone, even the PKK. Anything to bail themselves out of the mess they had made."

Danny shook his head.

"What a fucked up situation, right? I mean, how in hell did the Kurds end up the only ones in the Middle East without their own country? They're the only sane ones of the bunch. Brave as hell and decent to the core."

Danny shook his head again and looked back out the window.

"Well, that's what you get for drawing up the Middle East on the back of a napkin. A hundred years ago now and we're still paying for that bullshit."

I stared at Danny's profile, starting to like him a bit. At least we had that much in common. Suckers for the underdog.

And yet I was restless. Danny looked over when I sat forward in my chair.

"Oh, that's right. You're just dying to go to hell."

He chuckled at his own joke, tossed back the rest of his coffee, added his empty mug to the general clutter and stood up.

"Didn't mean to delay you but it's a waste of time, trying to fly out of here during rush hour. We'd just be sitting out there on the tarmac waiting. Things should have calmed down a bit by now."

He waved towards the back door and had me go ahead of him. Out in the hangar, Danny passed me and opened the door of his Cessna.

"Drop your pack inside and slide that hangar door shut for me, once I clear it. It'll lock itself."

I went outside and pulled the collar of my jacket up against the cold. High, gray clouds were streaking in from the west. The sky was starting to look bleak now. Some kind of storm was moving in.

Inside the hangar, the propellers sparked to life with the quiet drone of a wind tunnel. A moment later, Danny was easing the aircraft forward. I stood back as he cleared the opening, then threw my weight into the sliding door. When I climbed into the plane, Danny watched over his shoulder to make sure I was locking the door properly.

I took my seat up front. He reminded me to buckle up with a smile. Otherwise he was all business, earphones on and talking to the flight tower. He eased the plane forward again and continued on a long, slow crawl up the tarmac. Then Danny parked to one side of the runway. A KLM 747 dropped in for a landing. A Turkish Airlines 737 took off, followed by an Air India flight.

"Things have calmed down quite a bit," he assured me.

And still we waited for several more minutes before Danny received clearance for takeoff. He brought the Cessna around slowly to the runway and punched the throttle, the props humming through the insulated walls of the plane like a finely tuned lawnmower.

As we ascended into the bleak, gray sky, my thoughts turned to Lydia and Christmas again. I could have been at home in my wool socks, sipping hot totties and watching her put up decorations. Instead, I was on this fucked up mission.

But those pleasant thoughts of her were quickly supplanted by that Dear John BS. And not that I wanted pity, but she might have considered how I had just lost Tom.

And with that, the nightmare returned. The knife at his throat. His violent but hapless struggle as the razor-sharp dagger ripped through his carotid artery and severed his esophagus, the head pulled back and the neck anatomy further exposed with each slice. Until, with a final thrust, the neck bone cracked and Tom's bloodied head was held aloft, the now limp body falling forward with a kick from his assassin.

It had happened so fast, and yet Tom had suffered. For how long? Who knew, but put a bullet in me. I would never be free of those images now. I would never know peace again, no matter how many of those bastards I executed.

I darted a glance in Danny's direction. He smiled back.

"Looks like snow later on."

Great, I thought. That's all I needed.

☐

Four

We traveled east with the arc of storm clouds steadily receding behind us. What had become a gray, bitter day in Istanbul was now nothing but blue skies up ahead.

"Looks like we'll outrun that storm for a spell," Danny said with a look my way.

"Yeah," I said, staring straight ahead.

He glanced at his watch.

"Should be getting in about noon or so."

I nodded.

Danny made several more attempts to engage me in conversation and finally gave up. I assumed he was getting the message. I had no interest in small talk. You may as well try to shoot the shit with a man on his way to the gallows.

Not that it put a damper on Danny's cheerfulness in any way. He went about flying the plane like he was whistling. He always seemed to be whistling.

Still, several times I sensed him darting looks my way. David had told him something. Just how much I couldn't say.

As we neared Incirlik, Danny called ahead to the flight tower, a call that quickly turned into a ribald exchange with the man on the other end. They had BS'd back and forth for half a minute or so when Danny let out a big laugh.

"Okay. I'll give you a call," he added before finally clicking off.

"Roberto Ramos," Danny said with a look my way. "I call him border trash. Straight out of Juarez. He must have been born in a whore house because he's always trying to drag me into the latest one he's found."

Danny looked forward.

"Hey, what do you say we head into town for a bite to eat before I fly back."

He glanced my way. I shrugged. I had about as much interest in going out on the town as I had in Danny's good-natured bantering. Plus, whatever protection I enjoyed as an American soldier at Incirlik, it would no longer apply once I left the base and entered the streets of Adana. To the Turks, I was just another wanted terrorist.

"Come on," Danny said. "We'll have a good time."

I shrugged and nodded.

"Yeah, all right."

I figured I owed him that much for giving me a ride. I just hoped like hell that I wouldn't come to regret it.

While Danny got back to flying, my thoughts turned to Emine. The poor thing, lying there night after night with lecherous old men humping away at her. Then the helplessness of Tom's final moments returned. The blood spurting out of his neck. His horrible gasping for air. His body reflexively writhing to get free, like a fish flopping out of water.

Christ. I was doomed.

I returned to the memory of Emine for salvation. We'd run off to the French Alps somewhere. Live happily ever after in a cabin nestled among snow-capped peaks. A fire crackling. Cowbells echoing merrily across the mountain valleys. The thought of going back to rescue her had taken on a life of its own in my head.

But first the mission. And then we'd see.

Danny called into the tower again, snapping me from my reveries. He was banking in towards the northwest outskirts of Adana at one thousand feet, all business now. The protocol for landing at Incirlik was a mile long, and in spades for

36

civilian aircraft, so there was no more talk of girls and whorehouses.

Danny kept banking until we were bearing northeast, with the runway straight ahead. It struck me how few military aircraft there were out on the tarmac. The Turks must have gotten their diplomatic shorts into a knot again, forcing the coalition to launch airstrikes out of Riyadh or Aviano.

It was always something with these people. They were dyspeptic. It was the fall of the Ottoman Empire. They had never gotten over it. And probably never would.

Danny brought us in for a smooth landing, then taxied back over his shoulder and onto the tarmac. Down at the far end of the runway, an Airman 1st Class appeared out of a large hangar and directed us with a pair of marshalling wands. Once Danny had brought us to a full stop near the hangar entrance, he killed the engines, unbuckled his seatbelt and jumped up with a clipboard.

"Time to bend over for these SOBs. You got your paperwork all right?"

I nodded and followed him aft. The airman was waiting for us outside and pointed towards the hangar.

"This way, gentlemen."

We were led inside to a makeshift office. A 2nd Lieutenant sat behind a desk going over some paperwork. He looked up at us, as animated as cold coffee.

"Your business, gentlemen?"

Danny handed him his flight manifest.

"Just dropping off my partner here. And planning to do a little R&R before heading back tonight."

Danny smiled. The lieutenant had a quick look at the paperwork and handed it back to Danny, without the smile. His attention turned to me. I handed him my Army ID and orders. The lieutenant scratched his forehead with one hand while going over them. He glanced up once and looked back at the paperwork.

"You know where to find your team?" he asked while handing the paperwork back to me.

"Can't say I do."

"Cunningham," the lieutenant said to the airman. "Show this man to his quarters."

"Just a second," Danny said. "We're both planning to hit the town before I leave."

The lieutenant looked at me.

"That's between you and your team."

"Yeah. May as well drop off my pack and check in with them first."

The lieutenant nodded and got back to his paperwork.

"This way, gentlemen," Cunningham said.

He led us outside to an open jeep. Danny jumped in up front.

"So, how long you been stationed here?" he asked as Cunningham was cranking over the engine.

"Just about a month now, sir."

"Where before this?"

Cunningham released the handbrake and drove off.

"Mannheim."

"Ah, yes. The fräuleins. So, which do you like more, Cunningham? German girls or these Turkish women?"

Cunningham glanced over with a smile.

"They both have their advantages, sir."

"That they do. That they do."

While their discussion continued, I stared off across the runway. Other than for a couple of parked C-130s, the airbase was eerily empty.

Just as well, I thought. Maybe I'd catch a break from the coalition airstrikes. They would only make my life more difficult. Maybe even put an end to it. There was no distinguishing one fool from another at fifteen thousand feet.

Wouldn't that be the irony. Just as I was about to rake a knife across al-Ramadi's throat, an airstrike puts both of us out of our misery.

Up at the north end of the runway, Cunningham pulled to a stop in front of a warehouse. He looked back at me.

"You should find them inside. Just knock on that door. Their quarters are way in the back. Want me to come along and introduce you?"

"No. I'm good, soldier."

I jumped out and grabbed my pack.

"See you in a few," I told Danny.

He smiled and went back to his banter with Cunningham. I knocked on the door and stood back to wait. After a long moment, a large black man with male pattern baldness answered. The name tag on his Army uniform read Robinson. His rank was specialist. He seemed kindly enough, if not particularly happy to see me.

"What can I do you for?" he asked.

"I'm with Tiger Force."

"Yeah? Well there ain't no Tiger Force around here."

Robinson stood there deadpan for a long moment before opening the door wider.

"They's in back, but you ain't never heard me say that."

He nodded for me to come in. I did and Robinson closed the door.

"This way."

I followed him down a hallway and into a voluminous storage warehouse. A younger black soldier was operating a hand lift near the end of the hallway, picking away at a mountain of boxed rations.

"Just came in this morning," Robinson said. "Don't know who in hell's going to eat all this shit, but that's our job. Make it all look neat and tidy."

He pointed down at the far end of the warehouse.

"See that door?"

I nodded. He nodded back knowingly and returned to his work. I headed off across the warehouse with a sense of being watched.

At the door, I paused. They probably had a code but hell if I was going to try and figure it out.

I knocked and heard locks being turned from inside a few seconds later. I counted three of them before the door cracked open. An unshaven man in his twenties peered out at me.

"Who are you?"

"Cole Jeffers. 5th SFG ODA."

"Yeah? Never heard of you."

A man in his thirties nudged him out of the way and held out his hand.

"Rob. David told me to expect you."

I shook his hand.

"Come on in," he said, opening the door wider.

A dozen or so young men were piled around on sofas and chairs behind him, phones and laptops in hand, surfing the internet, playing video games and generally screwing off. If not for all the camo gear and weaponry lying around the room, it could have been a frat house.

"Men," Rob said. "This is Cole. A friend of an old friend. He'll be hitching a ride with us down to Mosul before moving on to his own op."

Everyone who wasn't already paying attention stopped what they were doing and stared. Rob quickly went around the room, offering up names. I mostly took in their faces. It was an icy reception, but understandable. You didn't trust anyone but your own when you were on a mission. And yet, it kind of pissed me off. Tasted too much of Lydia's rejection.

I don't know how to say this, Blake, but...

Yeah, put me in your little box. You're always doing this. You're always doing that.

Listen, soldier, I reminded myself. Lock that shit down. You never went out on an op, dragging along your personal problems. That was the easiest way to get yourself killed.

"Hey. Aren't you a bit old to be playing with guns?" one of the men said.

That was met with snickers. Rob gestured for everyone to cool it.

"Have a seat," he said to me.

"Actually, I have a ride waiting for me outside. Going into town."

"Yeah, no sweat."

Rob led me to a room off to the side.

"That's your bunk. Feel free to drop your pack if you want."

"Yeah. Just as soon drop my tactical vest too while I'm at it."

"Sure, whatever. Your gear's safe in here with me."

I pulled off my jacket, set the vest on the bed with my pack and pulled the jacket back on.

The team was all eyes when I reappeared.

"What, you come with your own private limo?" someone asked.

"Yeah, the shit rations around here aren't good enough for you?"

I looked from face to face.

"The truth is, I'd just as soon get on to wasting some hajis. That or just kick back until I can, but the pilot who gave me a lift down here insisted on showing me a good time."

I shrugged.

"And being the gentleman that I am, I figured I owed him that much."

Met with more cold stares, I started for the door.

"Fuck it," this Hispanic looking guy said. "Let the man enjoy himself. You never know when it's going to be your last supper."

"Hey, tear off a little piece for me while you're at it," someone else said.

A burst of laughter dissolved back into more grumbling. Rob joined me at the door.

"Don't be too late. You think they're edgy now. Wait until wakeup call at 0500. You come in here after midnight and you won't know what pissed off is."

I nodded. Rob smiled and opened the door.

"Go. Have some fun while you can."

I stared back, getting more pissed off by the minute. Sure as hell, David had been talking to Rob behind my back too.

"I'll be back early enough," I told him and went out the door.

A moment later, I heard it close behind me, muffling the sound of those gung-ho boys inside.

Hell, that was me twenty-five years ago. Hungry for pussy, itching for war and otherwise dying for some way to prove myself in this crazy, mixed up world.

Robinson and his pal were still tucking away crates of boxes with their hand lift as I crossed the warehouse. They made a point of acting like I wasn't there.

I had started down the hallway leading to the exit when I heard Robinson say, "No, sir. Ain't never heard me of no Tiger Force. And don't never wanna hear me nothing about no Tiger Force. No sir."

I smiled. A wise man, he who wants nothing to do with trouble.

Outside, Danny and Cunningham were still gabbing away. Danny looked over his shoulder as I jumped in back.

"All set?"

I nodded.

"Good. Cunningham here got clearance to take us into town."

Cunningham released the handbrake and sped off in the open Jeep. I huddled up in my coat, cursing both of them. You had to be some kind of fool, driving around in an open Jeep in weather like this. We should have caught a taxi at the main entrance. It felt like snow.

Meanwhile, Danny and Cunningham were up there chirping away.

Still grousing, I turned my focus to the mission ahead. Where to find these ISIS bastards? In the dead of winter, they were probably hunkered down in the home of a poor Syrian family, the husband and sons baking bread over a fire while the men fucked their wives and daughters in back. God, I hated the very thought of them.

Then Tom was back. I couldn't help but imagine his regrets in those final moments. Why did I come here? Why why why? The mind would be searching desperately for a miraculous rescue, when none was forthcoming. Just the sting of the knife at your flesh and your brief but crazed struggle as they opened up your throat like a pig.

And despite all that, I felt no pity. Why? Because of Tom's girlish shrieks? Christ, who wouldn't have squealed under the circumstances?

I shook my head. Face it, Blake. It's hopeless. Thinking a bloodbath will cure your lust for revenge when probably nothing short of death will exorcise those demons now.

I looked up to find a city skyline approaching from across the river. It was dominated by a mosque and its accompanying minaret, both of them higher than any of the surrounding high-rise buildings. These people still viewed life in the manner of our own medieval traditions. Nothing taller than a cathedral, nothing greater than God. My great disgust for organized religion aside, such humility wasn't the worst thing that could happen to this world.

Cunningham had quickly motored across the river on the low bridge and was passing alongside the mosque. Danny looked over his shoulder at me

"The Sabanci Mosque. The biggest in Turkey."

I nodded.

Danny looked forward again and said something to Cunningham. I heard Cunningham say something about the Sheraton Grande. Danny laughed at him dismissively.

"Christ, Cunningham. We're not looking for corporate school girls."

Cunningham flashed a sheepish smile. Danny pulled out his phone and made a call. It quickly became apparent that he was talking to his buddy Ramos again. Danny laughed several times and got off.

"You know where the Mall Market is?" he asked Cunningham.

Cunningham nodded.

"Drop us off there. That's where my buddy's going to meet us."

"You got it, chief."

Great, I thought. Ramos and his whorehouses. So why drag me along? Danny and Ramos already had each other.

Cunningham turned left at the far end of the mosque grounds and into the bowels of the city. Tenement buildings quickly swallowed the sky. They were giving the projects in the Bronx a run for their money.

Cunningham turned right into a commercial district. More apartment towers loomed up from behind the store fronts. The streets steadily grew narrower as he zig zagged into the city, until we were negotiating a winding, cobblestoned lane with white plaster buildings closing in around us.

Cunningham pulled to a stop at the outskirts of a small square and pointed.

"It's right on the other side of those buildings. Don't make me drive in there. It's a traffic nightmare."

"No problem, buddy."

Danny shook his hand and jumped out. I climbed out and shook his hand too.

"You guys have any problem getting back on your own?"

"No. Our buddy Ramos will get us there. About three in the morning."

Cunningham laughed.

"Just make sure that desk jockey back there got our clearances down to the gate. I don't want to be screwing around with paperwork in the middle of the night."

"You got it, boss."

Danny shook his hand again.

"A pleasure, soldier. And if you ever find yourself in Istanbul, look me up. I'll show you a good time."

"You got it."

With a final wave, Cunningham muscled the Jeep around in the narrow lane and headed back the way we had come. I looked at Danny.

"We're not heading back at three in the morning. *I'm* not heading back at three in the morning. Reveille's at five with Tiger Force and I've already been warned about coming in late."

Danny smiled.

"Let's just see what happens."

"There ain't no seeing what happens. I've got about six hours, max, and then I'm heading back. With or without you. Nine o'clock tops and I'm out of here."

Danny put a hand on my shoulder.

"Whatever you gotta do. Let's just go have a good time."

Five

Danny pointed down a darkened passageway between two buildings. A cook stood outside the back door of a café, a cigarette in his mouth, watching us. A dog poked around in the trash near his feet. You could count the rib bones through the poor creature's hide.

"Hang on," I told Danny and pulled out my money clip.

Seeing me approach, the cook took the cigarette out of his mouth and nodded his chin. I pointed at the dog and held out a $20 bill.

"You want to feed?" the cook said.

I nodded. He went to take the bill but I pulled it back and gestured at the dog again. The cook stared for a moment before tossing his cigarette and going inside. He returned a minute later with sliced beef piled on a piece of waxed paper. I nodded and he tossed the meat on the ground. I handed the cook the bill and encouraged the dog our way. Wary at first, it was soon gobbling down the beef. I petted its back before joining Danny down the alleyway.

"Got a soft spot for the lost and downtrodden, huh, my friend?" he said.

"We're brothers in arms."

Danny smiled and patted me on the shoulder.

The alley soon dumped us out into a bustling, cobblestone square. Directly across the square, another alleyway wound out of sight, lined with street vendors. Men were gathered at an outdoor café by the entrance, with others loitering around the fringes, their eyes on who came and went from the bazaar, especially if they were women.

"There he is," Danny said with a wave to a young man standing off to one side of the square.

I followed Danny that way and stood back as the two men shared a boisterous greeting.

"Oh, this is Cole," Danny said. "On his way down to Mosul on a mission."

Ramos shook my hand.

"Good luck with that shit. I was there right after the invasion. Nice place then. Ain't so fucking nice now."

I nodded. Ramos studied me before looking back at Danny.

"All right, you crazy son of a bitch. What have you got up your sleeve this time?"

"Oh, you're going to love this place. Beautiful young women. Young and beautiful and eager to please. Only the locals go there."

"Yeah? So what are we doing there?"

"Don't worry. They love Americans. They love our money anyway."

Ramos raised his eyebrows at me. Danny smiled and waved.

"Lead the way, you depraved heathen."

Ramos glanced at me again before heading towards an arrow shaped building at the east end of the square. A long, straight commercial street led back towards the Sabanci Mosque to the left of the building, a winding, residential lane disappeared off to the right. As we neared the building, Ramos gestured towards the winding lane.

The two of them went ahead, gabbing away about life and love and war. I fell behind, my eyes alert for every possible danger. We passed two older women dressed in black, standing by a doorway. They reviewed our passage dourly. A curtain parted in a second story window to our left, revealing a young woman's face. Then an unseen hand pulled the curtain back down. With a look up, I noticed the arc of dark storm clouds was now bowing across the sky overhead.

My mind had started to drift.

Lydia. Emine. A Christmas Day long ago in the Smoky Mountains.

The mission, Blake. The mission. You have to stay focused.

Then Tom's death was back. The fool. Had to be a big wartime correspondent and stumbled into a den of fanatics. That's all it really amounted to. Wrong place, wrong time. The equivalent of a Neolithic hunter stumbling unawares into a pride of lions. The rest of the tribe would muse somberly around the fire that night. Well, Gork had it coming. Should have been paying better attention.

Tom should have been paying better attention. That's all.

Better yet, he should have stayed home, writing opinion pieces about corruption in government, instead of turning himself into a pawn for one of their videos. We had bombed the crap out of them and they had no other form of revenge.

The horror movie of his final moments resumed in my head.

"Noooooooooooo!"

Oh, yes, Tom. These boys in their sweat soaked sandals aren't screwing around. They're going to slice your head off, and right now. You play around with lions and you get eaten.

Ramos started up a walkway between two buildings, yanking me from my thoughts. We were in an impoverished neighborhood now, block buildings without plaster. Even a small mosque down the street looked sad and destitute.

Danny had followed Ramos up the walkway. I stood back on the street while Ramos knocked.

Some moments later, a buxom woman in her fifties cracked the door and peered out. Ramos said something to her in Turkish. The woman looked warily at me and back at Ramos. After another long moment, she opened the door halfway and Ramos nodded for us to join him inside.

We passed through a vestibule and into an expansive but dimly lit parlor. It was littered with sofas and chairs, the sofas and chairs littered with men and prostitutes. The women already paired up with men hardly noticed our entrance. The free women were all eyes our way, some smiling, some not.

The madam encouraged us to have a seat and said something in Turkish to Ramos. He replied and waved us over to three chairs in a corner.

"She's bringing us Raki. You know it?" Ramos said to me.

I nodded.

"Good shit," he said. "She said theirs is made from figs."

While we got comfortable, six women drifted our way. Quickly, we each had two of them draped around our chairs. The one to my left started running her fingernails through my hair. The other one put her hand inside my jacket and rubbed my chest. By the looks on their faces, they could not have been happier.

The one running her fingernails through my hair said something to the other one and they giggled. I looked from face to face. Ramos was right. These were young and beautiful women but I wasn't in the mood. I did not want to spoil the memory of Emine. She had come to represent purity to me. A golden thread leading back from my descent into hell.

The madam arrived with a silver tray and delivered the Raki. Ramos and Danny saluted the madam and drank. I tried mine. It was good. Sweet, but tart and warm. Like swallowing a thousand warm summer days.

The two women on my chair kept talking quietly and giggling over my head. Danny and Ramos headed off towards the back rooms with their four women. Danny saluted me on his way out.

My ladies eyed me expectantly. I responded with another sip of my drink. That led to an exchange of shrugs.

The madam returned moments later.

"You are fine?" she said.

I nodded.

49

"And...?"

She waved at the two women. I shook my head. She spoke sharply and the two women reluctantly abandoned their posts on my chair.

"Another Raki?" the madam said.

I nodded and she left.

I had been sitting there for nearly an hour and was working on my third Raki when Danny and Ramos finally reappeared from the back rooms. Danny was all smiles.

"Done already?" he said.

"Dude, he hasn't even moved," Ramos said.

I stared at him without responding.

"All right. Fuck it. The guy doesn't talk. Let's go get something to eat. I'm starving."

He went off to find the madam. Danny patted me on the shoulder.

"Got a gal back in the States, huh?"

I stared at him too.

"It's all right. I understand. We've all been there."

I let Danny believe whatever he wanted to believe. I wasn't pissed at him. You couldn't help but like the man. If he wasn't being cheerful, he was being kind, and perhaps even wise. But Ramos was another story.

He had settled up with the madam and returned.

"Let's go," he said.

Danny patted me on the shoulder again and followed Ramos. I downed the rest of my Raki and left a tip for the ladies. The madam had a frown for me on my way out the door. As customers went, there had been better ones.

Outside, the day was quickly fading to dusk.

"I still can't believe you didn't nail those two dolls," Ramos said with a look over his shoulder. "Shit, that one brunette was just my type. Sweet little compact body. I was ready to get going again, just looking at her."

I stared back without answering. In my world, you did not talk about women as chattel, even those engaged in the world's oldest profession. They were still human beings.

Ramos glanced over his shoulder and looked pissed to see me falling behind. Screw him. I fell even further behind, just to piss him off more.

Walking along, I remembered Emine's desperate reach of a hand as I got up to leave. The poor sweet creature. She filled me with noble feelings. There was an impulse to rush back and rescue her. If not for the mission, I would have done just that.

We had walked for maybe half a mile and seemed to have grown lost among the winding back streets when I heard the sounds of the city over the rooftops. Danny and Ramos turned a corner up ahead. Danny waved to me before disappearing.

I turned the same street corner and found them standing on the sidewalk of a bustling commercial district, waiting. As I joined them, Ramos pointed at a café a few doors up the street.

"This place'll do."

I followed Ramos and Danny inside. The place looked like any small-town America café, except the tables were made of wood, not Formica, and they were playing Turkish music.

While I sat there staring out the window, a snow flurry fluttered by. It was quickly followed by another one, and another.

"Here comes the snow," Ramos said.

"Yeah," Danny said. "I'd better get on my way soon, before it really sets in."

"Just spend the night."

"Naw. I like my own bed."

"Shit. You'll just run into hell if you head back now."

"Don't you worry about me."

Danny quickly had a radar map pulled up on his phone.

"There. It's already clearing back in Istanbul. All I need to do is run south for a hundred miles or so and circle around this shit."

I saw the arc of the storm on his screen, slowly pushing down from the northwest. Mosul would be buried in snow by tomorrow morning. And with that, Christmas was back. Hot totties in front of a fire, carolers and skating on the village pond.

But a few days ago, there was only revenge in my heart, as if my very existence depended on it. Now all these other sentiments were seeping in. I just wanted to live in peace. Let's just take that ride back to Istanbul with Danny and spirit Emine out of Turkey. Screw the mission.

No, goddamn it. You owe it to Tom. Wherever the hell he was now, let him know that you had returned the favor. Carve Saleem's throat open while his pals sat there wetting their pants.

I smirked to myself, picturing the scene.

"What?" Ramos said.

I looked his way.

"Nothing."

He stared, nodding his head.

"You don't talk much, do you."

I glanced Danny's way. He put a hand on Ramos' forearm.

"Don't pretend to know another man's business."

"What? I'm just wondering if this guy has a problem with me or something."

Danny gestured at Ramos with his right hand. He added a smile but it didn't much change Ramos' attitude.

"Fine. Fuck it," he said. "You're right. Anyone going into Mosul these days has got to be in one fucked up state of mind. Lo siento," he said to me.

It was supposed to be an apology. We both knew it wasn't.

I looked at Danny. He was serious now, checking his watch and trying to get the proprietor's attention.

"You know what you want?" he asked me.

"I don't care."

"Döner kebab?"

"Yeah, fine."

"Ramos?"

"Yeah. Shit. That's fine with me."

He slapped his menu shut.

The proprietor's wife arrived with a pitcher of water and left moments later with our orders for kebab and three beers. Danny checked his watch again.

"I told you. Stay," Ramos said.

"What? And listen to your bullshit all night?"

Ramos smirked.

"Shit. I'm ready to go back and bang that brunette of yours," he said to me.

I nodded, wanting to kill him. Fifteen years on the frontlines will do that to a man. Killing became your default answer to many things. If I ever caught the man talking about Emine in that way, I would take his head off.

I drummed my fingers while watching the snow come down outside. Ramos went back to talking about his adventures in bed. Everything about him made me want to leap across the table.

Danny glanced my way and changed the subject. Now they were talking about their adventures in the Iraq War. Danny made it sound cheery. He made everything sound cheery.

The meal came and we ate mostly in silence. Ramos stole repeated glances my way. Then Danny was hurrying to pay the tab. The snow was coming down in earnest now and gathering on the sidewalks.

Outside, it felt like Christmas in New York, shoppers coming and going from store fronts, rushing to get home at twilight with their treasures. All the scene lacked were Christmas lights. Christianity was prevalent in Turkey but you didn't flaunt your beliefs. So were persecution and torture.

"Which way to a cab?" Danny said.

Ramos pointed down the street.

"Next block."

We walked along with me next to the store fronts and Danny serving as a buffer in the middle. I had my attention on a man across the street. Tweed sports jacket, camel hair overcoat, no packages and no other seeming agenda, other than to keep pace with us. I cursed to myself for having agreed to this excursion in the first place. Just like in Istanbul, there were surveillance cameras all along the streets of Adana and apparently it hadn't taken long for an algorithm down in the bowels of some intel boiler room to match my face.

Ramos noticed me noticing the guy shadowing us and said, "What the fuck?"

"Think I'll do a bit of Christmas shopping," I told Danny.

Danny winked and gently prodded Ramos down the sidewalk.

"What the fuck?" Ramos said again. "What did you get me into here? I've been stationed at Incirlik for two years and haven't seen this kind of shit once."

I stepped into a gift shop and was met by a slim woman in her mid-thirties. She was wearing a cashmere sweater and smelled of fine perfume. She was one of those women who burst with femininity and raw sexual energy, though her face was coarse and she was not particularly attractive.

She smiled at me from among the wares.

"May I help you?" she said with a smoky Turkish accent.

"I'm shopping for my wife. A little something from Adana."

A man looked up briefly from behind the counter and went back to counting receipts. I assumed him to be the woman's husband.

"As you can see, we have many beautiful things," she said.

"Yes, I can see that."

I picked up the figurine of a sea sprite and stole a furtive look out the storefront. Whether or not the man could see through the reflective glass from the opposite sidewalk, he was staring my way and showed no interest in Danny and Ramos as they headed down the sidewalk. This was all about Blake Peters.

"That's a lovely piece" the woman said. "The artist is from Yalikavak. You can see there are several other pieces to the set."

I nodded.

"I'll take this."

"A perfect choice."

I glanced around the shop while she took it behind the counter. There were subtle signs of these people being Christians. Besides, the woman would have been wearing a hajib if they were Muslims.

"Is this a Christmas present?" she said while ringing me up.

I nodded.

"How nice. I'll be happy to gift wrap it for you…"

"I'm sorry," I said and reached out with a hand.

The man looked up.

"Please. Just a bag will do."

The woman did as asked. I pulled out my money clip and counted out more than enough to cover the gift.

"You can keep the change."

I placed the figurine inside my coat with a quick glance over my shoulder. Their eyes followed mine.

"Would it be all right if I used your bathroom?" I said, turning back.

The wife looked at her husband. He studied me for a moment before nodding subtly.

"Please," she said and waved me towards an opening.

I followed the woman into the back of the shop. She opened the bathroom door and turned on the lights. When I glanced out towards the street again, her eyes following mine, and again when I looked at the door leading out back.

"I'll leave you alone," she said.

Her return to the front of the store was executed as if I did not exist.

I closed the bathroom door from the outside and went to the back door. When the deadbolt clicked loudly, I froze.

Seconds later, I heard the front door fly open and a man's voice bark sharply at the couple. I unlocked the doorknob, slipped out into an alleyway, closed the door behind myself and ran towards the nearest corner. The snow was falling hard around me.

My options were limited. Hide in a dumpster. Climb up a fire escape to the rooftops. Try back doors until I found one unlocked. Not particularly fond of the first two choices, and seeing little time for the latter, I raced on in full flight, hoping to disappear around the next street corner before I was spotted.

A hundred yards down the alley, I heard a voice call out and looked back. The man in the overcoat had exited the shop and was coming my way, a gun in one hand and a phone to his ear with the other.

I continued running at full speed, and cursing Conway in the process. Had to go hit the town with that prick, Ramos. I cursed myself for letting those two get me into this situation.

Sprinting on in the falling snow, the next corner seemed to be moving farther away, not closer. When I finally reached it, I had another quick look back, taking comfort in one fact. That man could never keep up with me on foot.

I had relished that advantage for all of two seconds when a Mercedes careened around a corner behind him and raced to a stop. He jumped in and the driver sped my way.

Well, shit.

With my options diminished even further now, I tried the first back door on my right, then the next one. It appeared I was still in a commercial district of some kind, with shops on the ground level and apartments above them.

After the third door failed to open, I resigned myself to the rooftops and started up a fire escape. Below me, the alley echoed with the sound of approaching tires in fresh snow.

I had scampered up to the rooftop and gotten one leg over the edge when the Mercedes spun around the corner. Four men jumped out and two of them quickly fired shots at me.

I ducked out of sight and ran in the direction of the next block. The buildings were wall to wall up to that point. Then I would be cornered.

Down in the alley, I heard voices and the sound of hard shoes dispersing. One man began beating on a door and shouting. Another one was racing down the alley, trying to outflank me. The third one was scampering up the fire escape at my back. The Mercedes had turned around and raced off in the other direction.

I came to the door of a roof access, found it unlocked and dashed down to the second story, and then to a window at the far end of a long hallway. The window overlooked a street of shops, all of them still open and catering to shoppers, despite the snow. There was a produce stand directly below me with a makeshift awning above it.

While forcing the double hung window open, I heard someone rush in down on the first floor and footsteps dashing up the stairs. I climbed out and was easing my way down the brick façade when my grip failed and I tumbled down onto the awning, and from there onto a table stacked with produce. There were screams and voices cursing.

I got back on my feet and ran towards a narrow passageway across the street. The Mercedes careened around the next corner with the man in the overcoat now driving it. I disappeared into the passageway with shots clipping off the stonework around my head. The Mercedes couldn't follow me, but someone on foot soon would.

I made it around to the next street and stood there under an overhang, thinking. Moments later, a thought came to me and I raced on, deeper into that labyrinth of back streets.

Eventually, I arrived to the door and knocked. The madam answered after several seconds. She did not look the least bit happy to see me.

I had bent over, trying to catch my breath and stood back up. When I glanced both ways along the street, the madam did so too before turning her attention back at me. I made an effort to shake off some of the snow and look presentable.

With another look up and down the street, she parted the door further and nodded for me to come in. The two young dolls who had been sitting on my chair earlier giggled upon seeing me. I nodded at them and the madam escorted the three of us off to a back room.

With the door closed, the young women backed me towards the bed, shedding gowns as they did.

Please forgive me, dearest Emine. I would rather be with you. Anytime…anywhere.

☐

Six

Time drifted by there in the room with the two women doting on me and all my focus on the people passing by out in the hallway. At one point, I thought I heard the voice of the man in the overcoat back in the reception area and reached for my Glock. The two young women watched me intently, intrigued more than alarmed. When the danger appeared to pass, they went right back to what they had been doing.

At the end of an hour, the madam knocked on the door. The two ladies got up on their elbows and giggled from across my chest. That brought an immediate bark from the madam and another knock on the door. The ladies were quick to their feet now and slipping into their panties. Hearing their whispered voices, the madam barked again and cracked the door open. The two women hurried that way, trailing gowns and kisses in my direction. The madam had another word for them as they disappeared. I called out before she could close the door. The madam stared with her hand on the doorknob.

"I need a taxi...Discreetly, please."

She stared for a moment longer before nodding and closing the door. I climbed out of bed and got dressed.

As before, my appearance out front garnered little attention. Between the dim lights and quiet Turkish music and all the petting, no one much noticed who came and went.

I found the madam and gestured at the front door. She nodded. I left a generous tip for everyone and went out into the cold. A taxi sat gathering snow in the narrow street. I climbed in and told the driver, Incirlik.

As he drove off, I pulled the hood of my jacket up over my head and got down out of sight. The driver looked once at me in the rearview mirror and returned to his own business.

The city passed by, completely transformed now by the snow. It was as if someone had waved a magic wand over Adana and turned it into a fairyland.

At the base entrance, I sat up and showed the guard my ID through the lowered window. He saluted and waved us in.

Once we were safely on the base, I looked over my shoulder. The man in the overcoat was sitting in the Mercedes across the street, glaring my way. The other three men were in the car with him.

No, they're not going to forget about you, Blake. Once you betray the Turks, they never do.

As a purely bureaucratic matter, I was now on American soil and would soon be out of the country, but their interest still troubled me. If I returned for Emine, spiriting her across the border into Bulgaria or Greece would already be a major bitch. Add these government pricks on my tail and I would be running a special op.

I made a mental note to sound Danny about a black-market passport on my way back. He seemed like a man who would know about such things. I also made a mental note to steer clear of the Turkish border. You could easily stumble from Kurdish controlled territory into Turkish hands without realizing it.

I turned forward, only to be faced with Tom's tortured death again. The poor fool. What disbelief he must have felt in those final few seconds, realizing the horror of what was to come. Oh dear god, please. Let there be some kind of miracle.

But no. They had dragged him back to his knees and promptly butchered his head off. The infidel had it coming. It was the will of Allah.

Well, I'd show them the will of Allah, all right. There'd be no turning the other cheek with me. I'd have my revenge, as sick and insane as the whole thing had become. I had already sensed that butchering Saleem would not displace the horror of Tom's final minute in my mind, that in all likelihood, I would soon be stuck with both horrors, but I could not seem to get the hatred out of my heart.

The driver looked over the seat and said something in Turkish, breaking me from my thoughts. I leaned forward and pointed at the other side of the airstrip, and kept pointing until we were at the far end of the base.

"Here," I said and motioned for him to stop.

I climbed out, left the driver his fare and tip, watched him drive off and looked up at the falling snow. The storm had started to wane.

After taking in the stillness of the night for a few moments, I walked over and knocked on the door. Hopefully Robinson and his pal were still up. A minute passed without a response so I knocked again. I was starting off towards the back of the building when Robinson finally answered.

We stared.

"I don't know me nothing about no Tiger Force," I said.

A whisper of a smile crossed his face as he parted the door.

"You catch on, brother. You catch on."

I went in past Robinson without responding. His pal sat at a table in a small office with the lights down low and a game of cards in front of him. It looked like gin. I headed down the hallway and out into the warehouse, accompanied only by the echo of my own footsteps.

At the door to Tiger Force, I paused before knocking. A chorus of grumbling instantly broke out. It was followed moments later by Rob's voice and the grumbling stopped. I listened to the door being unlocked and it opened.

"Hey," he whispered and parted the door. "Everyone hit the sack early."

I looked at my watch. It was a few minutes past nine-thirty.

"You're good, you're good. Come on in."

A couple of the soldiers had their heads up. Rob relocked the door and gestured towards his room. A final chorus of muttering followed us through the door. Rob closed it and waved at the bed. He had set out a sleeping bag for me.

"Make yourself at home. The bathroom's in there if you need it."

"Thanks."

I retrieved the toiletry kit from my pack and went in to brush my teeth and relieve my bladder. I returned to find the room darkened and Rob already tucked away in his sleeping bag.

"Good night," he said.

"Good night," I said.

I stripped down to my camo shirt, pants and socks and climbed in. The unspoken nature of my mission hung in the air. Rob hadn't asked but I could sense his mind working.

I lay there with eyes open, seized by the usual horrors. Tom's shrieks of agony and final desperate struggle, his gasps turning to the grotesque sounds of a man drowning in his own blood. Then the twitching and contortions of a body that was only acting reflexively now, the blood splotched head held up defiantly, so suddenly dead and lifeless.

I rolled over, trying to escape the images but could not. What manner of being would perform such an act? You want him dead? Just shoot the poor son of a bitch. But no. They had to make him suffer.

I finally found sleep; a restless, tormented sleep filled with feverish dreams. The women I wanted. The women who no longer wanted me. The men and forces in life that kept getting in my way.

Then I heard Rob quietly calling my name. I acknowledged him and rolled over. Goddamn it. It was way too early.

While Rob used the bathroom, I lay there thinking. My enthusiasm for the mission was waning. It had been something of a fever the past few weeks, but now, with the field of battle drawing nigh, I found myself questioning my own sanity. David was right. The coalition forces would be bombing the crap out of ISIS soon enough. Why did I care?

But I had come too far and had too much on the line to turn back now. I was in this until the bitter end.

When Rob left the room, I went in to use the bathroom. The boys of Tiger Force were milling about restlessly and being their usual wise asses when I joined them.

"Hey, did you get any last night, grandpa?" one of them said.

I sat down without answering.

"Can he still get it up?" another one said. "That's what I want to know."

I made a gesture to suggest, halfway. That got a roar.

"Hey, how does that Viagra shit work, anyway?"

I made another halfway gesture, to more laughter. Late-forties, a few gray hairs and I had to put up with this crap.

A colonel had come into the room amidst this banter and cornered Rob. They both looked my way once and resumed their conversation.

When the colonel left, Rob came over to me.

"Looks like you attracted a bit of attention in town last night."

"Yeah? And?"

He shrugged.

"Nothing, I guess. They're just up Colonel Brand's ass so he's up mine, wanting to know who the hell you are and what the hell you're doing here. I told him what David told me. You're on a covert CIA op and he let it go, with a caveat. Get your asses in the air and out of Turkish airspace before he catches anymore flak about this."

He patted me on the shoulder.

"Just thought you'd better know."

"Thanks."

"You ready to push out?"

I nodded. He gave me another pat on the shoulder and headed off to his room. A few moments later he reappeared with his gear.

"Okay, boys! The bird's on the tarmac! Grab your gear and let's get airborne!"

The young men responded to the announcement by jostling with each other to be the first one out the door. Rob followed his men and I followed him up the C-130 ramp in silence. The middle of the fuselage was jammed full of palleted supplies. Our mesh jump seats were in front. I settled into one of the last empty spaces, leaned back against the wall and closed my eyes. It was good to be going. Anything to blot out all the other crap. I liked remembering Emine. The rest was a nightmare.

A few minutes later, I felt the plane taxiing backwards. With no windows, you didn't know where you were going. Just somewhere.

After a long, slow journey down the tarmac, the pilot made a turn, the engines roared to life and the plane rumbled and shook as we picked up speed. Then came that sense of weightlessness as we went airborne.

The jokes and wisecracks continued on unabated. It was getting on my nerves. I tried to picture myself twenty-five years earlier. I honestly couldn't remember being a jock like these young soldiers, but maybe I had been.

Feeling the plane level out, I opened my eyes. The young man seated across from me was staring.

"So seriously," he said.

"Seriously, what?"

"Where did you break your cherry? In the Gulf War?"

"No. 'Nam, actually."

"Bullshit."

"Well, how old do you think I am?"

There were a bunch of wisecrack answers, most of them in the eighty to ninety year range. I nodded. I wasn't going to dignify this crap with an answer.

"Then the Balkans, huh?" somebody else said.

I glanced his way.

"That was some gnarly shit, right?"

I nodded.

"You dust a lot of those fuckers?"

I shook my head and looked down.

"Then what did you do?"

I looked back up.

"I was sent in to fix things, mostly. Most of the killing had been done by the time I got there."

"So, you were like a diplomat?"

I shrugged.

"Sort of."

"Was it as bad as Iraq?"

I shrugged.

"Different."

"How so?"

I considered his question.

"The Serbs were a nation state. You're talking an army with tanks and artillery and planes. You weren't running around trying to hunt down hajis in a hole."

"Shit. ISIS had tanks and artillery and shit and we kicked their asses."

I nodded.

"ISIS just stole all that shit from the Iraqi army," someone else said.

"You mean they kicked their asses and took it from them," another one said.

The first young man was still staring at me.

"Why don't you want to talk about it?"

I shrugged.

"Fine. I don't care. And I don't care if those Serbians had an atomic bomb. From what I've heard about them, I'd have been dusting those fuckers left and right."

I nodded. The young man kept staring.

"Well, didn't you?"

"It helps if you understand the history."

"What's that supposed to mean?"

"It means, if you knew the history, you'd know that the Croatians were the bad guys during World War II. Doing the same shit to the Serbs that the Serbs were doing to the Croatians in the nineties. Murder. Rape. Genocide."

"No shit," another one of the young men said. "You mean the Serbs were just trying to get even."

I shrugged.

"Well, which is it?" the first young man said.

I looked back at him.

"Which is it? I'll tell you which. That shit goes back centuries, just like in Iraq. You fucked with my ancestors? Then I'll fuck with yours. I watched those people killing each other until it dawned on me one day. There ain't no getting even. There's just peace. Or starting the next war."

"No shit," someone said. "They had a blood feud going, just like the Sunnis and Shi'ites?"

I nodded and closed my eyes.

"So how do you know all this shit?" the first man said.

I cracked my eyes to look at him.

"From reading books."

He stared as if he didn't like my answer.

"You should try it sometime," I added.

That got a big laugh out of his friends.

"Fucker," he said.

I nodded and closed my eyes again, chewing on my own words. There ain't no getting even.

An hour and a half later, the pilot backed off the engines and we started our slow descent into Mosul. I had been chewing on my own words the entire way. There ain't no getting even.

Finally, we were on the ground and dragging our gear down the ramp. The base was buried in snow, with a harsh wind whistling among the low-slung buildings and the temperature in the twenties. The tallest thing in sight besides the flight tower were the hardened aircraft bunkers. Snow had been bulldozed away from the entrances and two airmen were busy preparing an F-15 for a mission. The jet looked as if it had been attacked by graffiti artists in a freight yard. Bob al-Kalamazoo was scribbled across the tail.

"You know where you're going?" Rob said.

"To the mess hall for a cup of coffee. And to make a few calls."

Rob nodded.

"You're welcome to join us."

"Thanks. I'm good."

"Okay…Well, best of luck with your mission."

"Yeah. Same to you."

He headed off with his troops.

"Hey, good luck, Gramps," one of them said with a wave over his shoulder.

I nodded my chin at him and headed off through the collection of tents and trailers and converted shipping containers that made up this makeshift base. The com center and commissary were off in the distance, and about the only thing that looked remotely permanent. A twenty foot high concrete barrier surrounded both of them.

On my way into the mess hall, I passed two soldiers digging out from the snow. Christmas and hot totties were back in my thoughts. So was Tom, though growing strangely distant now. Something was changing. Maybe I had just tired of my own madness.

I found the coffee inside and quickly doctored up a cup with cream and sugar. There was worse coffee in the world.

I found a table off in a corner and called Faisal's number. After several rings, a deep, soft spoken voice answered in Kurdish.

"Faisal. This is Cole Jeffers."

"Ah, yes, Mr. Cole. I have been expecting you."

His English was clear but heavily accented. A woman would have found it charming.

"Are you at the base?" he said.

"Yeah. Just got in."

"Ah. Then I presume you want me to come and retrieve you?"

"That was the general idea."

"Yes, then. It will take me most of an hour to be there."

"Okay. Just call when you get near. I'll grab some breakfast while I wait."

"Very well. I shall see you in a short time."

"Thanks. See you soon."

I hung up, frustrated by the delay but somewhat reassured by Faisal's demeanor. He appeared to be rational enough. I had feared some unhinged fanatic, working for the Americans while secretly planning jihad. Not that I could blame anyone for having a less than stellar opinion of the gringos, but I didn't want to be shot in the back.

The Twelfth Commandment

☐

Seven

I went through the breakfast line and returned to my table with a plate of scrambled eggs, sausages and flapjacks. My force field was up, head down. Anyone passing by would know in an instant. No use in trying to shoot the shit with this man.

The memo appeared to have gotten around the mess hall until near the end of my meal, when a soldier sat down opposite me. To his credit, he had done so at the far end of the table.

Aware from the man's fatigues and insignias that he was a fellow Army Ranger, I glanced that way and received a subtle nod. Good. We seemed to be on the same wavelength. No one had joined him so I took him to be a lone runner like me.

I was taking another bite of my eggs when the ghastly images of Tom's final bloodbath did a reprise in my head. I swore under my breath and headed for the trash with my plate. You may as well have squirted ketchup all over my pancakes.

While dumping the remains of my meal, I stole another glance at the man. His head was down and focused on his meal. No sign of him being interested in me, and yet I had a funny feeling that David's hand was in this somehow.

I went out into the cold morning, walked around to the lee side of the mess hall, found a crate to sit on and got comfortable with my back against the wall. The sky was clear, the distant sun faintly warm on my face.

I checked my phone for the time. Almost 1100 hours. Impulsively, I also checked for messages. Nothing. Love did strange things to a man. You kept wanting the woman who was no longer any good for you. Once you had tasted their sweetness, they remained deep in your soul, long after the warmth from their hearts had melted away.

Maybe I just hated defeat but scenes of conciliation played out in my head. Lydia and I would patch things up and live happily ever after.

My phone rang before I got too far with that. It was a blocked number. I answered it.

"Yeah."

"Just called to wish you a happy holiday," David said.

"Yeah. Same to you."

"You on that hunting trip?"

"Sure am."

"How's things at the cabin?"

"Cold. It snowed last night."

"Well, at least the deer will leave tracks."

"So will the hunter."

"That's true...Okay, listen. I got a call from that guy you bumped into the other day and he's fishing around, making trouble. Anything that I ought to know?"

"No. I'm guessing it's all about the company I keep."

"Yeah, well, thanks to you, he's now making trouble for me."

"Sorry to hear it."

"Yeah. You and your damned rebellious streak."

"Somebody has to root for the underdog."

"Yeah...Well, look. Be sure to avoid his neighborhood. Next time you see him, there's going to be big trouble."

"Like I didn't know that already."

"Don't get smart...I'll check in with you in a few days. See if you nabbed that buck."

"You know where to find me."

"Yeah. Right around the corner from death and mayhem."

I didn't answer.

"Okay. Back at you soon," David added and hung up.

I closed the screen and considered David's words. God, how I hated the Turks. At least the men in power. Having gone off the reservation the way I had, I had found myself on the wrong side of a diplomatic pissing contest, with the Turks pressing the issue all the way up to the State Dept. Forget dishonorable discharge. I could have been court martialed, and nearly had been.

And still I had no regrets, and would do it all over again, in a heartbeat. If I hadn't helped Firat and his people escape down the mountain, they would have been slowly tortured before a final bullet in the head. It made me sick, the way we treated the Kurds. Set them up again and again, only to turn around and stab them in the back.

I looked back out at the tarmac, watching what passed for thrills at a military airbase. Trams coming and going. Mechanics servicing airplanes. Three of them were at work on a nearby C-130. An A-10 Warthog came in for a landing and taxied over to a hangar. Another C-130 took off, loaded down like a Christmas goose.

I sat there for the next half an hour with my mind bouncing around between Emine and Lydia and Tom's final horror. I was doing my best to stay focused on Emine and not having much luck with it. Finally, my phone rang. It was Faisal.

"Are you here?" I said, answering his call.

"I am outside the gate."

"All right. Hang loose. I'll be there in a minute."

I got to my feet, circumvented a couple of soldiers shoveling more snow and headed off through the maze of makeshift buildings. The din of military activity went on everywhere around me, though of necessity, more at the pace of molasses in the bitter cold. In most cases, it was hard to tell who was doing what, or why, but you knew it involved being neat and orderly. That was the lifeblood all military operations. Nice and neat and orderly. Always had been. Always would be. It was even how they trained you to kill another human being.

After a sizable hike, I arrived at the main gate and flashed my ID on the way past the guard. That earned me a salute from the private manning it.

I spotted a white Isuzu SUV parked a hundred yards down the road. David had definitely gotten the car right. Battered and sand blasted by the desert winds.

The man sitting behind the wheel noticed my approach and climbed out, bracing himself against the cold. He was wearing a threadbare wool sports coat and cabled sweater.

I assumed it to be Faisal. With his tall forehead and short, scraggly beard, he had the air of the academic. He was tall and lanky and slightly stooped at the shoulders.

Faisal al-Khabur. Faisal from Khabur. His ancestors had hailed from that area but I found it difficult to imagine Faisal living there now. Khabur was a bleak, provincial outpost and Faisal did not look to be the bleak, provincial type.

All in all, he appeared to be a good soul, not that being one would do much good where we were headed. I could imagine a few situations where it would have an upside, but a lot more of them where it wouldn't. Whatever else you could say about Faisal, it did not appear that he knew how to use a gun, and that was of far more importance to me at the moment.

"I am Faisal," he said as I walked up.

"Cole."

Faisal offered his hand and waved me towards the driver's seat. I waved him back before he could get around the front of the Isuzu.

"You drive."

"Ah, very well," he said.

As I opened the shotgun side door, I glanced back at the gate and spotted the Ranger who had been sitting across from me in the cafeteria, talking to one of the guards at the gate but stealing looks my way.

Goddamn it, David. Leave it alone. I came here on a do or die mission. There's no need for you to babysit me.

I climbed into the front seat and set the pack at my feet. Faisal climbed in opposite me and went about performing various safety measures. Seat belt on, rearview mirror adjusted, side mirrors checked. In the middle of nowhere, he was practicing for his driver's license.

He glanced at me and my idle seat belt and was about to pull around in the road when I stopped him.

"How much did David tell you?"

Faisal searched my eyes.

"That you were looking for a man."

"Did David tell you who?"

Faisal shook his head.

I unzipped an arm pocket and pulled out the photo of Saleem. Faisal stared at it for a moment before looking up again. I studied his response. Something was going on in there. I wasn't sure what, but it was there, and he was not particularly good at disguising it.

"Do you know who that is?" I asked him.

After a long moment, Faisal nodded.

"Do you know where to find him?"

Faisal studied me for a moment, released the brake and turned around in the road.

"If he is anywhere," Faisal said a few hundred yards farther ahead. He looked over and met my eyes. "And can be found, it will be somewhere near Deir ez-Zor."

"Then we'll need to head south," I said, pulling out my map.

Faisal shook his head.

"No. Daesh still controls everything from Deir ez-Zor to Haditha, and from Al Hasakah to Palmyra. The safest way is from the north."

Faisal pointed at Khabur on my map.

"We must cross into Syria from there."

"Shit, that's two hundred miles out of our way. Anyway, I don't want to be anywhere near the Turkish border."

Faisal snapped a look at me while driving.

"If you want to find this man…And live to tell about it, that is the only way. The road is open to Qamishli. If we try to drive in from the south or east, we will only run into the retreating Daesh forces. It will be a suicide mission."

Faisal drove ahead some distance before glancing at me again.

"Even from the north and west, it can be very dangerous. We may need to take backroads at times, and in some places, there are none. We will be finding our way across open country."

"Okay, let's say you're right. Can you get me there?"

He stared for a long moment and looked forward again without answering. I continued staring for another long moment before doing the same.

Okay. If I got his drift, he knew the lay of the land better than me, so I could either accept his help or get there myself. There was nothing more to say.

We drove along in silence, heading northwest. The terrain was red and bleak. It could have been Mars, except for the snow. I continued chewing on this Turkish border business. It smelled like trouble.

Ten miles up ahead, we entered a hilly terrain that was as red and bleak looking as the flat terrain we had just left behind. Ten minutes later, we were circumventing Mosul. It looked like the battered remains of Berlin after World War II. Wrecked building after wrecked building with mounds of bricks and cinderblocks lying around their bases. It was a wasteland.

Passing the city, we crossed the Tigris and headed due north on Route 2. Just north of Hatarah, we came to a checkpoint.

"Kurds," Faisal said without looking at me.

I had already known as much by the uniforms.

He slowed to a stop alongside the guard and rolled down his window. The two of them were quickly talking in Kurdish. I recognized that much. Kurdish sounded more like Persian than Arabic. Whether they were speaking in the Sorani or Kurmanji dialect, I could not tell, but they had spoken like old friends.

Then the guard glanced at me and said something to Faisal. I was already getting out my military ID when Faisal turned to ask for it. The guard took it and did a double take at both me and the ID.

"Where are you going?" he asked in heavily accented English.

I pulled out the CIA card and handed it to him. The guard took that ID with another double take, then shuffled the IDs back and forth in his hands before passing them back with a nod. The Kurds trusted the CIA more than they did the US military, and they trusted the US military more than they ever should have.

As I was putting the IDs away, the guard said something to Faisal and Faisal darted a look at me. Then those two were talking again. With a final nod at me, the guard waved us on.

I sensed Faisal stealing more glances at me as he drove along. The guard had told him something. I wondered what.

The road turned west and soon brought us alongside a lake. I checked my map and saw that it was actually the Tigris. Not being familiar with the terrain in this corner of Iraq, I assumed that the river had been dammed somewhere out of our sight.

Farther ahead, the road turned due north and we drove with the snowcapped Zagros Mountains looming off in the distance. My mind was back to its pinball machine of thoughts and memories. Tom. Lydia. Emine. Making love. Christmas by the fire. Rejection. Anger. Revenge. Back and forth, up and down, round and round.

And just what had that guard told Faisal back there?

Then I was back to Tom's final few seconds on this earth, to that moment of disbelief and horror, when he had lurched away from the knife in revulsion, only to be dragged back to his knees. Tom would have had those few fleeting seconds to realize there was no changing things. And yet no doubt his mind had gone on disbelieving. This can't be happening. There has to be some kind of escape.

But those men had no mercy and the knife had taken its first, deep slice at his throat.

Fuck.

Faisal seemed to sense my tension and glanced over at me. I did not bother looking back.

A mile south of Bassetki, Faisal bore left on Route 2, away from the mountains, then five miles farther on, left again onto a dirt road. We jostled along with the mountains off to our right now. Khabur was fifteen miles ahead, where the Tigris entwined with and demarked the northeast corner of Syria.

Nearing the river, we saw signs of more Kurdish forces. An artillery position had been set up near the base of the bridge. Faisal turned left a few hundred yards shy of the bridge and worked his way back through a maze of dirt streets. You were reluctant to call the mud block structures we passed homes. They mostly lacked windows and the entry doors were thrown together with rickety planks of wood.

Faisal eventually drove in among the trees lining the river and pulled to a stop at one of the mud block structures. I checked my watch. It was getting on towards two o'clock.

"We stay here tonight," Faisal said with a look at me. "It will be a long day tomorrow. Best to think and plan before moving on."

He got out and headed for the front door. I did not like this much but got out and joined him. Faisal yanked the front door free and set it to one side. It had been jammed into the mud block opening without hinges.

"Please," he said, waving me inside. "I will gather some wood."

I set my pack inside the door, went around to urinate against the backside of the building and followed Faisal down among the trees. There were oaks, mostly, with dead branches and acorns littering the ground. In a matter of minutes, we were both carrying a sizable load of brush and firewood back to the house.

Inside, Faisal shoved the makeshift door back in place and went to work getting the brush lit in his fireplace. While he did, I broke the branches down into more manageable pieces. Before long, the fire had cast a warm glow in the room.

"I'm sorry," he said on his way to an improvised kitchen. "There is not much to eat. Rice. Flatbread. Some cheese." He searched among the plates and bowls and baskets on his shelves. "Here. There are two tomatoes. Ah, and a green pepper."

He shrugged.

"We will have something. I will get the rice started."

He uncovered a large drum of water, dipped a small pot into it, added some rice and took the pot over to a cooking rack above the fire. Back in the kitchen, he filled another pot with water.

"Best if I boil this for you. You will not want to drink our water. Tea?" he added over his shoulder. "Or I have coffee."

"Tea sounds good."

He added a teapot to the fire and returned to the crude countertop in his kitchen. There was a sink and a drain pipe that went out through a hole in the wall. I assumed right into the soil.

I yawned, exhausted from the road and early start.

"Please, make yourself at home," he said.

I did on a threadbare sofa in front of the fire and stretched my legs out, yawning again. With eyes closed, I heard Faisal chopping away and thought of Lydia. Tom was there too, with his final shrieks of agony. I really only wanted to think of Emine and went to work on how to steal her away. It would not be easy. The madam no doubt considered her a precious commodity and would miss her within minutes, and that was assuming I could ever get her out of the building.

I chastised myself for being distracted and tried to refocus on the mission. How was I going to find Saleem al-Ramadi? And outwit his ragtag army of fellow jihadists? As ragtag as they were, they were not to be trifled with.

I glanced over at Faisal. I needed the man but wondered just how much he could be trusted, and how useful he would be in battle. Someone with military experience would have been preferable. I felt like I was dragging a high school teacher into war. I pictured him freezing at the sight of an enemy gun.

I looked out the solitary window. The shadows had grown long. It was that hour when men searched their souls. I had no interest in searching mine. I had to do what I had to do. There was nothing left of me now but hatred and revenge.

Sitting there with my eyes closed, I sensed Faisal approaching and opened them again. He had a pan with the chopped tomatoes and bell pepper in it. As it began to sizzle, he added a spice that sent a burst of curry like scent through the room.

I looked again out the window at the darkening afternoon. Then Faisal was hurrying over to his kitchen with the rice and sautéed vegetables. He had left two pieces of flatbread on the grill. The bread quickly browned on one side so I got up and turned them.

"Thank you," Faisal said when I delivered them to the kitchen.

He ladled half the rice and vegetables onto a plate, added a thick slice of cheese and handed me the plate with a shrug.

"It is not much."

"It's fine. Thank you."

"Please, sit down. I will join you in a moment."

I took my plate and piece of bread and went back to the couch. I had started to eat when Faisal came with a tray holding his plate, two cups and a jar of honey. He sat on the floor, poured hot water into the two cups and handed one of them to me.

"Honey," he said.

"Thanks. In a minute."

I dug into the meal. When I wasn't looking at the food in front of me, I was staring into the fire. At one point, Faisal paused from his own meal to toss a few more branches onto the flames.

When my meal was done, I added honey to the tea and sat there sipping it quietly in the dimly lit room. There was an urge to ask Faisal about his life but I dared not go there. I would be inviting scrutiny of my own, and that was another thing I did not welcome.

But of course I wondered. What had brought him to this place? A home, as sad as it was, without a wife and children? Or even a photo of them?

There was every sign that this place had been a casualty of war, but a casualty of what specifically? I remembered the look of loathing on Faisal's face when I had showed him the photo of Saleem al-Ramadi. Faisal knew something, but it was not something he wished to discuss.

"Let us see your map again," he said, breaking the silence.

I had been thinking to pull it out myself and did so. Faisal moved closer in the flickering light and pointed.

"I know Daesh still holds Al Hasakah. But these towns to the west?"

He shrugged.

"It is day to day. We are safer taking this route. To Tell Beydar. Then south from there. Raqqah is free, but we will only know where the occupied line is as we draw nearer to Deir ez-Zor."

He shrugged again.

"But you know the area?" I said.

Faisal studied me for a moment before gathering up the dirty dishes and heading to the kitchen.

"My wife's family was from Raqqah."

He looked over his shoulder once and turned to washing the dishes. The question of what had happened to her and the rest of the family now hung in the air.

☐

Eight

I was staring into the fire when Faisal returned from the kitchen.

"You are welcome to the bedroom. There is a mattress…"

I waved him off.

"The couch is fine."

He went off to the bedroom and returned with a blanket and pillow. For all that was third world about this place, the blanket and pillow were respectably clean and sanitary looking. He held out his hand again, this time with some tissue paper.

"My apologies. There is no working toilet. Anywhere out in the woods will do."

He went to the front door, removed it and disappeared outside. A minute later he returned.

"And you?"

I nodded and got up.

"I will make coffee in the morning," he said before returning to the bedroom and closing the door.

I waited to hear if he would pray. I had assumed he was a Muslim but had yet to see him get out his rug and bow to Mecca and all that shit. I wasn't sure why it concerned me. Probably I just didn't trust Muslims. They were known to take off people's heads and blow things up.

When no sounds of praying were forthcoming, I went out to drain my bladder again and shoved the door back into place. There was a pause before sitting down on the sofa, not wanting to sleep with the vest on but not entirely certain I wanted Faisal to see how well I was armed. At least not yet.

In the end, I decided it was best to get that out of the way. Faisal had to know I was packing all this weaponry, just as I had to know if he was capable of using it, and willing to do so.

With the vest off, I pulled the Glock from my waist holder, placed it on the floor by my side, stretched out and covered myself with the blanket. The fire was nearly down to embers. I stared into it, thinking.

At last, it was time for action. Everything had been a dress rehearsal up to this point. By tomorrow afternoon, we would be somewhere near Deir ez-Zor, and hopefully closing in on Saleem al-Ramadi. My mind was driven to game out various scenarios, even though I knew from much experience that it was pointless to do so. Things never played out the way you expected, and yet my mind went on envisioning this and that battle scene.

In the final smoky version, I had Saleem gagged and tied to a chair while slowly sharpening my knife in front of him. Then I was out.

When I reawakened, there was a sylvan light in the room. I checked my watch. A bit past 0400. The moon must have been out.

Knowing I would not sleep again, I got up, shoved the Glock back into my waist holster, grabbed Faisal's tissue papers and went to the door. It took me most of a minute to remove it quietly.

Outside, I watched and listened for any signs of movement before being satisfied and disappearing off into the brush.

Back inside, I quietly returned the door to its place in the opening and went to start a fire. There being no quiet way to go about breaking up the brush and branches, I soon heard Faisal stirring. A minute later, he appeared, dressed but looking groggy. Still no prayer rug. So maybe he was a Christian. Or just done with god, like me.

"I will make coffee," he said.

I nodded. He had started for the kitchen when his eyes snapped in the direction of my vest. His gaze locked onto the Sig and ammo clips, then onto me, before continuing on his way. I finished starting the fire and headed for the kitchen. We passed each other as he headed to the fireplace with a coffee pot and a pan of water.

I drew water in another pot and splashed some on my face. When Faisal returned, he had a bar of soap and a towel. Our eyes met.

"Thank you."

"I was heating water for you," he said.

"It's all right. This is fine."

While I washed my face and chest, Faisal took the last two pieces of flatbread to the fireplace. Faisal was crouched down in front of the fire when I returned to the sofa. I grabbed my vest and pulled it on. Faisal darted another look my way. I unzipped the money belt around my waist and counted out one thousand euros.

Seeing me offer the money, Faisal held up a hand.

"No," I said. "There are no guarantees that I will return from this mission alive."

"The same is true of me."

I went over and stuffed the money into his shirt pocket.

"Just in case. And if necessary, you know where the rest is. If I'm dead and you're still alive, the money is yours."

I stared at him for a moment before continuing to get dressed. Faisal had browned the bread and gone off to the kitchen. I joined him. Our eyes met.

"Have you ever used a gun?" I asked while taking my piece of bread on a plate.

He gestured at the honey and poured me a cup of coffee. I spread some of the honey on my bread while continuing to look at him. He finally looked back and shook his head

I added some of the honey to my coffee and drank. The coffee was strong, strong enough to want the honey.

Before I could speak again, Faisal pointed at the fire and started that way with his own coffee and bread. He sat on the floor by the fire. I sat on the sofa.

"Would you?" I said after a moment.

He glanced at me.

"I don't know."

"If it was his life or yours?"

He searched my eyes before answering.

"I don't know."

I studied him while he stared into the fire.

"There will probably come a moment when both our lives depend on it and I need to know what to expect from you."

It took a moment before he looked back at me.

"It will be easier, knowing it is your life I am saving."

"Okay. Let's leave it at that. I watch your back and you watch mine."

He nodded.

"Fine. I watch your back and you watch mine. Isn't that what all good soldiers do?"

I acknowledged his point with a nod.

Later, Faisal went out to clean things up in the kitchen. I noticed the sky growing light through a small window high up on the wall. The morning had come alive with birdcalls. One of them was shrill and repetitive, the other one nasal and intermittent. Faisal noticed me listening.

"The Dead Sea Sparrow," he said. "That is the busy one. The other is the Black Francolin."

"Thank you. I had never heard them before."

I joined Faisal out in the kitchen. The water he had boiled for me was still sitting in a pot on the counter. I used it to refill my water bottle and went back to pull on my vest and coat.

Faisal joined me.

"I am ready to go," he said.

I pulled the Glock from my waist holster and removed the ammo clip.

"Like this," I said, showing him how to insert it. "Hard. Like you mean it."

I aimed the gun at the wall and pretended to fire with both hands.

"If it ever comes to that point, you don't think or you'll be dead."

He stared without emotion. I put the gun away and patted him on the shoulder.

"Just remember, if it ever does come to that point, it's because there's a man in front of you who'd just as soon cut your head off as look at you. So it's that or you kill him first."

Faisal nodded and pulled on his coat.

"Are you ready?"

"Yeah."

When he removed the door, I went around to empty my bladder at the back of the building. The Dead Sea Sparrows flitted about me. I looked for the Black Francolin but did not see one.

Faisal had the motor running when I returned. I climbed in and he pulled around in the yard, heading back the way we had come.

The nearby hills were splotched with snow. The snow covered mountains rose up behind them.

At the main road, Faisal turned left and we were soon backed up in a line of cars and trucks waiting to cross the river. The pontoon bridge was low to the water and the river ran brown beneath it.

Only one vehicle was being allowed to cross at a time so some minutes passed before we had inched our way to the front of the line. A truck rumbled over from the Syrian side and the guard waved us forward. While he and Faisal talked, the guard lowered his head to look at my face. Then he had a final word for Faisal and waved us on.

The bridge jostled this way and that as we crossed. Then we were at the other side and the guard waved us through without a word. They were all Kurds, so if we had been cleared on one side, there was no reason to check us any further.

We drove north through farmland, fallow with winter. Beyond the fields, the land along the river was lush with more oaks and pines and an abundance of shrubs.

Ten miles farther on, we came to the small village of Zuhajrijja and the road jogged west. Another ten miles farther on, we came to Al-Malikiyah and the road turned to the southwest. We saw Kurdish troop movements outside that city and their fortifications. A whitewashed church stood above the ancient walls, crowned by a minaret off in the distance, a reminder that everyone had once gotten along around here without cutting each other's heads off.

Two miles past Al-Maadadah, the main road turned due west with Qamishli an hour's drive straight ahead. I pulled out my charger, plugged it into Faisal's UBS connection and my phone into the charger. He turned on the radio and we went along with Arabic music playing. I was reminded of driving down through Mexico as a young man. The song had always seemed to be the same somehow. A man was in love. A man had been abandoned. Love was the same bliss and heartache, no matter the language or culture.

At Qamishli, Faisal suggested we stop for something to eat.

"We will not have much chance the rest of the day."

I shrugged, impatient but knowing he was right.

He pulled off the road and into a district of nice shops and restaurants. Nusaybin and Turkey were but a few miles to our north. I saw another church with women walking by it in hajibs. You would not have thought that war existed. If it did in these parts, it was due to the Turks and Kurds. They were at each other's throats as much as anyone.

Faisal parked in front of a restaurant.

"This will do."

I followed him into the long, narrow dining area. It was mostly empty at that hour. I checked my watch. Too early for lunch but that was what I wanted. I told Faisal to order for me and went off to use the bathroom. Faisal went off to use it when I returned. I sat there drumming my fingers, nervous about being this close to the border and eager to move on.

The waiter eventually returned with something that resembled chicken dumplings. Roasted tomatoes and peppers and rice were on the side, and more flatbread. The food once again smelled of curry. Imagining it would be the last time I saw one for a while, I ordered a cold beer. Faisal had tea.

I ate quickly and stared out the front windows while he finished. He saw me checking my watch once and hurried to finish too. When it came time to pay, I waved him off and left ten euros for a tip. The owner followed us out, bowing profusely and instructing God to watch over our every deed.

We started out of Qamishli with the radio still on and more Kurds pining away about love and heartache. The road ran straight out of town for five miles before turning southwest towards Tell Beydar. We were roughly three miles down the road when we saw a Toyota truck go by the other way with two men in it. I noticed Faisal glancing in the rearview mirror and looked back too. The driver had quickly braked to a halt and turned around.

"What's this?" I said.

"Turks."

"You're sure?"

Faisal nodded.

"Goddamn it." I got out both my Glock and Sig and checked the magazines. "This is exactly why I didn't want to be anywhere near this goddamned border."

Faisal kept glancing apprehensively in the rear-view mirror.

"Would you really shoot them?" he said with a look at me.

"You bet your ass. I'm pretty sure this isn't a welcoming party."

The driver quickly caught up with us and sped by in the other lane.

"Stop, stop!" I yelled at Faisal when the driver braked to a halt a hundred yards ahead. "Now lock your door and don't do a thing until I tell you. I'll handle this situation. And leave the car running."

Both men got out with HK33s pointed at Faisal. I darted a look at him. What the hell? Why were these men so interested in my Kurdish translator? Well, we'd have to sort that shit out down the road somewhere. Whatever their interest in Faisal, sooner or later they were going to figure out who I was, so I could pretty much count on being dragged off to one of those infamous Turkish prisons, never to be heard from again, and that wasn't going to happen.

I rolled down my window and quietly pulled on the lock handle so that the door was ready to swing open freely. Then, at thirty feet, one of the soldiers appeared to recognize me and began talking rapid fire into the receiver on his shoulder. The other one had started around towards Faisal's door and was waving for him to get out of the car.

I placed my left hand on Faisal's thigh, holding him back. My eyes were on the soldier with the radio. He had stopped talking and was now drifting cautiously my way.

Meanwhile, the one on Faisal's side of the car had grabbed the door handle and was trying to open it. With my eyes on the soldier in front of me, I flung my door open and fired both weapons simultaneously, one over the top of the vehicle and one through the rolled down window. The soldier on Faisal's side of the car went down without a shot. The other soldier had gotten off a spray of bullets in my direction before collapsing. I reflexively checked to make sure I wasn't hit anywhere before rushing over and adding a bullet to his brain cavity. I did the same with the other soldier and hurried back to the Isuzu.

"Go!" I yelled at Faisal, jumping in.

He sat there staring forward with both hands on the steering wheel.

"Go!!!" I yelled again.

He finally stepped on the accelerator. I killed the radio and watched over my shoulder. We were roughly half of a mile down that flat, straight road when I saw a black SUV pull up to the scene. It braked to a stop and two uniformed men jumped out from the front seat. Then a third man climbed out from the back seat, but nonchalantly, and wearing the red beret of an OKK officer. He walked over to one of the slain soldiers and looked down before focusing his eyes on our fleeing car. Then, just as nonchalantly, he walked back to his vehicle, pulled out a speaker and began talking into his radio.

Even at that distance, I had recognized him. Colonel Arslan. The bastard.

"Step on it!" I told Faisal. "This situation is now so totally fucked up, I can't even begin to explain it."

I kept looking back until we had taken the road to Tell Beydar, all the while stealing glances at Faisal. How the fuck had those men recognized him?

Finally, I spoke.

"What the hell was that all about, Faisal? Why were those men so interested in you?"

"Because I am Kurdish."

"Yeah? And so what? They pull over every Kurd they see these days?"

He glanced at me quickly.

"I don't know."

"Faisal. Don't fuck with me. Those men knew you. Now how?"

"I have lived in this area for many years. So they know me."

"And what? After all these years, they suddenly decide to take you in?"

"I don't know."

"You don't know."

Faisal glanced at me while driving.

"What do you want me to say? These men are no good. And they were in Syrian territory. They had no business running these patrols."

He did a double take at me.

"And they knew you too."

I stared.

"Yeah, the Turks know me too but you still haven't answered my question."

He glanced at me again.

"So if you know the Turks, then you know what happens when men like this take you in."

"Yeah. They throw you in a hole, never to be heard from again and you still haven't answered my question."

Faisal darted another look at me.

"I told you. I am Kurdish and they want to kill us all. They would never do it in plain sight because of the Americans. Like in a café or marketplace. But on a road like that? With no one watching?"

He shrugged again and let that gesture finish his thought. Hardly satisfied, I was about to grill him again when my phone rang. I saw the blocked number and answered it.

"Just checking in on me?"

"Just checking in, my ass. The word's out that somebody's been shooting wild turkeys out of season."

"Whoa! Wait a minute! Are you telling me that this shit's already come over the wire?"

"Not exactly front page news, no. I just heard some chatter. Like you can probably expect to see some wild ducks flying overhead any minute now, shitting on your head."

"Son of a bitch."

"Yeah. Better take cover. And I mean fast. I'll call you back in an hour and we'll finish this conversation."

The phone went dead. I ended the call and stared out at the barren countryside.

"Okay, Faisal. We need to find someplace to hide. I just got word that we can probably expect a Turkish airstrike."

Faisal did another double take at me.

"What have you gotten me into?"

"What have I gotten *you* into?! What have you gotten *me* into?! That shit never would have happened if they hadn't recognized you! And it sure as shit wouldn't have happened if you hadn't dragged my ass up here to the border in the first place!"

"And we wouldn't have been at the border if it wasn't for this mad scheme of yours."

"Yeah? Well you know what, Faisal? You can get out any time. In the meantime, let's quit screwing around and find some kind of cover, before both of us end up burnt flesh…We'll finish this conversation later."

"But hide where? Where are we going to hide in this countryside?"

"I don't know. Look for a tree. A barn. Anything. Just keep your eyes open and make it fast."

A half mile farther ahead, I pointed at a farm on our right.

"There. That'll work."

Faisal looked at me hesitantly.

"Just pull over, Faisal. I'm not going to shoot anybody. We'll just tell whoever it is that the Turks are after us and offer them a few hundred euros."

Faisal reluctantly turned onto a washboard road. The house was two hundred yards off. A large, open shed stood behind it. I spotted the farmer out in a field to the right of the house and waved at him.

"What do you want me to do?" Faisal said.

"Just drive around to that shed."

I kept waving until the farmer started our way. Faisal drove around in back. The shed had a corral underneath it filled with goats.

"Shit," I said and jumped out. "Go on. Get things arranged with this guy."

The farmer appeared as I was opening the double gate to the corral. He quickly protested. Meanwhile, the goats were trying to get free. I waved emphatically for Faisal to drive the Isuzu through the open gate. A mad scramble ensued with the farmer and I trying to keep the goats from escaping or being run over. Finally, the Isuzu was underneath the shed and the goats safely back inside the gate. I stood there with my money clip out and goats bleating around my feet.

"Ask him how much he wants."

Faisal spoke to the farmer. The farmer looked at me and my money clip and held up three fingers.

"Fine," I said and peeled off three hundred euros.

The farmer looked less than satisfied but took the money and tucked it away. Just then, I heard a jet scream by overhead, followed by another one. When I peeked out to have a look, the farmer went off at Faisal with both arms flailing. It didn't take a rocket scientist to figure out what he was saying.

"Fine," I said and peeled off two more bills from my money clip.

The farmer continued protesting. I tried two hundred more but it failed to quell his indignation. Exasperated, I peeled off three hundred euros more.

Okay, I gestured.

Still looking less than satisfied, he finally nodded. A thousand euros just to keep the old man quiet.

"Now tell him to go on about his business," I told Faisal.

The farmer listened to Faisal and went out the gate with a final look back our way. As he disappeared around to the front of the house, I heard the jets go overhead again and peeked out. They were low enough to make out their markings. I looked over at Faisal and shook my head.

"What?" he said.

"What? You don't have to tell me your whole life's story, Faisal. I just need you to be straight with me."

"And you should be straight with me."

"Yeah?"

"Yes."

"Okay, fine. We both have a history with the Turks. Now is there anything else I should know about you?"

"Nothing. We both have a history with the Turks, as you say."

"And that's it?"

"Yes."

"Okay. Then no more surprises, please. I don't know what kind of man you think I am but I don't particularly like killing people. Only when it's absolutely necessary."

□

Nine

While staring at each other, my phone rang again. It was David.

"You someplace safe now?" he said when I answered.

"Yeah. Safe enough. We're under a shed here."

The jets passed overhead again just then.

"You hear that?"

"I sure do."

"So? What's up?"

"Well, are you alone?"

"Not exactly."

"Probably best if you were."

"Okay."

I waved for Faisal to get into the Isuzu. When he failed to move, I gestured more emphatically. As he climbed in, I jumped the corral fence and moved off to the far end of the shed.

"Okay, shoot."

"Well, first thing, let's clear the air about this wild turkeys business."

I glanced Faisal's way and spoke quietly.

"Look, David. I told my hunting guide, I don't want anything to do with wild turkeys. I don't want to go anywhere near wild turkeys but he insisted that it was the only way to find my buck so we headed north and the next thing you know, we've got a couple of these park rangers running us down on the road. And guess what? Turns out the park rangers know my buddy here from somewhere in the past."

"You get that first hand?"

"I didn't have to. These two rangers show up and head straight for him, not me. And while I'm trying to figure out what that's all about, one of them recognizes me, I'm guessing from that hunting trip three years back, and all hell breaks loose. And I'm sure you can piece things together from there."

"I can piece things together from there, all right. I just got a call, telling me to rein in whoever's behind this shit. And that's putting it mildly."

"Hey. You set me up with this guide and now I'm wondering what I've gotten myself into. Like who the hell is he and who's he been working for? There's some kind of history there. I just don't know what."

David was silent. I looked back at Faisal. He was watching me.

"Well?" I said to David.

"Yeah. You may be right. I'll look into it. In the meantime, you may want to terminate his contract."

"Oh, great. Then what do I do?"

"I can probably find you another man out of Raqqah. I'll let you know. In the meantime, no more fucked up situations, please. You're using my hunting cabin so all this shit comes back at me."

"Trust me, my friend. That was the last thing I wanted."

"All right. I'll get back to you as soon as I have more intel."

"Roger that."

I ended the call and stood there thinking. The jets flew by again, but searching farther to the south and east now.

Goddamn it. I went back to the Isuzu. Faisal and I exchanged looks as I climbed in.

"Okay, I need to know two things, Faisal."

He stared.

"Do you really think you can help me find Saleem?"

After a moment, he nodded.

"Okay. And do you think you can do that without stabbing me in the back."

"Stab you in the back? I would never stab you in the back. What kind of man do you think *I* am?"

"I don't know, Faisal. I just sense there's something you're not telling me and it makes me uncomfortable. Like another shoe might drop any minute now."

"You want to hear my whole life story? You want to tell me your whole life story? Or do you just want me to help you find this Saleem?"

I nodded and pulled out my water bottle. While I was drinking, Faisal pulled out his. He had filled one with the leftover tea from that morning.

The jets flew overhead another time. I sat there weighing my options.

Half an hour later, it struck me that I hadn't heard the jets for a while and climbed out. More time went by without any sign of them. I jumped the fence and searched the sky but nothing. I waved for the farmer to come help us with the goats.

Five minutes later, Faisal was driving away with a final wave for the old man. The old man still appeared to be indignant. Screw him. A thousand euros. I doubted he had ever seen that much money all at once in his entire life.

Back out at the road, Faisal turned right, heading south. I watched the red, barren terrain pass by, lost in thought. Occasionally we passed a house back from the road but all in all it was a bleak land, and even more so in winter.

We reached Tell Beydar with neither one of us having said a word. I seemed to remember Tell Beydar being an archeological dig but saw nothing to suggest archeology. We did pass a large cluster of what appeared to be petroleum storage tanks. Otherwise, the village was a blip on the map.

Faisal stopped at a two pump gas station outside of town. While he fueled up, I used the outhouse in back. When I returned, I found Faisal off at a distance, talking to someone on his phone. I watched him, wondering just what the hell this man was up to.

Faisal played dumb when he returned. A man in a truck had pulled to a stop at the other gas pump while I was waiting. I told Faisal to ask him what he knew about the area. The two of them talked. The man had wary looks my way as the conversation continued.

I climbed into the Isuzu and waited. Faisal climbed in a minute later and looked over at me.

"What did they say?"

"It is as I thought. Al Hasakah remains in Daesh hands. And the road from there all the way down to Deir ez-Zor."

I pulled out my map and Faisal pointed.

"He said it was best to go on past Tall Tamr and turn south here at this road. From there? Who knows? It is possible we will have to take more back roads and ask as we go."

I studied Faisal.

"What did he really say

He started the engine.

"That it would be better if we did not go that way at all."

"I can leave you in Tall Tamr, if you want. I seem to remember there being a casino."

Very subtly, Faisal smirked, checked his rearview mirror, released the parking brake and pulled back onto the road. I stole furtive glances his way as we motored on. Maybe it was only the Turks and the trouble was behind us now, but there was more to Faisal than met the eye. Who knew what? Or what might come up next? I hated the idea of leaving his body by the side of the road, but if it came to that, I would. Nothing was going to get in the way of my mission.

Some miles farther ahead, signs of commerce began to appear alongside the road, first a shop that sold and patched tires, then a small market, then a café. Being on the main road to both Aleppo and Homs, as well as to Tall Tamr, it was to be expected.

Before long, the bustle of civilization was everywhere and Tall Tamr appeared on the horizon like a mirage, all green and verdant along the Khabur River. We passed by brilliantly white plaster buildings, adorned with palm trees and fountains. It was like a Syrian Vegas, and seemingly untouched by war.

Then five miles past the river, the barren red terrain had surrounded us again. The only remaining signs of civilization were the supply trucks coming and going and coalition forces parked here and there alongside the highway.

So why hadn't they already pushed the final twenty miles down to Al Hasakah? David had said the Americans were about to bomb the crap out of these people. There had to be some reason for the delay.

As we neared the road east to Deir ez-Zor, I had Faisal pull off to the side of the road and got out my map.

"There," I said, pointing. "I want to go this far south and see what's up."

Our eyes met.

"I think we should go on to Raqqah for the night and try to learn more about Daesh movements before approaching ez-Zor."

"We can still reach Raqqah from this direction. I want see. Let's go."

Faisal stared at me with one of those looks that you always remember when it's too late. When you're looking back and wondering why you hadn't listened to your own gut before disaster struck. And yet I was determined to press forward and pointed again.

Faisal let his gaze linger for another moment before pulling the car back onto the road. I folded the map and leaned back in the seat. Here and there, we passed a home with a well and crops growing around it. Sometimes it was a gathering of homes and fields of crops.

Then we entered a terrain of rolling hillocks, the hillocks all bunched together closely so that we went along rising and descending swiftly. There was not a sign of civilization anywhere around us.

A few miles farther ahead, I noticed Faisal glancing in the rearview mirror and looked back. A black SUV had appeared over a hillock, a mile or so behind us. I watched it quickly gaining. Soon, they were only a few hillocks back; close enough to tell that they were all bearded and wearing black.

I got the Sig out, cocked it and looked back again.

"Maybe we should have gone straight to Raqqah," I said.

Faisal darted a look at me.

"What do you wish me to do?"

"Don't know yet. Let's see how many of them there are first."

We had driven another half a mile when the SUV came over a hillock and was on our tail. I counted three men, and not your typical ISIS trash. By the brand new Suburban alone, you knew these men were somewhere higher up in the food chain.

The driver quickly sped alongside us and the other two men started shouting through their open windows, pointing for us to pull over. When Faisal failed to slow down, the two men pointed their AKs. Faisal was glancing nervously between them and the road ahead.

"What do you wish me to do?" he said again.

"Stay calm, first thing."

"They are going to shoot us."

"They're not going to shoot us. They want me alive so they can videotape taking my head off."

I pulled the Glock out of my waist holster, cocked it out of sight and set it on Faisal's lap.

"Remember 'you watch my back and I watch yours'?"

He nodded.

"Well, this is where it gets real, partner."

He glanced at me.

"So here's what we're going to do. Once you pull over, one of them will come to your door, one of them to mine. The other one will stand in front, covering for them. Whatever they say, let me get out first. As soon as you hear my door close, you open yours and shoot the man on your side. I will take it from there. Just make sure you hear my door close first. I need to have a clear shot at the man in front."

I waited until Faisal met my eyes again.

"And make sure you kill him. If it's possible, put a bullet into his head. If not, shoot for the heart. And if he's not dead, keep shooting until he is. You have thirteen rounds in there."

A hail of bullets went off just then and both of us looked that way. The men had shot over the top of the car and now had their rifles pointed at the tires. Faisal gestured to let them know, okay.

Our eyes met again.

"Calm," I said. "Pretend it's all happening in slow motion."

After a moment, Faisal nodded and started to slow down. I shoved the Sig back into my vest holster.

Once we were stopped, the driver pulled his SUV around in front of us, blocking our way, and all three of them jumped out. We watched them approach our car warily with their AKs pointed.

As expected, one man came towards Faisal's door and one towards mine. Both of them were shouting in Arabic and waving the barrel of their guns. I held up my hands in mock surrender and started to open the door. The man kept yelling while backing away.

Once I was out of the car, he gestured for me to turn around. I stole a glance at the man in front of the car before pushing the door shut. Faisal's door opened in that instant and the Glock fired, distracting the man behind me. I used that split second to spin and put a shot into his forehead. The man at the front of the car had gotten off a burst of fire from his AK before I fired at him. By the time the first bullet struck his chest, I had fired three more times, hitting him twice more in the chest and once in the face. He was on the ground, moaning and reflexively trying to reach for the AK.

I got down in a crouch and peeked under the car. The other man was lying dead at Faisal's feet. His AK had never gone off so Faisal's aim must have been true.

The man next to me appeared to be dead but I stood up and put another bullet into his brain cavity, just to be sure. Then I walked over to the man lying in front and kicked the rifle out of his reach.

When I stood over him, he tried to spit through the blood in his teeth. Had it not been for Faisal being there, I would have made him suffer. Instead, I calmly pointed the Sig at his forehead, paused long enough for him to contemplate his fate and pulled the trigger.

I looked back at Faisal. He was staring down at the man he had killed. There was a single red hole in his forehead. The Glock hung limply at Faisal's side.

I went over to him and our eyes met. I took the Glock from his hand and shoved it back into my waist holster.

"You're hit," I said.

Faisal looked at his left arm. He had taken a bullet roughly six inches below his shoulder. I quickly ripped a piece of cloth from the dead man at our feet and tied off Faisal's arm.

"Are you okay?"

He stared at me vacantly.

"Come," I said. "We need to get out of here. Gather up the guns and ammunition and throw everything into the back of the Isuzu."

I had to encourage him with a pull on his right arm.

While Faisal gathered up the weapons, I walked over and rifled through the clothing of the man out in front of our car. Everything about him suggested that he was the leader. Having found an iPhone, I used it to take pictures of all three men, then dragged the bodies to the side of the road and pulled their car out of the way.

Before returning to the Isuzu, I checked in the back of the Suburban and found a crate of bullets. Faisal was behind the wheel when I walked back. I set the crate in the backseat.

"Better let me drive."

He stared for a moment before scooting over. I handed him the iPhone

"Check for any recent texts and phone calls. I want to see if this guy was in contact with Saleem."

Faisal searched my eyes before taking the phone and scrolling through the text messages. He had gone forward several messages when he quickly scrolled back towards the top with a look of concern.

"What?" I said. "Is there a message from Saleem?"

Faisal looked at me and nodded.

"Yes, but there is more."

"Like what?"

He turned the phone screen towards me.

"This message?"

"Yeah?"

"It is in Turkish."

"In Turkish? So what the hell does it say?"

"It's a description of where to find us."

"Where to find us? And does it say who it's from?"

"No, it's a blocked number but it seems to have come from the military."

"Why do you say that?"

"From the way it describes our position. 'Have taken road south, eight kilometers due west on M4 from Tall Tamr'."

I looked over my shoulder and all around me, puzzled.

"The man at the gas station, maybe?"

"No," Faisal said. "He did not follow us."

"Then maybe somebody else did."

"I don't remember there being any cars. Definitely not when we pulled over to consult the map and made our turn."

"No, you're right. I remember a couple of trucks going by but…"

I had been sitting there puzzled for a few seconds more when it suddenly hit me.

"Son of a bitch!"

I quickly started the engine, dropped the Isuzu into gear and sped off with a look up through the windshield.

"What?" Faisal said.

"Colonel Arslan. He must have sent a drone to search for us."

"I don't understand. If there' a drone, why not just send a missile down to kill us?"

"No...no. He could claim jurisdiction up by the border but not this far south. Besides, a drone strike would be too obvious. It would have to be a state actor. And there would be markings on the bomb. It would all point back to the Turks."

"But sending Daesh to kill us? How does that make sense?"

I looked over at him.

"You have to be kidding me, Faisal. You know the Turks would get into bed with anyone to have their way...Anyway, let's get back to those hostiles we just wasted. You say they were communicating with Saleem."

He nodded.

"And what did the text say?"

He shrugged.

"It seems that this Turkish person had provided Saleem with our location and he forwarded it to those men, because they were already on their way back to Deir ez-Zor. And then they messaged Saleem back, saying that they had spotted the infidels and were closing in fast. And Saleem had texted them back, saying that he prayed for Allah to be with them and that it would please the prophet Mohamed very much to have more infidels to behead. And then..."

"And then we wasted them...All right. Attach the photos I took and tell that SOB, 'I just sent your friends to hell so you'd better come looking for me yourself next time. That or send better men'."

Faisal stared again before typing the message, then paused with another look at me before hitting the send button.

It took a minute but a message came back.

"It's a video," Faisal said.

"So play it."

He did and we watched Saleem brandishing his knife and shouting into the camera.

"What did he say?" I asked when the video was done.

Faisal shrugged.

"He is coming to cut your head off, basically."

"Good," I said. "Now break up that phone and start throwing the pieces out the window."

Faisal did as instructed and rolled the window back up when he was done. We drove in silence for a spell.

"We need to find you a doctor," I said with a look at him.

I handed him my map.

"Show me the way back to Raqqah."

☐

Ten

Some miles down the road, the hillock country gave way to the same bleak, reddish terrain. I saw peasants here and there, working the parched land.

We soon reached a crossroad heading south towards Raqqah and the Euphrates. I turned right with a glance over at Faisal. His head was back and his eyes closed. His face had grown ashen. No doubt the adrenalin had worn off and the pain was setting in.

I stole another glance his way as I drove. Well, whatever there was to Faisal's past, we had been through battle together and were brothers now. Anyway, he needed that bullet removed and I owed him that much.

Driving along, I smelled the approaching river well before I saw it. The scent of reeds and things rotting came on the wind. For all that was barren about the desert, it was antiseptic.

There was again a mirage like sense of an oasis rising up on the horizon. Then I saw trees and signs of civilization off in the distance. Faisal sensed the change too and opened his eyes.

"How do you feel?" I said.

He placed his palm to his forehead.

"There is fever."

I nodded.

"We need to get that bullet out of you. Didn't you say you had family in Raqqah?"

"If they are still there, they would be in Al-Mashlab."

"Where's that?"

"Up ahead. In the southeast district."

"Do you have an address?"

"I can find it. Follow this road. It's near the edge of the city."

We passed through farmland and increasing suburbs for ten miles. Then the city skyline rose up in the distance. As we entered the outskirts of the city, I looked at Faisal.

"Is this Al-Mashlab?"

He nodded, looking saddened to see in ruins.

"So which way now?"

He pointed left and right until we had come to a stop in front of a five-story apartment building. The roof of the building was gone and little remained of the walls.

"This?" I said again.

He barely nodded. I pulled on the parking brake and got out my phone.

"All right. We need to find a doctor. A clinic. Anything. Do you have any ideas?"

"There was a family doctor, but who knows in this destruction?"

I had Googled a map of Raqqah as he spoke and saw that there was a hospital about three miles from our present position. Or there had been a hospital. I was not too keen on the idea of walking into one, given all the potential scrutiny, but Faisal's wound wouldn't wait. We needed to get him fixed.

I had released the parking brake and started slowly in that direction when a burst of gunfire went off in the distance. It was followed by several more in rapid succession. Faisal had closed his eyes and opened them again.

"I thought the coalition forces had already taken the city."

"That is what I had been told."

"Well, somebody didn't get the memo."

We listened to what sounded like a running battle now, and in the general direction of the hospital. With increasing concern, I continued forward, turning this way and that amidst the ruined city, working my way towards where I hoped to find help, only to spot a barricade, roughly five hundred yards farther up a long avenue. I stopped and stared. The two soldiers manning the barricade were staring back.

"They look like coalition forces," Faisal said.

"Yeah, looks that way to me."

I reached over the seat, grabbed my pack and dug out the binoculars.

"Americans," I said, setting the binoculars down and looking over at Faisal. "It's probably our best shot at getting you patched up. You have a problem with that?"

"No. Do you?"

I shrugged.

"A little, yeah, but I don't think we have much choice."

I stared forward again.

"Look, once we get close, I'll go up on foot and see what I can find out. You stay in the car. These boys are probably plenty nervous about the idea of a suicide bomber driving up."

Faisal leaned back and closed his eyes again. I eased forward at ten miles an hour. At 300 yards, the two soldiers pointed their weapons. I rolled down my window and waved, then pulled to a stop at 100 yards and slowly got out with my hands in the air.

"Jeffers, captain! 5th SFG ODA! Here with a man in need of medical attention!"

"That all sounds real good!" one of the soldiers yelled back. "Now you just keep coming forward with your hands up in the air!"

At 50 yards, the soldier told me stop.

"Now open your jacket."

I did.

"And the vest."

I did.

"All right," he said, waving me forward. "But slowly."

"ID?" I said from 20 yards and pointed at one of my zippered pockets.

The soldier nodded and I got it out. They both had their eyes more on me than the ID as I continued forward.

Finally, when I was close enough for them to see, they both quickly saluted.

"Sorry, sir. Just being careful. There's still a lot of hajis running around this place."

As he said that, we heard more gunfire in the distance.

"Understood, soldier. What the hell happened? I thought you boys had this city mopped up."

"Mostly, but there's still pockets of those hostiles here and there. Like to nuke the goddamned place but we've got orders to protect the civilians."

I looked around at the wasteland.

"Who the hell would still be living here?"

"Enough of them. The poor SOBs don't have much of a choice. Boxed in by Assad on one end and ISIS on the other. If they're lucky enough to get out of here, they end up in a refugee camp, that or a leaky boat across the Mediterranean."

We stood there staring at each other.

"Cole Jeffers," I said, holding out my hand.

"Oh yeah. Private Cooper. 1st Brigade Combat Team, 25th Infantry."

"Private Stanley," the other soldier said, shaking my hand.

"So what do you got?" Cooper said, nodding his chin back at the car.

"Kurdish guide. We ran into three hostiles back up the road and he took a bullet for me."

"Whoa, sir," Stanley said. "So did you waste them?"

I nodded.

"He killed one. I killed the other two. Anyway, I need to get that bullet out of Faisal's arm. You guys happen to have a medic handy?"

"Yeah, sure. We're bivouacked in an apartment building around the corner. You'll need to clear it with Sgt. Benson but I'm sure he'll be glad to help."

"Okay. I'm going back to grab the car. You boys show me where."

"Will do, sir."

Back in the Isuzu, I glanced over at Faisal. His head was against the headrest with his eyes closed and jaw clenched. I patted him gently on the leg.

"Hang in there. These boys are going to help get you patched up."

I started the car and eased forward until I was in front of the barricade. Cooper and Stanley moved it to one side and allowed us to pass. Cooper came up to my open window and lowered his head to have a look at Faisal.

"I'll walk you in, sir. Somebody's bound to get itchy, seeing a strange vehicle."

"Thanks."

Cooper went out ahead on foot. I eased forward behind him. At the next corner, Cooper turned right. A hundred yards farther up the street, he waved me to the curb.

"Ranger. 5th SFG ODA," he told the two soldiers guarding the entrance. "His guide took a bullet. Is Polanski inside?"

One of the guards gave him a thumbs up.

"And Sgt. Benson?"

The guard gave him another thumbs up. Cooper waved for me to join him. I got out and went around to give Faisal a hand.

"I snatched three AKs and some ammunition from those hajis," I told Cooper with a nod at the back cargo area. "I'd like to keep them if nobody minds."

"I'll make sure they don't go nowhere," Cooper said. He called to one of the guards. "Gage. Show these men where to find Polanski."

Cooper saluted me and I saluted back.

"Better get back to my post, sir. You're in good hands here."

I was giving Faisal a hand up the steps when he froze in place. I followed his gaze down the block. A young boy was standing about a hundred yards off, staring back. He was a handsome young lad, no more than eight or nine years old, with hair and clothes all disheveled.

"We call him our little rascal," Gage said. "Lost his whole family in a bombing raid. Won't let anyone near him. The local aid people caught him once but he just escaped and came back. I guess he believes his family's going reappear someday. We leave food out for him and stuff. Gave him some blankets and clothes. Sad, but what are you going to do?"

Faisal stood there, still frozen in place. I shook him gently.

"Hey, partner. Better get you inside."

Faisal came along, but with his gaze still fixed on the kid. I looked back once before we disappeared inside. The boy hadn't moved.

"This way, sir," Gage said. "HQ's in the basement." He led us down a hallway and then down a flight of stairs. "Polanski!" he called out.

"Over here!" Polanski called back.

We found him in a makeshift med ward, bandaging up a soldier's foot.

Gage introduced me and Polanski saluted, then had a closer look at Faisal's arm.

"Bullet?" he said.

I nodded.

"Okay. Have a seat and hang loose. I'll be done here in a minute."

I helped Faisal get settled onto a cot and looked back at Gage.

"If you're done with me, sir, I'll be heading back out front."

"Just one more thing, soldier. I didn't see many vehicles out on the street. You have some kind of underground parking nearby?"

"Yeah. Next building over. That's where we keep most of our rigs."

"So, would you mind…"

"No problem, sir. I can move it down there for you. Are the keys still inside?"

I nodded.

"I'll let Sgt. Benson know you're here."

Gage saluted and left

I had been standing there for another minute when I felt a shadow over my shoulder and looked back. A tall, sandy haired soldier was standing behind me, high cheek bones and intense, narrow set eyes. Everything about him shouted Scandinavian roots. Pale skinned, taciturn, sensible and straightforward. His ancestors had herded reindeer and fished for herring.

"Sgt. Benson."

"Captain Jeffers. 5th SFG ODA."

He saluted.

"Private Gage told me you were here. What's going on?"

"My guide here took a bullet. Just looking to get him patched up."

Benson had a look at Faisal and back at me.

"If you don't mind me asking, what's your mission?"

"I'm really not at liberty to discuss that, sergeant."

I unzipped one of my sleeve pockets and showed him both IDs. Benson gave special attention to the CIA credential before handing it back.

"You at liberty to tell me how this happened?" he said with a nod at Faisal.

"We were coming down from the Turkish border and ran into an ISIS patrol. Three of them."

"I take it that you terminated these hostiles."

"You would be correct in that assumption."

"Okay. We patch up your friend. Then what?"

"We could use something to eat and a place to sleep for the night."

Benson nodded again.

"Take care of your friend here and have someone find me. We'll see what we can do about a hot and a cot."

"Thanks, sergeant."

Benson nodded and left. I sat down with my back against the wall and waited. A few minutes later, Polanski was sending the soldier off with his wounded foot.

"All right, let's have a look," he said to Faisal.

Polanski rolled his stool over and had a cursory look Faisal's wound.

"You real fond of this sweater and coat?" he asked.

"They are the only clothes I have."

"Oookaaayyy. Let's get these off of you then...Hey, Barnes!" Polanski called over his shoulder. "Get me some fresh swabs...And, hey! Bring a blanket too!"

I stood up and gave Faisal a hand with pulling the coat off and the sweater up over his head. He winced but otherwise didn't let out a sound.

Faisal unbuttoned his cotton shirt with his right hand. Barnes returned with the blanket and swabs.

"Please," Faisal said.

I helped him remove the shirt and Barnes placed the blanket around his naked chest. Polanski probed gently around the raw wound.

"Missed the bone. That's good."

He looked up into Faisal's eyes.

"I'm going to have to dig it out. I can give you some morphine and a local but I don't really have a way to knock you out. Not without sending you over to our field hospital."

Faisal glanced at me. I made clear with an imperceptible shake of my head. No. Faisal looked back at Polanski.

"It will be all right."

"It's going to hurt."

Faisal nodded.

Polanski dug around in his medical cart, produced a vial of morphine and a syringe, gave Faisal a shot of that and dug around again for the local. With another look into Faisal's eyes, he began to prick gently around the wound with his needle.

"All right," he said, setting the needle down. "Let that local set in for a minute. I'll go sterilize some instruments."

Polanski went off to the other end of his med ward. I grabbed a chair and sat down at Faisal's side.

"You did good, partner."

He stared back.

"I'd say you deserve a medal but I'm guessing that's not what you want to hear."

He stared back.

"Look. I can understand how you feel, killing people, but men like that? They'd just go on killing more innocent human beings. The world's a better place without him in it."

Faisal had started to say something when Polanski returned with a tray of instruments and swabs.

"Let me see your eyes?" he said, sitting down next to Faisal. "You feeling the morphine yet?"

Faisal nodded.

Polanski probed around the bullet hole.

"Feel that?"

Faisal shook his head.

"All right. Best to get this over with."

He held out a wooden tongue depressor and Faisal clenched it between his teeth. Polanski poured some antiseptic onto several swabs, cleansed the wound, had one more look into Faisal's eyes and began to probe. Faisal jerked when the forceps penetrated his flesh but did not say a word. I held his other arm. His entire body had knotted up from the pain.

Polanski was in there a good thirty seconds before retracting the bullet with his forceps.

"All done," he said, dropping it onto the tray. "You okay, buddy?"

Faisal nodded. Polanski applied more antiseptic, wiped that entire area of Faisal's arm clean and began to apply a bandage.

"You allergic to penicillin?" Polanski asked him.

"I don't know. I don't think so."

"Probably not. I'll give you a supply. With a wound that deep, it's probably best."

Polanski finished the bandage and went off with his dirty tray. He returned a minute later with a prescription bottle.

"Two a day until they're gone. Otherwise, you should be good to go."

"Thank you," Faisal said.

"No problem."

"Sgt. Benson said to find him when we were done."

Polanski pointed.

"See that man at the desk over there?"

I nodded.

"Check with him. He'll know where to find the Sarge."

"Thanks. And thanks again for taking care of us."

"No problem."

Polanski rolled off with his stool. I stood up with a hand on Faisal's good shoulder.

"Wait here. I'll arrange things. Probably best if you stay off your feet for a spell."

Faisal nodded and closed his eyes. I walked over to the soldier at the desk.

"I'm looking for Sgt. Benson."

"Captain Jeffers?"

I nodded. He saluted.

"The Sarge said you'd be looking for him. Through that door over there. You should find him behind his desk."

I worked my way through the human traffic and tapped on Benson's door. He looked up from some paperwork and waved me in.

"Have a seat."

I did. Benson studied me.

"Your man all right?"

I nodded.

"Thanks for your help."

He nodded.

"These hostiles you wasted today. You happen to gather any intel while you were at it?"

I shook my head.

"Phones? Anything?"

I shook my head.

"Didn't figure I had time for any of that. Middle of the road and who knew what else might be coming up on our tail? They could have been part of a caravan for all I knew."

"You had time to gather their weapons."

"They were lying on the ground so we grabbed them and got our asses out of there."

Benson kept staring.

"Look, you want answers? Their bodies are probably still lying there, five miles up the Tall Tamr road. Their SUV too."

"Fair enough. Anything else I can do for you besides a hot and a cot?"

"Well, I was wondering why you boys haven't pushed all the way down to Al Hasakah yet."

He nodded his head slowly while studying me.

"Those decisions are made higher up the chain of command. I'm sure they have good reasons. I can tell you this much. ISIS is down to its last stand and a wild animal is dangerous when cornered."

"They could just as easily use the opportunity to melt back into the countryside."

"Your concerns are duly noted, Captain...So, any idea where you're headed next?"

"Not sure. Depends on what I learn here."

"Not much to learn."

"Okay."

"Is that it, then?"

I nodded. Benson nodded back and stood up.

"I'll show you to the mess hall."

I followed him out the door.

"Talmadge," he said to the kid at the desk. "Have someone arrange a room for the captain here. Two cots. And make sure there's a heater in the room."

"Yes sir."

"Oh, Sergeant. One other thing," I said. "Any way you can have someone clean up my partner's coat and sweater? It's the only thing he has to wear. I hate to give it back to him with all that blood."

Benson looked at Talmadge.

"Consider it done, sir," Talmadge said.

Benson waved me down a hallway. We passed a number of small rooms that mostly served as storage, then came to what looked like a small auditorium at the other end. There were scattered tables and a handful of soldiers eating.

"Harris in there's the cook. Might not be much left at this hour but whatever he's got, you're welcome to it."

Benson led me back to Talmadge's desk. Another private stood there with him.

"Carpenter here will show you up to a room."

"Thank you, Sergeant."

He studied me for a moment before heading back to his office. I looked at Carpenter.

"I understand you have someone with you, sir."

"Yeah. Show me the room and I'll come back down to grab him."

We passed an elevator that no longer functioned and started up a wide, stone staircase.

"Down here, sir," Carpenter said on the second floor. "Figured you'd prefer being as close to ground level as possible."

He looked over his shoulder.

"Not that we've had any incoming lately, but you really don't want to be anywhere near the roof."

Three doors down, he pushed one open.

"I dug up two extra blankets but this propane heater will keep you plenty warm."

I had a look around and nodded. The windows were boarded up with plywood. Otherwise the room was intact.

"Bathroom?" I said.

"Oh yeah. There's a john down the hall. The water doesn't work but there's a barrel of water and a bucket. You know the drill."

"Yeah, thanks."

"Anything else, sir?"

"No, this is fine. I'll head down with you and grab my translator."

We started back the way we had come.

Down on the first floor, I thanked Carpenter and Talmadge again and headed off to the mess hall. The cook was cleaning up tables when I walked in.

"Good evening, sir. What can I get you?"

"What's simple, soldier?"

"Well, I've got chicken and some of that local flat bread left over. I could whip you up a sandwich of sorts easily enough."

"Sounds good. Can you make it two? I've got a translator. Just had a bullet dug out of him but I suspect he's going to have an appetite before the night's through."

"You got it, sir."

"All right. I'll take him up to our room and come back."

Faisal appeared to be asleep when I sat back down next to him. After several seconds, he opened his eyes and looked over at me.

"How are you feeling?"

"Better. Thank you. Thank you for taking care of me."

"Yeah. I watch your back, you watch mine."

Faisal stared back with a deep unspoken sadness. I was reminded of that ragamuffin kid outside. Why Faisal had fixated on him was one more question that wanted answers, and one more question I wasn't going to ask, lest the questions turn back on me.

"So, listen," I said. "The sergeant provided us with a room upstairs. Let's get you settled and I'll come back down to grab some food."

I helped Faisal to his feet. He still had the blanket wrapped around him.

"Looks like someone already came by to grab your coat and sweater."

"Yes, thank you again."

"Yeah. It's not exactly a great look, you walking around like you've been bloodied in a battle."

Faisal wobbled a bit on his feet.

"You all right?"

"Yes, yes. It's only the morphine. It has made me sleepy."

"Yeah, but thank god for that crap, huh?"

"Yes. Thank god."

I helped Faisal up to the room and pointed down the hallway.

"There's a bathroom at the end, and a barrel of water."

"Thank you. I think I will go there first."

I watched to make sure he was all right on his own before heading back down to the mess hall. Ten minutes later, I was settling in with our sandwiches, two bottled waters and two cookies.

The room glowed dimly from the propane heater. We ate in silence. The boarded up window stood as a reminder of the destroyed city outside.

Faisal set his sandwich down after a couple of bites.

"For tomorrow," he said and pulled the extra blankets over him.

He lay there with eyes closed, looking weary of me and the mission and the world in general.

After a moment, he opened his eyes and said, "Thank you," again.

I nodded.

While finishing the sandwich, my thoughts turned to the events of that day. I felt no particular remorse for wasting a couple of Turks. What I didn't like was this Colonel Arslan following me around. He was way off the reservation, which suggested that this had become personal. The man had said as much, the last time we had parted. And even that didn't bother me much. It was the part about him providing intel to ISIS that troubled me. In my efforts to find Saleem, that could definitely become a problem.

As to Saleem, his completely unhinged display of rage today was revealing; not at all like the bloodless man who had impassively taken Tom's head off. It figured. I knew the type and had seen them in every combat zone, from the Balkans to Iraq to Afghanistan. Real tough, until you got them alone in a room somewhere. I couldn't wait to see him tied up in a chair. Show him the video of Tom's last minute on earth. Let that sink into his zealotry riddled brain while I sharpened my knife. I'd show him about taking people's heads off.

I looked over at Faisal while he slept, feeling a twinge of guilt over my earlier thoughts. I had considered dumping his body by the side of the roadside somewhere. Had he sensed that? And realized how close he had come to death? I still had major questions about his past and worried that it might somehow jeopardize my mission, but we were brothers in arms now and nothing could change that.

☐

Eleven

I had opened my bottle of water and started to drink when Faisal's voice broke the silence.

"Why?" he said.

I finished the drink and looked over at him. He turned his head to look at me.

"Why what?" I said.

"Why are you so intent on killing this man?"

Faisal's face glowed from the flames. I stared back, annoyed by his question.

"He killed someone dear to you," Faisal said, answering for me.

I kept staring. Faisal turned his face back towards the ceiling.

"There are many here who have suffered the same fate. Whole families stolen from them. Everything lost in this war. Their homes. Their livelihoods. It is the sorrow of a thousand lifetimes. All in one heart."

I kept staring, not at all keen on where this discussion was headed.

"It is all right," he said after a spell. "I understand. Hatred is a powerful flame. So powerful, it can consume even the best of men."

He looked over at me one more time before closing his eyes. I sat there chewing on his words. Hatred is a powerful flame. Okay. Well let me tell you what I hate, partner. I hate people saying shit like that. I already have enough crap rolling around in my head. I don't need to be chewing on someone's sermon.

Alone, I found my thoughts in the usual pinball machine. The memory of Emine was my only lifeline. God, the way her hand had reached out desperately as I got up to leave.

Don't worry, darling. You don't know it yet, but I'll be back to save you. I'll sweep you far, far away somewhere, where we can leave this mad world completely behind us. As soon as I'm done washing my hands in blood.

I looked over at Faisal. Hatred is a powerful flame. Okay, my friend, but please don't meddle with this fever inside of me. You get in the way of my mission and you'll find yourself dead.

I went to use the bathroom before crawling into bed. Faisal appeared to be out when I looked over at him. I wondered again about his back story. No wife, no kids, a life seemingly in ruins. Something terrible must have happened. Then why wasn't he angry and filled with vengeance like me?

Off in the distance, I heard several bursts of gunfire. Somewhere out in that ruined city, men were fighting. A thousand years these people were known to hold a grudge. A thousand years, waiting to repay the last slight.

So what's the difference between you and them, Blake? A thousand years? A different god? I was working on that question when weariness overcame me and I finally fell asleep.

When I reawakened in the morning, Faisal wasn't there. I assumed he had gone off to use the bathroom and lay there waiting for him to return. When he did, it was with two coffees. He handed me one along with several packets of cream and sugar.

"I remembered you liking it sweet."

"Yeah, thanks."

I took the sugar and creamer, added two of each and had a big gulp.

"I see you got your coat and sweater."

"Yes, thank you. A soldier dropped them off early this morning."

He showed me how the blood was gone, then fingered the bullet hole.

"And how's your arm?"

"Much better, thank you."

We stared. The grim events of the previous day still hung in the air.

"Have you eaten?" I asked.

"No. I waited for you."

"All right. Let me use the bathroom and we'll head down to grab some grub."

Faisal was sitting on his cot when I returned. He stood up and joined me on the way downstairs. Talmadge saluted as we passed by his desk.

"Did you get a good night's sleep, sir?"

"Yeah, thanks, soldier."

The corridor leading down to the mess hall was crowded with passing soldiers. Inside, we grabbed two plates and got in line. There were scrambled eggs, hash browns, bacon and pancakes. I grabbed a little of each and headed for a vacant table. Faisal joined me a moment later, with everything but the bacon.

So maybe he was a Muslim. Or a Reformed Muslim. Whatever it was, I still hadn't seen him pray.

Our eyes met several times while we ate. Finally, Faisal wiped his mouth and spoke.

"What is the game plan for today?"

I looked up from a bite of pancakes. The game plan. I had to force back a smile.

"Head south."

"And then?"

I shrugged.

"I don't know. We'll have to see what happens...Look, I wouldn't be upset if you opted out right here. I imagine I could get you on a flight back to Mosul."

Faisal stared for a moment and returned to his meal. I shrugged and returned to my own.

When I was finished, I wiped my mouth and stood up.

"I'll be back. I need to talk with the sergeant."

Talmadge saluted again when I walked up. I returned the salute.

"Where can I find Sgt. Benson?"

"I believe he's out in front, sir."

I thanked him and headed up to the first floor. Benson was standing in the street when I walked outside. The SUV we had encountered on the road was there too, along with a transport truck. The three dead bodies were in the back of the truck. Benson stared as I walked up.

"This look familiar to you?" he said.

I nodded. He kept staring.

"And you're saying you just stumbled into them."

"Actually, they overtook us on the road. Had us pull over. And then…"

I shrugged. He nodded.

"Hell of a catch."

"Why?"

"That one there's Abu Muhammad al-Aaloua. Third or fourth in the ISIS leadership hierarchy, depending on how you're counting."

I shrugged again.

"I didn't bother getting their names and ranks before I shot them…You got a problem with any of this, sergeant?"

"I don't, but there's an American journalist who probably would. If he still had a head to complain with. They took it off last night and posted a video inline, saying it was revenge for what the Americans did to their people yesterday."

I stared.

"You have any idea how they knew this encounter went down? Or that it was done by Americans?"

I shrugged.

"Called ahead when they spotted us? I don't know."

"Yeah. I found three bodies but only two cell phones. And neither one of them had anything on it about spotting you."

"I don't know what to tell you, Sergeant."

Benson nodded his head and pulled me aside.

"Look. I'm catching flak from the people above me, wanting to know just who the hell you are and what you're doing in our theater of operation."

"And like I've already said..."

"Yeah, I know. You're not at liberty to discuss your op with me. Well let me level with you about something, captain. You wanted to know why we haven't already pushed down to Al Hasakah? It's because we received some intel a few weeks back that ISIS has been working on a chemical weapons program. We don't know what or where or when just yet, but let's say we lay waste to some target with a drone strike and it happens to be a chemical dump? We could be laying waste to the entire countryside, villages included."

"Yeah. Sounds like bad business."

"Real bad business...But you don't know anything about that."

"Not a thing."

"But if you did happen to learn something, I'd be the first one to know, yeah?"

"Absolutely. If I heard any shit like that, I'd pass it straight up the chain of command."

Benson kept staring and nodding.

"You mind me asking where you're headed?"

"I guess south. Any fresh intel you can share with me about the road from here down to ez-Zor?"

"Not much. It's like everywhere else around here. Mostly clear." He pointed his chin at the three dead bodies. "Until it isn't."

"All right, Sergeant. Guess I'll grab my guide and be on my way. Any chance you can have our rig dragged back up here street side?"

"It'll be waiting for you by the time you return."

"Thank you."

He turned his attention back to the SUV. It was getting a going over while Benson watched.

Back inside, I grabbed Faisal and a handful of bottled waters on our way out the door. The truck with the bodies was gone by the time we walked outside. The Isuzu was fifty feet up the street.

"Thanks again for the hot and the cot, Sergeant."

He saluted and watched us walk by.

"You okay to drive?" I asked Faisal as we neared the Isuzu.

As I had started around towards the shotgun side, Faisal stopped in his tracks. It was that young boy again, standing down the street and staring back.

Faisal started up the street towards him. The boy remained motionless until Faisal was within a hundred feet or so and then fled into the bombed out wreckage of an adjacent building. I walked down and gently placed a hand on Faisal's shoulder.

"Come, my friend. We've got to move out."

Faisal kept staring at where the boy had disappeared.

"Come," I said again. "We can't save everybody."

I pulled on Faisal's arm and he reluctantly came along.

"You're sure you're okay to drive?" I said.

He nodded.

"All right. Give it a go but if you're arm gets sore, just let me know and I'll take over."

Faisal went through his ritual of checking mirrors and buckling up before making a U-turn in the road. He kept looking in his rearview mirror, his mind obviously still on the boy.

As soon as we were safely out of Benson's sight, I had Faisal pull over and went around to the back. Faisal studied me when I climbed back in with one of the AKs, the crate of bullets and several empty ammo magazines. I set everything at my feet and waved at the road ahead.

"You know the way?"

"The road is better on the other side of the river. Do you think the drone is still watching us?"

"Doubt it."

I looked over at him.

"I had them park the Isuzu underground last night. They were bound to lose interest. Besides, a drone can't stay aloft forever."

I waved at the road ahead again.

"Let's just keep moving. That's our best defense."

Faisal pulled back onto the road. I checked the action on the rifle and got back to loading magazines. Faisal stole another glance my way while driving.

At the base of the bridge, we came to a checkpoint. I set the rifle down at my feet and got out my ID. Faisal took it and handed it to the soldier at his window. The soldier had a look and quickly saluted.

"Sorry, sir. Be on your way."

"Thank you, soldier."

Faisal handed the ID back to me and started across the long bridge. I tucked the ID away and resumed filling empty magazines. The river wound off to our east and west in a shroud of trees and farmland, the land around it starkly rich and fertile compared to the utterly barren terrain just beyond it. It was as if the gods had dipped their brush in green paint and swept a meandering line across the desert. The river explained Babylon and empires.

At the far end of the bridge, Faisal turned east and we wound alongside the river. Several small villages came and went. Then Faisal took a crossroad away from the river and got onto the main highway.

My phone rang a minute later. It was a blocked number. I answered, expecting it was David.

"Yeah."

"What the hell's happening down there? Did you hear that heads are rolling?"

"Yeah."

"Yeah? And so?"

"So, shit happens."

"Shit happens. Well, forget the game warden and folks hunting without a license. I'm about to have the interior secretary up my ass."

"A buck went wild on us so we shot it."

"Shit…Look, my friend. I don't mind you using my cabin, but when it starts causing me trouble, that's the end of it. Understood?"

"Sure. But listen, there's more."

"Like what?"

"Like we had another wild turkey flying overhead late yesterday. A headless turkey, if you get my drift, and that turkey was busy warning that buck about us being here. Are you with me here?"

There was silence.

"If I get your meaning, it doesn't make any sense."

"Bullshit. Just go back three years and think common foes."

"Well, if that's true, we've got a whole new set of problems, don't we?"

"You do, not me."

"No, we both do, partner."

"Well, whatever. Back to the headless turkeys."

"Yeah. I'll look into it. In the meantime, get your quota and get out of there. Any more shit comes back my way and I'm out of options. Understood?"

"Understood…Anything more on that other issue?"

"Nothing yet."

"Okay."

There was more silence.

"I'll be back at you as soon as I know something."

After a moment, the line went dead. I set the phone down, ticked off about the ass chewing but understanding David's position. It was one thing to catch flak about some Turk mischief up by the border. Everyone knew the Turks were ruffians. Always causing one diplomatic scuffle or another. A few months earlier, a gang of them had roughed up a group of peaceful protestors outside their DC embassy. The Turks knocking Americans around on the streets of our own country? When it went viral, you could have lynched one of them and not found much sympathy. But when hajis started beheading Western journalists and care workers? And sending out videos of it? That was front page news and a real burr in the saddle of the spy agencies.

Faisal looked over at me. I glanced back while pulling out my map. I already had Saleem's attention. My focus now was on leaving some more tracks. With any luck, I could guide the rat right into my trap.

At Madan, Faisal stopped again for gas. I got out my photo of Saleem and had Faisal show it to an old farmer fueling up next to us. The farmer immediately grew wary.

"Ask if he's seen him."

Faisal said something in Arabic and the man said something back. He looked from Faisal to me and waved his hand to the east. I studied his eyes for a moment before saluting him. He said something else to Faisal before returning to his old truck. There were more wary looks our way as he drove off.

"What did he say?"

"That they have all fled further east."

"In other words, he hasn't seen anyone lately."

"Something like that, yes."

"Okay. Let's go."

"Did you want to follow the river or…"

I looked at the map and out at the terrain. A line of hills buttressed the river south of Madan and stood between it and the main highway. Civilization and attention lay close to the river and a man like Saleem would want to avoid attention, especially this close to Raqqah. I pointed at the barren terrain away from the river.

"This way," I said and refocused on the map.

The small village of Al Tebni was roughly twenty miles ahead. After that, the next sign of civilization would be Al-Masrab, which was barely ten miles this side of Deir ez-Zor. If I wanted to lay a trap, it would have to be well before we got to that point. Otherwise we'd be running an op in ISIS' backyard.

I pulled up a map of the area on my phone and zoomed in. There was a small village called Halabiyah. It straddled the Euphrates and was five miles back up the road from Al Tebni. I kept an eye out for signs and pointed at the turnoff when we came to it.

"This way," I said.

A half mile on towards the river, we came upon a small mosque to our right. I motioned for Faisal to turn in.

"Go in and tell them that we're waiting to meet someone and just need a place to rest and get out of the cold for the day."

I handed Faisal 100 Euros.

"Tell them thank you to God and all that in advance."

Faisal hesitated.

"What?" I said.

"You will be leaving a trail for Saleem."

"That's exactly what I'm trying to do."

With a long look my way, Faisal got out of the car. I watched him disappear into the mosque. A few minutes later, he was backing out of the door. A man followed Faisal outside and appeared to be in cordial spirits until he saw me. Then his face turned to stone. By his long beard and cap, I took him to be the Iman. There was little question whose side he was on.

Faisal climbed back in.

"What did he say, Faisal?"

"He says there's an abandoned house about a mile up the road. No one will bother us there if we just go in to rest for a while."

Faisal started the car and sped off nervously, without his usual fussing over mirrors and such. I met the Iman's stare as we pulled away. It was the look of a man who would gladly remove an American from his own head.

I turned my attention back to Faisal. Okay. What the hell was that all about? My gut instinct told me that Faisal already knew the Iman. His mysteriously missing wife and family were from this area. That would explain how. But why the nervousness?

Well, the two of us were just going to have another little chat. Once again, there seemed to be something the man wasn't telling me. Something definitely didn't smell right here.

A mile up the road, Faisal turned left onto a dirt road and followed it away from the river. The farther we drove out into the wilderness, the more I began to feel this was a setup. We had gone nearly a mile when an abandoned house came into view, a few hundred yards back from the road. Faisal took the turn and headed that way.

I held out my left hand.

"Slowly. Let's drive past the house from a distance."

The front door was closed but did not appear to have a lock. The glass was gone from all the windows. There were no cars or signs of anyone around.

"Okay, go back to that side with no windows," I said.

He did and parked where no one could see us from inside.

"Wait here," I said and got out with the AK.

With one eye on Faisal, I had a quick look at the backside of the building. Nothing. I went back around to the front, ducked beneath one of the broken windows and paused beside the door before kicking it in.

Having cleared the inside, I walked back out to the car and confronted Faisal.

"What exactly happened back there?"

"What do you mean?"

"I already told, Faisal. Don't fuck with me. Something was going on back there between you and that Iman. Now spill it."

Faisal stared back for a long moment.

"He knows my wife's family."

"Yeah, I figured. So you knew this Iman before you went in there."

"I had never met him. I only knew of him."

I kept staring.

"What?" he said.

"What? I told you to be straight with me and you keep doing shit that makes me doubt your loyalties. That's what."

Faisal looked indignant.

"What happened to, 'I watch your back and you watch mine'?"

"Yeah, well, it's a nice slogan but it doesn't mean shit if you don't mean it."

Faisal kept staring.

"What?" I said.

"Maybe the words you speak mean nothing to you, but each word that comes from my mouth is sacred to me…"

"Then why didn't you tell me you knew that man before you went in there?"

"I was hoping he wouldn't recognize me."

"You still should have told me!"

Faisal stared back. I gestured at him emphatically.

"Answer me!"

"I told David that I would look after you. And I gave you my oath. You watch my back and I watch yours. I may not like this…scheme of yours…but I gave my word and that is that."

I studied him.

"Yeah, okay. I guess I'll just have to trust you."

"I wish you would."

"Yeah, fine. So let's get set up."

I strapped the AK over my shoulder and went around to the back of the building, feeling worse over my outburst than about anything else. I sensed Faisal's approach and looked back at him.

"This looks good. No other farmhouses around."

I pointed at a small hillock in the distance. There were two oaks and a terebinth for cover.

"Let's gather up our gear and set up among those trees."

We went back to the Isuzu.

"Please take the keys," I told Faisal. "If someone comes, we don't want them driving away with the car."

Faisal did that and joined me in back.

"Here. Takes these rifles."

I grabbed the box of ammunition and my pack and we headed off towards the hillock. I dropped the ammo and pack at the base of one of the oaks and looked back at the house. We had a good line of sight but would be exposed. I moved things farther to the other side of the hillock and looked again.

"This is good. Might as well get comfortable."

I sat with my back to the terebinth and checked my own weapons to make sure they were working properly, then the AKs. Then I started filling more magazines with bullets.

"I can help," Faisal said.

I tossed a few of the empty mags over to where he was sitting. Faisal pulled the leftover sandwich out of his coat pocket and had a bite. When he saw me look, he gestured with it. I shook my head.

"I have these too," he said and pulled out the two cookies.

I took one of the cookies and got back to work.

Once we had all the mags loaded and a fresh one in each AK, I retrieved the SBR from my pack, assembled it and checked the sight while firing twice at the house. Then I pulled out my binoculars and surveyed the surrounding area.

Satisfied for the moment, I went off to urinate and sat back down against the tree with eyes closed. It was cold but pleasant. Birds sang out in the fields. From the sounds of it, they were more Dead Sea Sparrows. The wind whispered in the trees above our heads. Life went on.

"What is your plan?" Faisal said after a minute.

"I don't know. Have to see who comes."

"You think someone will?"

I looked at him once.

"Are you kidding? You saw the look on that Iman's face. He'd pay to watch me beheaded."

"And then what?"

I opened my eyes.

"Kill them. All but Saleem. Assuming he's here. If not, I'll leave one man alive who will tell me where Saleem is."

I held Faisal's gaze for a moment before closing my eyes again.

"I told you. You don't have be involved. Take the Isuzu and go back home if you want."

When he did not respond, I looked at him again.

"What?"

"And how will you get anywhere without it?"

I shrugged.

"There'll be at least one vehicle here by the time I'm through. Assuming I'm not dead. And if I am, who cares? Anyway, I saw that look on your face back there when you had to kill a man. I understand. Killing's not for everyone."

Faisal stared without answering.

"What?" I said again.

"You are wrong. I was not revolted because I had killed a man. I was revolted because I was glad to see him dead. And maybe because I had found pleasure in killing him."

I stared back, thinking again of all the things I had wanted to ask Faisal — about his wife and children and everything — but once again decided to mind my own business, lest he start prying around in my private affairs.

"Some men deserve to die," I said and scanned the terrain with my binoculars again.

Seeing no signs of dust or approaching vehicles, I set them down and closed my eyes. It would be better to have the cover of darkness but I was eager for action, no matter how this situation played out.

☐

Twelve

An hour passed, the afternoon shadows grew long and I had felt myself growing sleepy when Faisal shook my arm.

"Someone is coming."

I quickly raised my binoculars and trained them on a plume of dust rising up from the desert floor. It was an SUV. As it drew nearer, I could make out five men inside. I checked farther back up the road and in the other direction but there were no signs of other vehicles.

I looked over at Faisal.

"What are you prepared to do here?"

"What do you want me to do?"

"I'm thinking to leave you here while I relocate to that gathering of rocks over there."

I patted the SBR.

"I'll see how many of them I can pick off with this. Meanwhile, you keep them pinned down from this location."

I shrugged.

"We'll have to see how they react once the fireworks go off. I expect they'll rush for the safety of the house first thing. Then start firing back. Are you all right with holding this position on your own?"

He nodded.

"Okay. However we do it, we need to neutralize them fast. Before they start making phone calls and we have a few dozen more scumbags breathing down our necks."

Faisal nodded in the direction of the approaching SUV.

"You should go."

"All right, but look. Hold your fire until you hear my first shot. Once they've searched the house and come back outside, that's when I'll start taking them out."

I patted two of the AKs.

"I'm leaving these with you. And you have the Glock."

I held his gaze for a moment, slung the other AK over my shoulder, grabbed the SBR and made a dash for the gathering of rocks. Having made myself comfortable, I watched the cloud of dust drawing nearer. The SUV kept appearing and disappearing over the lay of the land.

When the driver came over the last rise and into full view of the house, he braked to a stop about two hundred yards up the road. A few seconds went by. Then the three men in the backseat piled out with their AKs and scurried off into the brush. I watched them come in and out of view as they worked their way towards the house.

Having reached the Isuzu, they looked inside before moving over to the adjacent wall of the house. One of them went around to the back corner and stood there watching. The other two disappeared around in front and out of my sight. A minute later, I heard voices and the two men reappeared. After some animated discussion, one of them walked over and waved to the driver.

The car pulled up and all five men gathered around it, talking. Then they disappeared around in front again. When they reappeared, it was to go around in back and search the terrain.

Saleem was not among them so I focused the SBR sights on the man who appeared to be the leader. Always best to cut off the head of the beast first, if possible. Besides, he didn't look like someone who would readily give up Saleem if tortured.

I pulled the trigger and the man crumpled to the ground. Faisal's AK had gone off with the sound of my report but he failed to hit anyone.

As the surviving men scrambled back around towards the front of the house, I fired on the trailing man and he went down like a horse had kicked him in the back.

Some moments later, the barrel of an AK appeared through the broken windows at the back of the house and an exchange of gunfire with Faisal followed. Then all was silent.

With no clear shot of my own, I dashed over to where the Isuzu was parked. Another exchange of gunfire went off as I did. Then all was silent again.

Crouched behind the Isuzu, I considered my next move. If correct in my assumptions, the men inside were dumb to my existence. There were no windows on this side of the house. They could not have seen me. That said, I was equally blind to them. For all I knew, they were scattering off through the brush from the far side of the house.

Then it occurred to me that Faisal would have fired if he saw anyone trying to flank him. That suggested they were all still inside.

I had a quick look that way and ducked back behind the Isuzu, again weighing my options. Haste could be deadly, but so could delay. The longer I waited, the longer they would have to call for backup.

Seeing little choice, I dashed over to the side wall of the building, eased down to the front corner and had a quick look. Nothing. I got out a flash grenade, slipped around to the front, ducked beneath the window and continued on to the front door. After a pause, I had a quick look inside. Again, nothing. There were intersecting walls blocking my view but I had to assume they were all huddled in the back room, looking out in the direction of the enemy fire.

With my left hand, I placed the grenade pin in my teeth, slipped inside and moved quietly to the nearest wall. There were whispered voices in the other room. Then they stopped. I pulled the grenade pin, counted to three and had started to toss the grenade when two of the men surprised me from the other end of the wall. I reflexively hit the ground and fired as the grenade went off, and kept firing in the direction of the two men until I realized that no one was firing back.

Stunned by the shock wave and half blinded by the dust and smoke, I sat up and had a look around me. One of the two men was moaning. He had taken a bullet in the face. The other man was missing half of his head. I pushed to my feet and peeked around the corner. The third man was lying motionless on his back but still had his AK in one hand.

I walked over to the man who was moaning, pulled out my Sig and added a bullet to his brain. He was quiet now.

I peeked around the corner again. The man was still lying flat on his back and seemingly out cold but you never trusted a man holding a gun in his hands, no matter how dead he looked.

I moved cautiously in that direction with my AK pointed and was nearly upon him when I heard movement at my back and spun around. Faisal stood there with his AK pointed.

"Well, fuck, Faisal. Don't ever sneak up on a man like that. You'll get yourself killed."

"I came to cover your back."

I saw the look of alarm on his face and heard an AK go off in the same instant. The smack of a bullet dropped me to my knees. I had unloaded most of a magazine on my way down. The man was definitely dead now. I gripped my side.

"Fuck!!!"

I ripped off my jacket and vest.

"You're hit," Faisal said, coming to my aid.

"No shit!"

I fingered the bullet hole in my flesh, just above the pelvis.

"Fuck!" I said again and felt around in back for an exit wound. It was there so at least the bullet wasn't lodged in my body. That much was good.

"Please go get my pack," I told Faisal. "It's behind those rocks."

He threw the AK over his shoulder and jumped out the broken window. I stared after him, astonished momentarily by his sudden agility.

I moved on to searching the three dead men. Faisal ran back in with my pack a minute later. I took it and dug out the first aid kit.

"Here," I said and pulled up my shirt. "Pour some of this antiseptic on the Z gauze and wipe the wounds."

Faisal paused with the antiseptic laced gauze in his hand before applying it. I grimaced and pounded the floor with one boot.

"All right. A bit of that anti-bacterial powder."

I stomped again from the sting.

"Okay, some more of that gauze."

He applied several pieces to both wounds. They quickly stuck to the blood. I leaned down and ripped the shemagh from around the nearest man's neck.

"Here. Make sure the gauze stays in place."

Faisal helped me with arranging things from the back and then I tied off the shemagh. Our eyes met.

"I am sorry," he said.

"Yeah."

"I was only trying to help."

"I know."

"It was to keep my oath."

I nodded and patted him on the shoulder.

"We need to get out of here."

Outside, I found the phone of the man who appeared to be the leader and went about taking pictures of all the dead men.

"Okay. Check for Saleem's number again."

Faisal quickly found it.

"Then send the pictures."

He did. It took a minute but Saleem texted back with another video rant.

"What's he saying this time?" I asked Faisal.

"Death to all the American dogs and he will personally be taking your head off. Basically that."

I nodded and took a picture of myself, flipping him off.

"Send that."

Faisal did.

Rather than wait for a response, I broke the phone apart and chucked the pieces here and there into the brush.

"Okay. We need to go see that Iman."

Faisal hesitated.

"Faisal. I would have questioned that hostile in there, but he's dead now. Anyway, that Iman prick ratted us out."

"He has family there. A wife and children."

"Well, I'm not going to randomly start shooting everybody. But I am going to get some answers, whatever it takes."

Faisal still hesitated.

"Faisal, I already told you. Either your loyalties are with me or you can hit the road. Now what's it going to be?"

"I already told you my answer."

"Fine. Then let's go. I'm sure these bastards called for backup so we'd better get moving before we have company."

We gathered up all the guns and ammunition on our way out to the Isuzu. While Faisal stored those things away, I checked the Land Cruiser and found an RPG launcher, some grenades and a SAKO TRG 42 sniper rifle with a sound suppressor. I had a look in the SAKO's scope and checked the action. That was a find. Rummaging around amongst the crap in the back, I found a box of ammunition for the rifle.

Faisal's eyes got big when he saw me walk up with the RPG launcher. I nodded.

"Yeah, that's right. I'm going to blow the shit out of something.

Faisal grabbed my arm as I was loading everything into the back.

"What?" I said.

"Why not take their Land Cruiser?"

I looked at it and back at him.

"I don't know."

"It's a better vehicle. Plus the drone, you know?"

"Yeah, fair enough."

I went over and turned the key to the on position. The tank was nearly full.

"All right," I said. "Let's do this."

We quickly transferred all the armaments and Faisal climbed behind the wheel. I had another thought, held up a hand and hurried back into the house. None of these men looked to be on a wanted list so I took their phones.

Outside, I had Faisal call me from one of the phones. When the call came in, I had him write down the number.

"All right. One second."

I went around to the Isuzu and climbed underneath.

"What have you done?" Faisal asked when I returned.

"I stashed that phone under the Isuzu. Whoever comes looking for us will likely take it and I might be able to use the phone to track them.

I grunted in pain, getting into the seat.

"We should go back to Raqqah and have you treated."

"Forget it. Come on, let's go."

Faisal started the engine and went through his usual ritual of checking mirrors and such.

"Goddamn it, Faisal! We're in the middle of fucking nowhere! Just drive!"

He looked at me once and turned the Land Cruiser around without a word. We had gotten some distance out towards the highway before Faisal spoke again.

"God hears those best who speak with a sweet tongue."

"Yeah?" I said, doing a double take. "Well I'll definitely have to keep that in mind when the live fire is going off."

When we came to the road, Faisal turned right, back towards the mosque and looked over at me.

"What is your game plan?"

"My game plan? Well, I'll tell you this much. We're not driving right up to the front door."

"So, what?"

"I seem to remember there being a little grove of oaks back up the road from the mosque."

"Yes, I believe you are right."

"Then we'll park there and decide what to do next."

"You don't know?"

"No. Let's just get that far and see how things look."

As we neared the grove, Faisal slowed down and pulled across the road. There was a village of homes farther up the road but no sign of anyone outside or around the mosque.

Faisal parked out of sight and looked over at me.

"What now?"

"Okay. First off, I don't know what you're going to tell this Iman but it has to be something like, our car broke down. I just need him out in the open where I can see him when I follow you in. Did you see any other men around while you were in there?"

Faisal shook his head.

"I did not see anyone. I only heard the women and children in back."

"All right. So let's assume we make it to the front door without being seen. Then you go in and get his attention. Now, if he comes out unarmed, you greet him pleasantly but if he comes out with a gun or anything doesn't seem right to you, you make it clear by the tone of your voice that something's wrong. Do you understand me?"

Faisal nodded. I had a thought and pulled the Smith & Wesson out of my ankle holster.

You still have that Glock I gave you, right?"

"Here in my waist."

"All right. Take this instead. It'll hide better in your waist band."

I checked the Smith & Wesson to make sure it was fully loaded and handed it to Faisal. I did the same with the Glock and tucked it into my waist holster.

"Now look, Faisal. If you feel your life's at risk for whatever reason before I come in, you shoot the bastard. If not, I'll be listening to the tone of your voice and come in behind you, ready to deal with whatever the situation is. Are we good?"

He nodded.

"All right. Let's do this."

We headed off through the small grove and stopped at the edge of the trees. The mosque was a hundred yards across a flat, dusty expanse. There were no windows facing us and no signs of anyone watching.

With a nod, Faisal and I dashed across to the nearest wall and paused to regroup. I heard the sound of chickens and goats and children's voices from inside an enclosure in back. A dog had begun to bark. I stared at Faisal, waiting to see if it raised any alarms. When it did not, I whispered.

"I'll be right outside the door when you go in. And as soon as I hear voices, I'll follow. Just make sure I know by the tone of your voice whether or not everything's okay in there."

He held my gaze before heading around the corner. I poked my head around that way and waited until he had disappeared inside before following him.

Standing by the door, I heard Faisal call out. Several seconds went by before a man's voice greeted him back. When Faisal returned his greeting in a pleasant tone, I took a deep breath and rushed inside. The Iman's eyes darted from Faisal to me and back again. Yeah, you prick. The tables are turned.

I motioned for him to hold his hands out. He did so slowly. I moved the rest of the way towards him, patted him down and found an AK hidden beneath his thobe. His eyes met mine as I took the gun.

"Let's go clear the rest of the building," I whispered to Faisal.

I was turning the Iman around when a teenage boy appeared from in back, saw there was mischief and reached for the AK slung over his shoulder. I unloaded with him calling out the prophet's name. He hadn't gotten off a shot off.

Three women quickly rushed out from in back, screaming and wailing over his dead body. The children were crying somewhere out of sight.

"Fuck!" I said and shoved the Iman onto a bench. "Do not let him move a finger!"

On my way in back, I yanked the oldest woman to her feet, pointed the AK at her head and motioned for the rest of the women to go out ahead of us. The next room was in chaos with more women wailing, children crying and the dog barking. I quickly shot the dog and pointed at a smaller room with the AK. When the women hesitated, I yelled at them.

"Get in that fucking room!"

Understanding the tone of my voice, if not my words, they began herding the children in that direction. With all of them inside, I waved my phone and pointed the gun at them.

"Phones!"

Reluctantly, the women began revealing their phones from beneath their robes. When one of the younger women failed to comply, I placed the barrel of my AK to her forehead. Instantly, there were wails and women dropping to their knees. I gathered from their begging that this woman did not have a phone. I looked from face to face before motioning for them to stay put and closing the door.

Having cleared the rest of building, I dragged the boy out of sight and returned to Faisal and the Iman.

"All right, let's get him in back."

Faisal spoke to the Iman in Arabic and he slowly got to his feet, his eyes focused on me the whole time. Every fiber of his being exuded hatred, for me and all Americans. I motioned again with the AK and shoved him towards the back. We passed the room where the women and children were gathered. You could hear the women crying and praying and trying to keep the children quiet.

"In there," I told Faisal, pointing at a room in the far reaches of the building.

I closed the door behind us and motioned for the Iman to sit down.

"All right, Faisal. This is what I want you to tell him. I'm going to ask some questions and if he cooperates, I give him my word, nothing will happen to the woman and children. But if he doesn't cooperate?"

I shrugged and waved for Faisal to translate. The Iman listened while staring at me. When Faisal was done, I pulled out the photo of Saleem.

"Tell him I want to know where to find this man."

Faisal asked him. The Iman's eyes went from the picture to me and back to Faisal. Then he said something in Arabic and shook his head.

"He says he doesn't know," Faisal said.

I handed the AK to Faisal.

"If he tries anything, shoot him."

I went around behind the Iman, pulled the bottom of his thobe up around his chest and tied it in a knot around the back of the chair. Then I pulled out my own phone and scrolled down until I had the video of Tom's beheading on the screen. I held the screen up for the Iman to see and clicked the start button. Soon I was hearing Tom's final, horrific screams. The Iman's eyes darted back and forth from my face to the screen.

"That was my brother!" I screamed at him.

I looked over my shoulder and yelled at Faisal.

"Tell him!"

Faisal stood there stunned.

"Translate!" I yelled at him.

He did.

The Iman looked perplexed at first, then indignant. He said something to Faisal and Faisal argued back.

"What?!" I said. "What did he say?!!"

"He asks, who is to answer for all the innocent Muslims the Americans have killed?"

"My brother didn't kill anyone!" I yelled in the Iman's face. "He was a fucking reporter! An innocent fucking reporter! He was only here trying to help you fucking people!"

"Tell him!" I yelled at Faisal.

When Faisal failed to speak, I yelled at him again and he finally translated my words. Hearing the Iman reply, I looked at Faisal.

"What?"

"He says that he did not kill your brother, so why are you punishing him?"

"You motherfucker!"

I smacked the side of his face with the butt of my AK.

"My brother didn't kill any Muslims! So why the fuck did you people kill him?!"

I pointed at the photo of Saleem again.

"Where?"

When the Iman failed to answer, I pulled out my knife and shook the photo in his face.

"Where?!"

When the Iman still failed to answer, I drove the knife deep into his right thigh and dug it around a bit as he screamed. The women and children were back to crying and wailing in the other room.

I pointed at the picture.

"Where?"

The Iman spit at me so I drove the knife into his other thigh. This time he choked back his scream, his neck bulging and torso convulsing.

"Where?!" I screamed again.

When he still failed to answer I pulled out my Glock and handed the AK to Faisal.

"Go bring me one of the children."

"No. I beg of you. Please don't do this."

"I said bring me one of the children!"

Faisal said something to the Iman in Arabic and the Iman looked at me.

"That's right, you two faced piece of shit. I'm going to start cutting their little heads off one by one until I get some answers."

When Faisal failed to move, I started for the door and suddenly the Iman was talking rapid fire in Arabic. I stopped and waited for Faisal to translate.

"He says he doesn't know for sure. Only a few people have this knowledge but he has heard there is a place, somewhere along the road from Deir ez-Zor to Al-Suwar. On the left as you are going that way and back among the hills, hidden from sight. That is all he knows."

I placed the barrel of the Glock against the Iman's forehead and stared into his eyes. He stared back and spoke again. I looked over my shoulder at Faisal.

"He says you may as well shoot him. You may as well kill all of them because if Saleem finds out that he has been betrayed, he will do far worse."

I looked back.

"Yeah. You sick motherfuckers. That's all you know. Fucking killing and revenge."

I raised the barrel above the Iman's head and fired several times. He recoiled from the shockwave and fell backwards in his chair. The wailing in the other room went ballistic. I started for the door.

"Tell him if he's lying to me, I'll be back to kill everyone here."

I heard Faisal translating my words as I crossed the hallway and opened the other door. The women recoiled at seeing me and covered their children. I fired a few shots over their heads for good measure. Faisal came rushing in and grabbed my arm.

"Please, let us go," he said.

"You tell them that if they call for help or say one thing about what's happened here, I'll be back."

Faisal quickly translated my words and pulled on my arm again.

"We must go, before someone discovers us."

I looked hard at all the women before following Faisal towards the front of the mosque. On our way past the kitchen, I stopped him.

"We'd better grab some food."

"There is no time."

"Faisal, wherever we're going next, there's not going to be anything to eat."

Exasperated, Faisal joined me in the kitchen and helped with throwing food into a flour sack.

"Okay, that is enough," he said.

I grabbed a case of bottled water and we hurried towards the front.

Before Faisal could walk out front the door blindly, I took the AK and had a wary look. An Isuzu pickup had just then braked to a stop and four men piled out, two from the cab and two from in back, all of them armed and rushing towards the door.

I waited until they were nearly upon us and gunned them down.

"Let's go!" I said and dragged Faisal behind me.

We ran past the bloodied bodies and off towards the trees.

Thirteen

Alerted by the gunfire, scores of people from the nearby village had spilled out onto the road and some of the men gave chase when they saw us fleeing. We cleared the trees and jumped into the Land Cruiser with the sound of angry voices closing in from behind us.

"And don't check the mirrors or I'll shoot you," I said as we piled into the front seat.

Faisal glanced at me once while starting the engine.

"Are you sure about this?" I said when he whipped the Land Cruiser around in a cloud of dust and headed towards the river. "Seems like we'll be boxing ourselves in."

Faisal didn't bother to look at me. I waited until we were well away from any nearby houses before tossing all the phones I had confiscated from the mosque. Faisal still hadn't explained where he was taking us.

A half mile farther on, he yanked the Land Cruiser hard left across the road and started up a sandy wash between two hills. I darted another look his way. Faisal seemed to know where he was going. Again, I wondered exactly how, and what else he wasn't telling me.

At the far flank of the hill on our left, he veered left again and followed another wash back in the general direction we had just come, only with a line of hills now separating us from the village. Farther on, we came to a washboard road. When that road led back to the highway, he crossed it and continued south.

Sandstone bluffs grew up around us, carved deeply from the rain. As the road wound deeper into the hills, their flanks increasingly closed in.

Then some ten miles farther on, we passed between two nearly vertical bluffs, their shadows looming over us for a few hundred yards before dumping us out into a small, cloistered valley, rich with date palms and fruit trees. There were fields that had once been cultivated but now stood fallow.

A respectable looking house stood apart from the groves, not only respectable for the Middle East, but for most any other part of the world.

A water tower stood next to the house with a ladder leading up to the top. I looked over at Faisal.

"What the hell is this?"

"What does it matter? We are here…And safe for now."

He climbed out and I climbed out with him.

"What do you mean, 'safe for now'? Are you saying that ISIS knows about this place?"

He nodded.

"Then they'll come."

He shrugged.

"I think so."

"And do you have any idea how soon?"

Faisal shrugged again.

"As soon as they learn about the Iman."

"Because the Iman knows about this place too."

"Yes."

"Then we'd better get ourselves armed up and ready for battle."

"Let us get things inside first. If you will bring the guns and ammunition, I will grab the food and water."

Faisal went about gathering up the food supplies. I stood there staring at him, pissed. Faisal kept playing coy with the facts and I didn't like it.

When he disappeared inside, I walked around and opened the back of the Land Cruiser. He was busy putting the food stores away in the kitchen when I walked in. I set the guns and ammunition down by the door.

A pall hung over everything now. I thought to say something but decided to leave it alone. What was the point? There would be more bloodshed by the time I was through. Anyway, I was still pissed about being kept in the dark.

"Do you wish to eat now?" Faisal said from the kitchen.

"Yeah. Best if we do. It's never good to fight on an empty stomach."

Faisal was soon chopping away in the kitchen. I went to the front door and looked out. The shadows were long. There was a chill in the air. I caught the scent of cooking and looked back. Seeing it was an actual gas stove, I walked around to the back of the building and found a large propane tank loaded onto the back of a flatbed truck and a generator next to the truck.

The place was ingenious. Early 20th century in its technology, but ingenious. I assumed this had something to do with Faisal's wife and her family. It couldn't be Faisal's family. He was from up north.

A glade stood between the back of the house and the groves. I had started out towards the groves, thinking to explore further, when I came upon four mounds, each with a gathering of stones at one end. So something had happened here. The only question was, what?

Faisal looked up at me when I returned to the house. I was listening to the bird calls outside.

"Is that the Dead Sea Sparrow again?"

"No. The Isabelline Wheatear. Actually, there are two calls. The Wheatear is the one down in the throat. The sharper call above it is the Black-winged Pratincole."

I nodded and looked down the hallway.

"Go ahead," Faisal said. "You are free to look."

I did, following a long hallway from bedroom to bedroom, the feel of each room like that of an old boardinghouse, the furniture dated and worn and spartan, but tidy. I went into

150

the bathroom and found an actual toilet with water in the tank. I urinated and flushed, then stood there mesmerized by the water swirling around in the bowl.

Back out in the kitchen, the air of gloom lingered.

"Guess I'll go gather some firewood," I said.

Faisal nodded without answering me. I went out the door and had been collecting dead branches out in the groves for a spell when Faisal appeared. I was watching a dove like bird darting among the trees.

"The Cream-colored Courser," Faisal said.

I looked at him.

"And you know all this…because?"

"From reading books as a boy. And of course, from living here."

We stood there listening to its high pitched cluck-cluck and mournful caw before gathering up more branches. On our way back to the house, we passed the four mounds. I pretended not to notice.

Back inside, I checked a weather station. There were some ominous looking clouds off to the northwest.

"Looks like snow," I said, tucking my phone away.

Faisal nodded.

"Maybe it is for the best."

I wasn't so sure about that. The storm might delay the inevitable, but if they came, it would be impossible to hide our tracks in freshly fallen snow.

"Let's just move on to getting ready," I said.

"We will eat first, and then prepare."

"Fine. Just make it fast."

While Faisal cooked, I went over to check our stash of weapons, making sure the action on each rifle worked and they all had fresh magazines in them.

A short while later, Faisal called to me from the kitchen table.

"Please."

I went over and joined him. He had sautéed onions and tomatoes and some cilantro with chicken. There was also a bowl of white rice and flatbread. I ladled some of the chicken over a bowl of rice and grabbed a piece of the bread. Faisal joined me with two bottled waters.

"There is a plum brandy if you would like."

I nodded.

"Maybe later."

We ate in silence. Whether real or imagined, I felt Faisal's ongoing disgust. I wasn't so sure it made sense to keep him around any longer. Why put him through what was to come? Saleem was close now. I could feel it in my bones. Our encounter would come soon enough and Faisal's only ongoing purpose would be to translate, and when it came to Saleem, I had no need for a translator. Play that video of Tom's death and sharpen my knife while that wretch sat there watching. That would say everything I needed to say to Saleem al-Ramadi.

Faisal got up with his plate. I followed with mine.

"All right. Let's get to this. Before the snow sets in"

"You are the professional. You must tell me."

"Okay. I considered moving that flatbed truck to just this side of the passageway and blowing the propane tank to hell with the RPG when their convoy arrived, but chances are they'll send scouts in first and then we'll have lost the element of surprise. It's probably best to appear unaware. Let them wander out into the open and cut them down from up in those hills. If anything, I'd hide the Land Cruiser. Maybe somewhere outside the valley. That way they might think we've gone off and let their own guards down a bit. Anyway, it's always good to have a plan B escape route."

"There is a place out beyond the valley entrance, off to the left. No one will see it there."

"Okay."

I grabbed my pack and pulled out the other two phones I had confiscated.

"Before we do that, help me to get these synced on Facetime. I'm going to place one of them at the entrance to the valley."

"Ah. A good idea," Faisal said.

I took one of the phones when he was done.

"You keep that one on you."

I slung an AK over my shoulder and grabbed two more of the rifles with my free hand.

"Probably best to leave some weapons in the Land Cruiser too. You never know when you'll find yourself empty handed."

Faisal started towards the front door with me. I stopped and glanced at his empty hands. After a moment, Faisal got the message and grabbed one of the AKs. We went out into the growing umbrage.

"Go ahead, you drive," I said.

I climbed in the shotgun side. Faisal started the Land Cruiser and headed back out of the valley. On the far side of the passageway, I jumped out. He drove on a short distance farther and turned left off the road. I watched until he had disappeared. The clouds on the western horizon had arced in closer and grown more ominous looking. A feel of snow was in the air; cold, like you had opened a freezer.

I turned to the rocks on my right and climbed up until I had found a small but deep crevasse, deep enough to keep the phone out of the snow. Using several small stones, I positioned the phone so that it was looking both off into the distance and down at the road. Anyone coming this way would be in our view, as long as the battery charge lasted.

Having a thought, I retrieved the phone, changed it to the low power setting and dimmed the screen before rearranging the stones.

Faisal reappeared a minute later.

"Check the other phone for the angle."

He looked.

"Maybe a bit to the right."

I adjusted things with the rocks and pulled my hands back.

"How's that."

"Good."

I climbed down and we headed back to the house. Halfway there, I felt the first snowflake on my face. Soon there were more of them, swirling about in the twilight. By the time we opened the door to the house, our jackets had a good dusting. I shook myself off and went to use the bathroom. Faisal was starting a fire when I returned. I glanced out at the darkening hills. If someone took that high ground and surrounded us, we would be sitting ducks.

"Okay, let's get back to our game plan," I said.

"That brandy?" he said.

"Sure."

Faisal waved at a chair by the fire and joined me a moment later with two aperitif glasses and a bottle of homemade brandy. He poured both glasses full, handed me one and held his up before drinking.

"Good," I said.

He nodded.

"So, your plan."

I explained at length how I saw this thing playing out. Faisal tossed the occasional branch onto the fire as I spoke. At one point, the wind stirred violently outside, rattling the front door and windows. I went to look. Four inches of snow had already gathered on the ground.

"What," Faisal said, seeing the look on my face as I sat back down

"This snow is not our friend. They'll see footprints heading off here and there and know where to find us."

I looked at the phone screen on Facetime. It was hard to imagine anyone coming in this storm. We most likely had until morning, or until the storm had passed, whichever came first.

Faisal tossed another branch onto the fire.

"I'm sorry," I said in the silence. "About the boy. Hell, I'm sorry about the dog."

I joined him in gazing into the fire.

"I probably would have killed them all...if not for you being there."

"I'm sorry about your brother."

Faisal met my gaze and looked back into the fire. I studied his profile. A thousand questions swirled around in my head.

"I won't ask," I said after a spell.

He glanced at me.

"I have nothing to hide. I just see no point in talking about it."

Faisal stirred the fire.

"Unlike you, I have no video of what happened, only a memory that plays every day in my heart."

"Daesh came here," I said.

He looked at me and nodded.

"I came back from Madan one day to find them here. Five of them. They had been chased south from Raqqah and somehow heard of this place. My wife's father was already dead when I arrived. He had protested their presence so they took him out back and shot him. My wife had been forced to make them a meal as she wept. Then nightfall came and they took her in back and used her. One by one. My daughter too. She was fourteen. My son was eight. He helped me out in the fields while a man watched over us with a gun. We were useful as long as we helped feed them. Then on the third day, they tired of listening to my son cry and shot him. And beat my wife for weeping over her son. And used her again and again as she wept. And I endured it all, hoping for one thing and one thing only. That I could somehow save her life, and that of my daughter."

Faisal sighed and drank down the rest of his brandy.

"Some days passed. I don't remember how many but I was out in the fields when I heard the men inside the house arguing and knew something was wrong. I should say, we had heard airstrikes in the distance for days and they kept growing closer so they must have known it was time to flee. Anyway, the man watching me had grown distracted by the voices so I hit him over the head with my shovel. Several times until I knew he was dead. Then I took his rifle and ran towards the house. The men were just then dragging my wife and daughter outside and forcing them into their SUV. One of them had come around the building, looking for the man I had killed, saw me with his rifle and started firing. I fired back and in all the confusion, my daughter and wife got free. They were running towards me when the men gunned them down in the back."

Faisal looked up at me from the fire.

"Like you, I had wanted to kill everyone and ran after their car, firing crazily, but they had already driven off beyond my bullets."

Faisal sighed heavily again and stared into the fire.

"I spent the rest of the day digging graves and burying the bodies."

The light from the fire danced on Faisal's face as he stared into the flames. I stared at him, unable to fathom his grief. Then I remembered the boy back in Raqqah and understood Faisal's fixation.

"I am truly sorry for your loss," I said finally. "But how can you not be angry. How can you not want to kill them all?"

He glanced up at me quickly.

"Who says I am not angry? I would kill them all, a thousand times over, if only it would bring back my family. If only it would make things the way they once were."

He looked back at the fire.

"But it won't. As much as I want these men to suffer, and as much as they deserve to suffer, my killing them would only make it worse. They would be dead and I would have become like them. A man possessed by hatred."

Faisal reached out his hand.

"I am sorry. I did not mean to…"

"It's all right," I said. "I know what I have become. And still I can't stop myself."

"I understand, I understand. Anger is like a fever and once started, hard to put out."

"But you did. I don't understand. How?"

"Reason," he said.

I shook my head.

"That is all I know, my friend…Let me ask you a question. All these men we have killed. Does it make you feel any better? Does it take away one ounce of the grief in your heart?"

I shrugged and looked into the fire.

"It's better than nothing. Better than watching that video over and over in my head."

"Then your solution is to go on killing and killing."

"I don't know. I will only know once I have repaid Saleem for what he did."

Faisal nodded and threw a few more branches onto the fire.

"I only know this for certain. It must stop somewhere." Faisal looked up. "I think your Jesus said something about it, did he not? Turn the other cheek? Take the smote out of your own eye? To do so is to carry the sorrows of all mankind in your chest, and yet it is the only way to stop the hatred."

There was silence.

"More brandy?" he said.

"Yeah, sure."

Faisal poured our two glasses full and held his up to me again. I did the same and drank. The liqueur was sweet and warm and good, like so much in this world, and yet I was consumed by everything evil in it. I looked over at Faisal with a renewed sense of sorrow for his fate. It increasingly seemed to be the fate of the entire world.

"I am truly sorry," I said. "For all you have lost."

Faisal stared back, the sadness of a thousand lifetimes in his dark eyes.

"Perhaps I should not tell you this, but your Saleem was one of the men who came here."

At hearing those words, my rage erupted anew. The heartless bastard. How could you not want to butcher him?

Well, if Faisal couldn't bring himself to do it, I would, for both us. And derive that much more pleasure doing it here, with the man knowing it was retribution for both his sins. To hell with Jesus. I was an Old Testament prophet. An eye for an eye. Fire and brimstone. There would be no turning the other cheek with me.

I had been there for quite a while, staring into the fire and dwelling on these thoughts, when my mind came back to the moment. I looked over at Faisal and held up my glass.

"To my partner. I'm sorry for having doubted you. I could not have asked for a more decent man to help me. I just feel like hell for having dragged you into this mess."

Faisal touched my glass and we drank.

"You did not drag me into anything, my friend. God called upon me to help you, so I am here."

"To help me with killing and maiming? That is not what you want."

"No. But it does not matter what I want. We do not choose what God will call upon us to do."

I shook my head.

"I don't believe God has anything to do with this. This is one man seeking revenge. And a not very good man at that."

Faisal stared.

"What?" I said.

"Either God is in everything, or He is in nothing. Each man must answer that question for himself."

I scoffed.

"That's exactly what those men out there think. Everything they do is the work of God, and look at them. Nothing but butchers."

"And if we do not fight them, then they win."

"Yeah? And what happened to turning the other cheek?"

"Keeping the hatred out of your heart is not the same thing as refusing to fight. Did not Jesus go in and wreck the temple?"

I looked into the fire, shaking my head.

"What?" Faisal said. "Do you not have any principles by which you live?"

I shrugged.

"Sure. The eleventh commandment."

"The eleventh commandment. And what is that?"

"When all else fails, fuck the first ten commandments."

A moment passed before Faisal laughed out loud.

"Oh, my friend. You truly are in trouble."

I shrugged.

"I'm doing the best I can…Anyway, like I said, I just hate having dragged you into this mess."

"No no, my friend. I watch your back and you watch mine."

"Yeah. There's that."

"Sometimes in this world, there is only that."

Faisal held out his glass again. I held out mine and we both drank. Time passed. My mind was fixated now on Faisal's grief.

"What did you do before all this," I thought to ask.

"I was a professor of history."

"Well that's a hell of a way for things to turn out."

He shrugged.

"Until these times, I had always thought of life as moving forward. Perhaps two steps forward and one step back, but always forward. Always evolving. Now, with all that has happened, the idea is hard to defend. It seems as if the world will go backwards for a thousand years now."

"You'd be hard pressed to convince me otherwise."

"Yes. It is for the simple people that my heart breaks. History has crisscrossed through this place for five thousand years and always the people are here, sewing crops and harvesting and believing in God."

We sat in silence again for a spell.

"Where did you teach, Faisal?"

"Ah, originally at Tishreen University. Do you know it?"

I shook my head.

"It is on the coast. A lovely place, and where I studied. And met my wife. Then Al-Furat University was founded in Deir ez-Zor, I received a position and we moved back here. And then..."

And then. And then I remembered Tom and what they had done to Faisal and the fires of hatred burned anew in me.

"Perhaps you would like to take a bath," Faisal said.

"Yeah. That would be nice. Is there hot water?"

"Warm, perhaps."

"Yes, I think I will, if you don't mind?"

"Please. There are fresh towels in the cabinet."

I stripped off everything but my shirt and pants and socks and grabbed my pack.

"Best keep an eye on the phone screen, Faisal. You never know."

"I will be watching."

In the bathroom, I undressed the rest of the way except for the bandage and climbed into the shower. The warm water felt heavenly. Once I had washed my hair and face and soaped everywhere else down, I unwound the shemagh. The wound was raw and sore but did not appear to be infected. I gingerly washed around both bullet holes and grimaced again while rinsing off the soap.

After drying off, I washed my shirt and briefs and socks, wrung them out, retrieved a fresh shirt and pair of briefs from the pack and pulled on the old pants.

"How is your wound?" Faisal asked as I hung up my wet clothes to dry by the fire.

"Okay. Help me to get some more of this antiseptic on the wound back here."

I grit my teeth from the fresh sting of it.

"I believe I have an elastic bandage somewhere," Faisal said.

He ran off and came back with one. I held the gauze in place over the wounds while Faisal wrapped the bandage around me several times.

"Here, the clips," he said.

I got things fastened and carefully pulled the shirt back into place.

"How is it?" he asked.

"I'll live."

I sat down with another grimace. Faisal stared at me worriedly.

"How's your wound?" I said.

"Sore, but there does not seem to be infection."

"Same here."

"Okay. Then I am off to wash up."

Alone, I took one of my morphine pills, pulled on a fresh pair of socks and threw a few more branches on the fire. All the while, the storm was clawing and whistling at the door and windows.

Faisal returned a short time later, drying his damp hair. He had his prescription of penicillin in hand.

"Please. You need these more than me."

"No, Faisal. Please, I don't want to…"

"No, please. Your wound is far more serious than mine."

I reached out for them.

"You're sure?"

He nodded.

"All right."

I swallowed one of the pills and chased it with the last of my plum brandy.

"Are you tired?" I asked.

"Yes. And you?"

"Not bad. Why don't you sleep and I'll take the first watch?"

"Very well. Wake me whenever you are ready."

"A couple of hours. We'll see how I'm feeling."
Faisal started off but stopped.
"Thank you, my friend."
"Thanks for what?"
"For watching my back."
"Well, we're definitely in it together now."
He nodded sadly and went off to sleep.

Fourteen

I got comfortable with my feet up, positioned the cell phone on my lap and lay there staring at the screen. The snowflakes kept blowing wildly this way and that, until, of a sudden, they would pause in midair, as if weightless. And then a fresh gust of wind would blow them wildly off in a new direction. On and on this ballet went, the snowflakes like dye markers, tracing each whim of wind.

Meanwhile, snow kept gathering on the road. I questioned whether anyone could find their way in this storm. The snow had so completely covered the road, it was impossible to distinguish it from the surrounding terrain.

I had been there for an hour or so when my phone rang. It was accompanied by a brief but all too familiar flicker of hope. Lydia? Calling to say that she was sorry and still cared?

But no. I saw the blocked number and answered the call.

"Yeah David."

"So you're still okay."

"Still okay."

"How's the hunting?"

"Sitting in a blind right now, waiting for a buck to appear."

"That seven pointer you saw last year?"

"Not sure about that. And you?"

"More flak. More guy's losing their heads. You know?"

"No. Hadn't checked the news lately."

"Well, maybe you ought to stay in touch. Forget about trouble with the interior secretary. The shit's coming down all the way from the top now."

"Sorry. Should be heading home soon."

"Well, it won't be soon enough for me...Your friend still with you?"

"Yeah, yeah. We're fine now. There's a story behind it. Turns out he had lost his wife and kids to this shit."

"Yeah?"

"Yeah. Enough to break your heart...Anyway, we're good. We're here using his blind."

"Okay. Glad to hear that's settled. I thought he was a good man."

"Yeah...But about those wild turkeys, you hear any more on that score?"

"It's a complete shitshow up north. Everyone with their horns locked. You may as well try to solve all the world's problems...But as far as anything else flying overhead? I don't think you need to worry about that for now."

"That's good to know."

"Okay, well, glad to hear you're all right but this hunting trip's got to come to an end. I need you back in town. And soon."

"I'll be on my way in a few days."

"Okay. I'll be in touch. And don't forget to check the news."

"Will do."

While waiting for more, the phone went dead. I clicked on a news site and scrolled down until I saw the article. Christ. Saleem had taken off another head. An aid worker this time. Poor fool. Over here out of the goodness of his heart and this was the thanks he got. Having his head handed to him.

The coalition forces had just raised the bounty on Saleem's head from five to ten million dollars. Dead or alive. I had been so obsessed with revenge, I hadn't considered that angle. I stood to get rich, just for killing the monster. The only problem was, I couldn't deliver him without his head. They'd have mine for war crimes.

While weighing all that, I felt myself growing sleepy and went off to awaken Faisal. He was dreaming. I could tell by his eye movements and sat down to wait. Sometime later, he grew calm, seemed to sense my presence in the room and awakened.

"Did you win?" I said.

"Ah. You were watching." He rubbed his eyes. "No. I'm not sure if we ever win in our dreams, but I was definitely not successful in this one. Maybe it's nature's way of conditioning us to our fate."

He stood up and I stood up with him.

"Thank you for letting me finish."

"You feel rested?"

"Yes, better. I will make some coffee."

"None for me. I'm off to get some sleep."

"Anything?" Faisal said as I headed into the bathroom.

"Nothing. I would have roused you if there was. Please do the same."

"Of course."

I used the bathroom and went to lie down in one of the back bedrooms. The pillowcase smelled of children, of summer days and growing pains and childhood dreams. I had rarely regretted not having kids, at least not that egocentric part of it — there, a chip off the old block — but was reminded right then of what a man missed when he failed to reproduce. A scraped knee, a new bicycle, the magic of a first Christmas, the constant sense of renewal and wonderment.

Reminded that it was only two days until Christmas, pain stabbed into my heart. Life was so much simpler in battle. You killed, or were killed. You survived or you didn't. There was no time for sentimentality. Adrenalin was the only emotion.

I lay there, wondering whether or not I was willing to give up my blood lust for ten million dollars. I felt denied, just thinking about it. The wind kept whipping around outside, and around my thoughts.

I fell asleep in darkness and awakened some hours later with the morning sun pouring in. The wind was still gusting hard but the storm had passed. The corners of the window were caked with snow.

I used the bathroom and went out to find Faisal sipping coffee by the fire.

"There is more in the kitchen," he said.

"Thanks."

It was black. I added honey and went to join him by the fire.

"I take it there's been nothing."

"Nothing."

We both looked at the image on the screen.

"Maybe we should send him another message," I said.

"I suspect he's already angry enough."

"Couldn't hurt...Well, I speak for myself. I want him to come but I'm not sure about dragging you into more death and destruction."

"Yes. I have thought much about my own feelings these past few hours. My desire has been not to bring more hatred into this world, but then I wondered. Am I simply being a coward?"

I glanced up from the fire, awaiting the verdict.

"Then I realized, a man must fight for what he believes in. I would not have gone chasing after these men, but if they come here, to my family's home, to what is cherished and sacred to me, then I must fight. I will not lie down like a lamb to be slaughtered."

I kept staring.

"I still feel like hell, Faisal. For having dragged you into this."

"No, no. You should not worry. As we say, it is written."

I smiled a bit.

"What?" he said.

"Oh. You just reminded me of a scene from Lawrence of Arabia. Do you know the movie?"

"No," he said. "Please explain."

I did.

"Ah," Faisal said when I was done. "You see? It was written."

"Yes, but I always remember Lawrence's words. *Nothing is written.* I suppose it's in our blood. Westerners, I mean. To think that we are always making choices, when maybe we're not."

"Yes. Who is to say?"

I continued staring at Faisal.

"What?" he said.

"Oh, just wondering. You speak as if you have religion but I've never seen you pray or do any of the other things that suggest you're a Muslim?"

"Again, I like your Jesus…"

"My Jesus?"

"Well, however you feel about it, he had admonished the faithful to be humble and pray in private, not on a street corner. It was to say that God already knows what is in your heart. Do you agree?"

"Yeah, I like that part. But I hate dogma. It makes my stomach turn."

"Then you and I understand each other very well."

"Ah. Then it is written."

He smiled.

"And so, my friend?"

"Oh, yes. About preparing?"

"Yes. You are the professional, so you must tell me."

"Okay, first thing, let's run the generator for a spell and charge up all our phones. And my charger. And while that's happening, I'll dig a path back out to the valley entrance. We need to swap out that phone for a freshly charged one. And then we need to dig a path out through the groves, and several of them going off in different directions from there. We want them to be guessing which way we've gone."

"Something to eat first?"

"Yes, please. What do we have?"

"Unless you want lunch, only some bread and honey. I am already heating the bread. No eggs. Our chickens were scattered long ago."

"The bread and honey is fine. And coffee."

Faisal went to the oven and checked the bread.

"It is browned. I'll prepare a piece for you."

"I'll dig a path out to the generator while you do that."

I got my coat on and forced the front door open. The snow drifts against it were two feet deep. Having cleared in front of the door, I shoveled my way around towards the back of the house. The day was bright and the snow crystals sparkled brilliantly against the sun.

With the generator running, I walked back around to the front and stomped my boots before going inside. Faisal had made fresh coffee while I was gone.

"Thank you," I said, taking the coffee and piece of bread.

I had a bite and a gulp of coffee before getting the phones charging, then quickly finished the rest of the bread and coffee.

"All right. I'm off to dig a path out to the entrance."

"I will dig a path out through the groves in a minute."

I nodded and headed out the door.

The day was crisp and cold but the distant sun still felt warm on my face. The light powder was easy to shovel and I went along with the crystals sparkling around me.

It took me fifteen minutes to dig down to the entrance. I dug past it another hundred feet before retrieving the phone from the cliffside and heading back to the house. Faisal had dug a path off through the groves and out of sight. I got the other phone charging and headed off to find him.

"Is this good?" he called out when we met.

He had dug out to the base of the hills in one direction.

"Yes, but let's branch off in several directions now."

Back at the point where the path exited the groves, I started a new path off towards the adjacent hills. Once we had five similar trails, I set the shovel down and started up into the hills on foot from the end of one trail. Faisal quickly got the message and did the same from another trail.

Once we had done the same with each trail, we stood back to examine our handiwork. Anyone looking for us would not be entirely certain how many of us there were or which way we had gone.

"All right," I said. "Better get back and deal with the phones."

"More firewood," Faisal said.

"Yeah." I looked around at the thick blanket of snow. "Probably should have thought of that before the storm, huh?"

"We could harvest some of these dead limbs from the trees."

"Sure. Let's harvest some dead limbs."

We walked into the grove, breaking off whatever dead branches we could reach. I had pulled up the hood of my jacket first thing but Faisal was without protection and looked as if someone had tossed a bucket of snow on his head by the time we met back at the cleared trail. I had to laugh.

"Here, let me help you," I said and dusted him off before starting back towards the house.

The day was lovely, silent save for the bird calls. What was to come seemed unimaginable.

Back inside, we synced up another one of the charged phones and I headed off for the entrance to the valley. A minute later, Faisal was on the other end of the line, helping me to get the phone properly pointed again.

"What now?" he said upon my return.

"Better get you properly outfitted. Is there a heavy jacket here you can use? Something with extra pockets?"

He went off to a back bedroom and returned with a wool lincd parka.

"Will this do?"

He showed me the zippered pockets both inside the vest and out. It also had a zippered pocket on each sleeve.

"That will do."

I took the jacket and loaded it down with six extra magazines.

"There. That should keep you out of trouble."

"What now?" Faisal said again.

"We wait."

"Ah. Then I will cook."

Not knowing what else to do, I followed him. Faisal was busy getting out everything we had taken from the Iman. There were onions, tomatoes, squash, peppers and chicken.

"I'm thinking to make a soup," Faisal said.

"Sounds good. What can I do?"

Faisal set the squash on a cutting board and handed me a knife.

"Chop this. I'll start with the onions and peppers."

"Okay. Any particular size?"

Faisal smiled.

"Not too big, not too small."

"Got it."

I placed the other phone on the counter where we could both keep an eye on it. The view from the passageway looked out over a terrain of rolling hills, glistening with snow and sunlight. Whoever came would have a hell of a time getting here. I still had my doubts that anyone could find the road.

I caught the scent of onions in hot oil and looked over. Faisal had moved on to chopping the peppers. I got back to chopping the squash.

Half an hour later, Faisal was adding seasoning to the pot of soup. I washed my hands and went to sit by the fire. We had let it burn down to embers in order to save firewood. Out of habit, I began checking and rechecking our weapons. One eye was on the phone screen as I worked.

Faisal joined me by the fire and sat there nervously playing with his hands.

"You worried?" I said.

He looked up at me.

"Of death?"

I nodded.

"No. I don't feel that I am but there are questions."

"Like what?"

"Moral questions. Philosophical questions."

"You do much of that and you'll definitely be dead."

"Ah. So you do not question what you're doing at all."

I shrugged.

"Sometimes. But if I get too carried away, I remember the eleventh commandment."

Faisal smirked.

"Well. I came here to take Saleem's head off and that's about as far as I want to go with any of this."

Faisal looked down.

"Sorry," I said. "I don't mean to disappoint you."

"It's all right. I'm not sure of anything anymore. For a time, after my family…you know…all I felt was pain. And anger. And I suppose a bit like you, wanting revenge. But one day, I found myself thinking, when did things become like this? How did this happen? And of course, I thought back to before the wars, before your country invaded Iraq, before Daesh, to when Hussein and Assad were in power. I remember studying at the university in Latakia and how we knew not to say certain things openly, but within these certain parameters, life was good. The cities were beautiful. Everything was clean and orderly. And functioned. Now, as one of your generals once said of Afghanistan, we've been bombed back into the dark ages."

He met my eyes and stared.

"Where are you going with this?" I said.

"I don't know. I suppose it is only to say, if we forget how it once was, we can never go back there again."

"Fair enough. So I figure, every time I waste one of these ISIS rats, we're that much closer to getting things back to normal."

Faisal looked even more saddened.

"What?" I said.

"No. It has come to me now that things will never be the same. I don't know what they will be, but never the same."

"Why don't you come to the States with me when all this is through?"

He shrugged.

"Perhaps."

"No. A man with your education could find work. And there are many refugees already there. You'd have some of your own culture around you."

Faisal nodded.

"Perhaps."

I studied him.

"Well, if you decide, just let me know. I'll be happy to sponsor you. I'm sure I can pull some strings. I'm sure David would be happy to pull some strings too."

Faisal nodded stoically. I got up and opened the front door. The sun was out and the day had warmed. You could see the snow starting to melt ever so slightly, the powder growing porous and icy looking. I checked the weather on my phone. The temperature was in the high thirties but the forecast was for more snow. They were expecting the storm to arrive by some time that evening.

Christ. I hadn't planned on all these delays. It just meant more time to sit around and dwell on my reasons for being here.

I closed the door with my mind churning through worst-case scenarios. If they showed up later today, Faisal and I would be fighting for our lives in the dark and a snowstorm. There were advantages to that, but a lot more disadvantages. Just being out in the cold would make things miserable.

"What?" Faisal said, seeing my look of concern.

"They're saying it may snow again. Later tonight."

"Then maybe they won't come."

I glanced at my watch.

"Maybe. Or maybe they'll see it's going to snow too and try to beat the weather."

"Perhaps they won't think of this place."

"No. No. You were right the first time. They'll hear about the Iman and come looking."

I looked at the phone on Facetime. Nothing but the snow covered terrain, as far as the eye could see. Well, hopefully they would check the other place first and grab the Isuzu. Funny how things turn out. I had considered David a nuisance. Now I was praying for his call so he could track that phone.

I was going on noon and I was out turning off the generator when I heard Faisal call.

"Someone is coming!"

I hurried back inside to look at the phone. Whoever it was, they were a good two or three miles out. All you could really see with the naked eye was a darkness on the horizon and snow crystals spewing up into the sky.

I grabbed my binoculars from the pack.

"I'm going down to have a better look. You stay here and get ready. I'll be back in a minute."

I ran off as fast as my feet could carry me.

Down at the passageway, I climbed up to where the phone was stationed and trained the binoculars on the horizon. Military vehicles of some kind. It was hard to tell from looking straight on but it appeared to be the Americans. I watched for another minute before running back to the house.

"It's the military, not ISIS. Could be worse. Could be better."

"Why would they be coming here?"

"Probably heard about the Iman. Maybe about that other business too. You have any reason to think they'd know of this place?"

"I have worked with others besides David but this place has never come up. Then, with your government, little is hidden."

"Yeah."

"Why? Are you worried?"

"Well, I don't exactly welcome the scrutiny. This isn't a sanctioned mission. Plus, word will have gone out among the villagers. Meaning, Saleem will likely hear about it and become more wary."

I looked at the phone screen. The dark mirage on the horizon kept growing larger.

"Let's get everything but these two AKs hidden away in a bedroom."

Faisal helps me with stuffing all the other weapons under a bed.

Fifteen minutes later, the faint hum of approaching vehicles broke the silence. Faisal and I stood at the door as the hum grew steadily louder. Then the convoy rumbled into the valley with a roar. There were two Humvees in the lead, followed by a transport truck and two more Humvees. The vehicles came to a halt and a few dozen soldiers piled out, along with Sergeant Benson. The platoon stood back at a distance as Benson walked up to greet us.

"Captain," he said with a salute.

I saluted back and shook his hand.

"How are you healing up?" he said to Faisal.

"Fine, thank you."

Benson nodded and looked back at me.

"So, what brings you out this way, Sergeant?"

"Trouble."

"What kind of trouble?"

"Local villagers turning up dead kind of trouble. Back in Halabiyah."

"Yeah? And you wanted from me?"

"Answers. Didn't figure I'd get any, but figured it was worth a try."

"And like I already told you, Sergeant. I'm not at liberty to discuss my mission."

"So you said…Well, I've figured out this much. You appear to be looking for Saleem al-Ramadi…And so am I."

I stared into his eyes, nodding.

"So what I don't understand, captain, is why aren't we working together?"

"And like I said…"

"Yeah, I know. You're not at liberty to discuss your mission."

I shrugged.

"Well, I'll tell you this much. I've been busy building up goodwill with these villagers for the past six months and somebody just set me back to square one. And that doesn't make me very happy."

"Understood."

Benson nodded and looked around the valley.

"Nice place. Nice place to set up an ambush."

He looked back at me.

"If someone was planning an ambush."

Benson took another visual tour around the valley and looked back at me.

"There's something else we need to discuss, Captain."

He nodded and led me away from the house. When we were out of sound range, Benson stopped to face me.

"It's about your translator there."

"Yeah? What about him?"

"He's on a wanted list by the Turks. For suspected ties to the PKK."

"With all due respect, Sergeant. Why the fuck would you care?"

"Personally, I couldn't care less but a Turkish patrol was ambushed up by the Turkish border three days ago with two men killed and we're catching hell about it. They seem to suspect your man was involved. And I suppose you too, by association."

"Yeah? So what do you want from me? Turn him over to you so you can turn him to the Turks? Sorry, but that ain't going to happen."

"Let me put it to you this way, captain. If it comes down to turning him over or having the Turks cut off our access to Incirlik?"

Benson shrugged.

"Sergeant. The man has saved my life. Twice now, so I figure I owe him my life in return. Meaning, anyone tries to take him in, it's going to be over my dead body."

Benson looked over his shoulder at his men and back at me.

"For now, I'm going to pretend this conversation never happened. But my advice to you would be, wrap up your mission, whatever the hell it is, and get your man back up to SDF controlled territory. If I see him again, I'll have no choice but to take him in."

Benson saluted.

"You have yourself a nice day, sir."

"Same to you Sergeant."

"Okay, men. Let's move out."

The platoon quickly climbed back into their vehicles. I walked back over to Faisal and watched the convoy turn around. There were several hard looks our way as the men motored off. Faisal turned to me once the convoy had disappeared from the valley.

"Is he angry with you?"

"Yeah, but a lot of people are angry with me. A lot of people are angry about a lot of shit in this world."

I looked over at Faisal.

"More to the point, my friend, it appears that our mutual history with the Kurdish rebels has come back to haunt us."

"Yes. I imagined it would."

"Oh, you did, huh? And just what do you know about me that you're not telling, Mr. Khabur?"

"I know of your history helping my people, that's all."

"You do, huh?"

"Yes. You are something of a legend, you know."

I scoffed.

"No. It was a noble thing you did. And we never forget a kindness."

I looked over at him.

"And let me guess. That's what you were doing back there at that gas station. Calling to check up on me."

"Yes. I wasn't sure what to do. I can't afford to bring more trouble to my people and you were becoming something of a liability."

I laughed.

"I was, huh?"

"Yes. But then I learned the truth and…well…I trust all is forgiven now."

"Sure, sure. So you mean, I don't have to worry about you stabbing me in the back anymore."

"No. And you?"

"No. I'd say you're safe…For now."

Faisal smiled acerbically. I looked off at the tire tracks in the snow.

"Well, whatever else there is to say, Mr. Khabur, Sgt. Benson just made it a hell of a lot easier for Saleem to find us."

"It is written," he said.

I smirked and headed back into the house.

The rest of the day dragged on, just watching and waiting. One o'clock came, then two. I kept hoping for David to call. Just when I needed the man, he couldn't be found.

I had been staring at the snowy landscape on that phone screen again when my own phone finally did ring. I jumped a bit, as always. You could never entirely prepare yourself for the unexpected.

"Yeah, David. I've been hoping you'd call."

"Yeah? Well, trust me. You really don't want to be hearing from me right now."

"Yeah, I know. Shit happens."

"Shit happens. I can't even begin to tell you how much flak I'm catching, trying to cover your tracks."

"Look, I'm really close but I need your help."

"And just what the hell have I been doing for these past two weeks?"

"A little more help."

"You're pushing me, buddy. You're really pushing me..."

"Look, David. I'm still in that blind, waiting for that seven pointer to show up but one of our guys here lost his phone. Thinks maybe he left it in a friend's car and the friend isn't answering. Wondering if you could track it for us."

"You really are pushing me."

"Yeah...You know, there's another snowstorm coming. Later today and into tonight. Would help a lot if we could find that phone first."

I gave him the number.

"All right. I'll see what I can do...When are you expecting to push out?"

"Tomorrow sometime. Better call and check in. I'll either have that buck by later tonight or it will be a major shitshow."

"All right. I'll see what I can do about moving some assets around."

There was silence.

"Get this done, partner. One more shitshow and you're on your own."

"You got it, chief."

"Okay. Back at you if I can find that phone."

Faisal had gone off to check on his soup. He glanced at me from the kitchen when I hung up.

"What was that?" he said.

"Oh, David. He's going to try and track that phone for us. The one I left under the Isuzu. Might give us a heads up on whether or not someone's coming."

"The soup is done. Did you want some?"

"Yeah. We'd better chow down. I've got a funny feeling that this battle is close at hand."

☐

Fifteen

We sat at the kitchen table together and ate. I quickly finished my soup and stood up.

"Do you have any other cold weather gear? Gloves? Scarves? Knit caps?"

Faisal got to his feet without answering and went off to the back of the house. He returned with several pairs of gloves, two scarves and a knit cap."

I took the gloves from Faisal and picked out a pair made of kid leather.

"These'll work," I said and tossed the rest of gloves onto the kitchen table. "That knit stuff will just get wet and soggy. How about thermal underwear?"

"Ah, yes."

He disappeared again and returned wearing a pair under his pants. He showed me.

"Good. Now let's get you all geared up before the shit hits the fan."

With Faisal's coat in place, I stood back and nodded.

"Khabur Force One."

A smile slowly crossed his face.

"You are pulling on my leg."

I smiled.

"A little."

I patted him on the shoulder and went out to the kitchen, digging around among the drawers for a knife.

"Here," I said, having found one that was compact and reasonably sharp. "If all else fails, you'll have this for close quarter battle."

I pretended to rake the knife across his throat and handed it to him.

"Or your own," I added. "You don't want to be taken alive by these assholes…I know I don't."

I patted him on the shoulder again, grabbed the phone and went to sit by the fire. After a moment, Faisal came over and stood beside me.

"What now?" he said.

I looked up at him and shrugged.

"We wait."

After a moment, Faisal returned to the kitchen. I heard him rummaging around out there and looked up. He had two sports drink bottles in his hands.

"These would hold soup." He unscrewed one of the tops to demonstrate. "If there is time in battle for us to eat."

"Probably not for that shit."

"Ah. Very well."

"Don't worry, Faisal. I've got plenty of jerky and protein bars for both of us."

He nodded and went about cleaning up in the kitchen. I glanced his way once. He looked a bit comical, all geared up for combat the way he was. The picture wanted a helmet.

Finally, he came over and sat by the fire, nervously driven to do something, when there was nothing to be done now except wait.

"Please," he said. "Let us go over everything again."

"All right. I'm going to take the high ground on that peak at the south end of the valley and you're going to take a position fifty yards to my right. Then we wait until they've checked inside the house and the surrounding area and start moving our way. You have to assume they'll get curious and start looking around."

"And if they don't?"

"I don't know. We'll cross that bridge if we come to it. The point is, we want them as far out in the open as possible. That way they can't quickly run for cover when we start firing."

"But I wait for your signal before I start."

"Yes, you wait for my signal...Look, like I told you, you're my cover. If you're firing while I'm picking them off with this SAKO, they won't know there's a sniper."

"But I fire in short bursts."

"Yes, but don't screw around. You're shooting to kill."

"I won't screw around."

"Okay. Then when I give you the signal, you leapfrog around to my left flank. Fifty yards or so. Whatever. Some distance. You just need to start firing again from a new position. That way they'll think there's more than two of us...We hope."

He stared.

"What?" I said.

"Does the plan ever change?"

"You bet...This is what we call game plan number one, which usually goes fubar within about five minutes."

"What is fubar?"

"Fucked up beyond all recognition."

"Ah. And if things go fubar on us? Then what?"

"Then we improvise. Look, the objective is to kill as many of these son of a bitches as possible while continuously moving so they're never sure just how many of us there are. Or where. Beyond that, our objective is to move steadily towards that Land Cruiser so our backs aren't against the wall if we get overwhelmed."

"Yes, we do not want our backs against the wall."

"No we don't. Anyway, I'll be picking them off with the SAKO as we go along and we'll see how things plays out from there. You can bet they'll be scrambling for cover with the first shots. Either back into the house or into the groves. But they'll regroup at some point and come after us. With a vengeance. You can bet your life on that."

Faisal stared into the fire, nervously playing with his hands.

"Look," I said. "Don't over think things. We have no idea how many of them there'll be. We may be totally outmanned from the start and have no choice but to run for it and live to fight another day. In battle, you just react to whatever's happening. Trust me, you'll be so pumped full of adrenalin from all the fireworks going off, you won't have time to worry."

Faisal was still staring into the fire.

"Just two other things," I said.

He looked back at me.

"First, we're still in agreement. If they all retreat to the house, I nail that propane tank with the RPG and blow them to hell."

"I have already told you. I can no longer live here. Someone will come along someday and build a new life in this valley but I would be haunted everyday by the memories I cannot forget."

"Okay. And point two. If Saleem comes here and he's in that house, it changes everything for me. Whatever it takes, I'm going to deal with that bastard face to face."

"So you have said."

"Even if it means to the death."

"So you have said."

"Well, I wouldn't blame you for taking the Land Cruiser and getting the hell out of here at that point. There's no need for you to stick around and fight to the death."

"No, my friend. I could never run away like that. What? And leave you here to fight on your own? No. I watch your back and you watch mine."

I smiled.

"You're a good man, Faisal. I hope we both live to see another day."

"If it is written."

I smirked. There was good reason to think that neither one of us would, but I had come here to finish something, and that was the way it was going to be.

We had been sitting there for a spell, watching the one phone on Facetime and talking occasionally when my phone rang. I saw the blocked number and quickly answered.

"What do we know?"

"That buck must be moving your way."

"You're sure of it."

"If that phone is any indication, damned sure of it. I've got him roughly ten clicks to your north and he's not alone."

"How not alone?"

"I'm counting three bucks. And multiply that."

There was a pause.

"Like you said, my friend, this is going to be a shitshow."

"I know."

"Maybe best to cut that hunting trip short."

"Not until I get that buck."

"You're a stubborn ass."

"I know."

"Okay. Here's to old times."

"Yeah. Thanks for the warning and I'll see you for New Year's."

"I'm holding you to it."

"Roger that."

There was silence and the phone went dead. I tucked it away in my vest and looked at Faisal.

"Time to move out, soldier."

"They are coming."

I nodded, pulled on my pack and started grabbing weapons.

"We have fifteen, twenty minutes so let's establish our battle positions, drop our auxiliary weapons and do a recon at the far end. I'd like to get a handle on just what we're facing before they pull in."

Once we had geared up, I headed for the door. Faisal paused by the kitchen.

"What?" I said.

"Maybe we should throw this food out. I do not wish to feed these men."

"Sentiment duly noted, soldier, but like I already told you. I don't want anyone thinking we're on to them. We dump the rest of that soup out in the snow and they're going to know something's up."

"Yes, yes. You are right."

"All right, come on. Let's move out."

Faisal closed the door behind himself and followed me around to the back of the house.

Off at the far end of the groves, where the trees gave way to a glade, I pointed left along one of the paths we had dug. Like all of them, it led up into the hills and eventually gave way to a jumble of brush and rocks near the summit. I scrambled up the last few feet and waited for Faisal.

"Go ahead and leave those two extra AKs here," I said when he joined me.

He set them down. I pointed back towards the house.

"There. From the house to the edge of the trees. That's where we make our first kill, before they can reach the groves. And we keep moving so they can't lock onto our position."

Faisal nodded. I headed off along the crest of the hill. It rose gently to a peak about a hundred yards to the north. I dropped everything there but one AK and continued north, descending now for roughly a hundred yards and then rising and falling gently as the crest arced steadily eastward.

Finally, we were looking back towards Madan. The snow had melted here and there, exposing rocks and shrubs.

Far off in the distance, you could see the greenness of the Euphrates, like a mirage on the horizon. I got out my binoculars and searched for any signs of their vehicles.

"Anything?" Faisal said.

185

I shook my head and looked down to where the Land Cruiser was parked.

"That's going to be a bitch," I said.

"Why? Because of the snow?"

"Yeah."

"It is a Land Cruiser."

"Yeah. I guess we'll find out what it's worth soon enough."

I turned the binoculars towards the west. The storm was coming. An arc of dark clouds had swallowed the sky in that direction.

How long before it got here? And to whose advantage?

I wouldn't be the first time I had fought in these conditions. David and I had been in a couple of shitshows together back in the '90s, up in the Serbian mountains. So bitter and cold, you considered yourself lucky to get out of there with all your fingers and toes still attached.

I focused the binoculars back on the road north.

"Still nothing?" Faisal said.

I shook my head.

"Here, you watch for a while."

I leaned back against a rock and felt the sun's faint warmth on my face. Ninety million miles away. One sun in a galaxy bursting with them, the galaxy but one dot in a universe strewn with more galaxies.

So what was I doing here? What was anybody doing here? Did Tom face these same questions in his final horrid moment of existence?

The images were back. I would never be free of them. Or of my hatred for his self-righteous killers.

I was trying one more time to hold Emine dear in my heart when I felt Faisal's tap on my shoulder. I opened my eyes, saw his gesture and took the binoculars.

At first, there was only a shimmering veil of ice crystals on the northern horizon. Then the hood of a vehicle appeared over a rise. It looked to be our Isuzu. A moment later, a Land Cruiser appeared, then a truck behind it, the truck bristling

186

with men in back and those men bristling with weapons. It was impossible to tell the precise number of men from that distance but I counted at least four in the back of the truck.

I lowered the binoculars and looked at Faisal.

"They are many?" he said.

"I'm guessing about fifteen. Six in the truck and maybe another four or five in each SUV."

I shrugged.

"It could be worse…There won't be nearly as many of them, once we get started."

I looked again with the binoculars. They were roughly two miles off. I tucked the binoculars away and patted Faisal on the shoulder.

"Better take our positions."

I ducked down in retreating, so as not to reveal myself and Faisal did the same. When we reached my post, I waved Faisal on.

"Get into position and call me. Let's make sure our coms are up and working…And make sure your ringer's on mute."

"I have already done so."

I nodded and watched him move out with a bit of a smile. He was the image of a green GI in an oversized helmet. You never knew how men would react in battle but I thought he would be okay. The man had reason in his head and courage in his heart.

I saw him settle into his position. My phone vibrated a moment later.

"Okay. We're good. You remember what to do?"

"Yes. A burst of fire. A short interval. Then another burst of fire and change positions."

"Yeah, well look. You're both covering for the sniper rifle and trying to kill the son of a bitches so don't get hung up on how many bursts of gun fire. Just make it short and sweet to conserve ammo and be ready to keep moving."

"Roger that."

I smiled.

"Roger that."

I hung up, got into a prone position with the Facetime phone screen next to my face, focused the SAKO on a rock to the left of the house and fired. The bullet kicked up some dust a foot to the right of the target. I adjusted the scope and fired again and hit the target square on.

Satisfied, I refocused my attention on the phone screen. The three vehicle caravan kept growing larger until I could start to make out individual faces. Was one of them Saleem? It was hard to tell. All their heads were wrapped in the traditional black shemagh of ISIS.

Strangely, all remained quiet until the vehicles passed by the phone. Then the convoy disappeared from view with a faint rumbling. I focused the scope on the entrance to the valley and waited but the vehicles did not appear. I looked up. All was silent again.

Okay, so they were being cautious. I should have known. These were zealous men, but not foolish.

Moments later, three men appeared on foot, sweeping the terrain with their AKs as they moved forward. Once they had established a cover position, the lead man waved and three more men appeared from the mouth of entrance, proceeding forward in the same classic search and clear formation. These men had been trained.

With the new team in a forward position, they gave cover as the first three men made a dash over to the walls of the house. One of them remained in my sights. The other two quickly disappeared around in front. A minute passed before those two reappeared from inside the house and waved in the direction of the entrance.

Within seconds, engines came to life and the convoy rolled into view, first the Isuzu, then the Land Cruiser and finally a Toyota truck. The vehicles parked in front of the house and more men piled out. I had counted a total of fourteen when the back door of the Land Cruiser opened and a fifteenth man appeared. I focused the scope on his head. I've got you,

Saleem. I could have ended his life right that second and felt a powerful urge to do so but stopped. The man deserved a slow and painful death and I was going to give it to him.

I did a sweep of the remaining men. They appeared to be discussing a game plan with Saleem.

I pulled back from the scope and looked Faisal's way. He was staring back at me. I gestured with two fingers at my eyes and looked back into the scope. The discussion was ongoing. Then Saleem said something and ten of the men started moving toward the groves. Saleem and the remaining four men disappeared back around to the front of the house.

The men coming towards us had roughly one hundred yards before they would disappear among the trees. I called Faisal.

"Yes," he answered in a whisper.

"Leave your phone on and when I say fire, fire."

"I am ready."

"Okay. Wait."

I set the phone down by my cheek and got focused on the man in lead. He would have the shortest distance to reach cover.

When they were roughly halfway between the house and the groves, I whispered, "Fire," and took my first shot. In that same instant, I heard Faisal's AK go off and saw the head of the man I had shot rock violently backwards. Three other men had been cut down by Faisal and the rest of them were quickly scattering for cover in a cacophony of curses and return fire.

"Fire," I said again and clipped one of them in the back.

"Okay, stop and relocate," I whispered and focused the scope on the downed man. He had fallen about thirty feet from cover behind the flatbed truck but was still moving. I put a bullet into his head and refocused on the grove.

"I am relocated," Faisal said.

"Okay. Hang on. I'm searching for the targets among the trees."

I pulled away, rubbed my eyes and looked back. The men Faisal had shot were not moving. That was good. We had quickly reduced their numbers from fifteen down to ten.

A minute went by before I spotted a man moving through the trees, and then another one, heading in the general direction of Faisal's previous position.

"Faisal," I said.

"Yes."

"Do you see anyone?"

"No."

"Okay. Next time I say fire, I want you to aim at the base of the hill, in the general direction of your last position, and from there into the grove."

"Okay. I will wait for your signal."

I swept the scope here and there through the groves and then back towards where I had last seen the men heading. Then I caught sight of two men again, pausing between two rows of plum trees.

"Okay," I said. "Get ready...fire."

I pulled the trigger with the bark of Faisal's AK going off in my left ear. The one man went down and the other one scrambled for cover.

Then I heard glass breaking and focused back on the house. Two of the men were firing wildly up at the hills through the windows. With rock and snow kicking up to my left, I ducked out of sight. The bullets continued for some seconds and stopped. I resumed searching the grove for the other four men.

"Are you okay?" I asked Faisal.

"Yes, I am okay."

"Do you see anyone?"

"No. Do you?"

"No."

That troubled me a bit. They might have retreated back the other way. I did not have a clear view from the grove to the south side of the house. But they could also be trying to circle around to my right flank. I couldn't see how but you had to consider every possibility.

I looked back over my shoulder. The storm clouds were closing in fast. The winter day was growing long. How much time did we have before it started to snow? Half an hour? Not long, whatever it was, and it would soon be dark.

I focused back on the house and the broken windows.

"Faisal," I said. "Stay focused."

"I am."

"There are still four men unaccounted for."

"I am watching for them."

"Okay. Next burst of fire, I want you to spray the back of the house. I'm going to try and pick off one of them through the window."

"I am ready."

"Okay."

I refocused on one of the broken windows, then the other. I had been back and forth several times when I saw a man peeking out cautiously from one side.

"Come on, you son of a bitch," I whispered.

"What?" Faisal said.

"Oh, just talking. I saw one of those bastards peeking out a second ago but he's being cautious. Just be ready."

"I am ready."

"Okay. Any second now."

I sensed the man lurking there in the shadows, looking here and there but just out of sight. Then the face reemerged.

"Fire," I said and pulled the trigger.

The jolt of the bullet bucked his head back and the body collapsed out of sight. There was yelling and cursing from inside the house and another spray of bullets wildly in the direction of Faisal's gunfire. Then all was quiet again.

"Seven down and eight to go," I whispered to Faisal.

"Yes. We are winning…What should I do next?"

"I don't know. You don't see any of the men who were down in the groves?"

191

"No. I do not see them."

I swept the scope back and forth in that direction but saw nothing. Something was off. The odds were definitely much more in our favor now but I still didn't like the feel of it. I couldn't account for four of the men and that continued to trouble me.

"Faisal," I said.

"Yes."

"Let's both move north about a hundred yards. Something doesn't smell right to me."

"I am moving now."

I searched the grove and the back of the house again before retreating out of sight and following Faisal.

Once we were settled into our new positions, I got out my binoculars and searched the valley, from the house to the groves and everywhere in between, but still no sign of anyone. The other men must have slipped back into the house somehow. That was all I could think.

I called Faisal again.

"Do you see anything?"

"Nothing."

"Yeah. Probably learned their lesson. They may even have figured out that they were being cut down by a sniper."

I refocused on the windows at the back of the house, then at the propane tank. About two seconds was all it would take for me to put an end to this shitshow.

"What are you thinking?" Faisal said.

"I don't know. Just keep your eyes open for any movement."

I hung up and refocused the binoculars on the house. What would I be doing if I were in Saleem's shoes?

A few seconds later, I jumped to my feet.

"What is it?" Faisal said, seeing me run by him.

"Nothing. Just keep your eyes on that house."

In a full gallop, I had reached that point where the hills jogged east and you could see back towards Madan when a man appeared over the crest, his head wrapped in a shemagh and his AK aimed at me. I quickly gunned him down but the report was met with many voices shouting and a barrage of return fire. I turned tail with bullets whistling over my head.

"What is it?" Faisal said when I reached his position.

"Saleem must have had reinforcements already coming!"

Two more men appeared over the hill in that instant, spraying bullets in our direction. I cut them down and dragged Faisal to his feet.

"Come on! Go go go! Retreat to the top of the hill!"

I followed Faisal for fifty feet and stopped to give cover. Men kept appearing from over the hill. It was like the gates of hell had been opened.

I turned and raced towards the top of the hill with more AKs going off. Down below to my left, I noticed men running my way through the groves. Saleem was among them, his eyes on me and his weapon firing.

Sixteen

Faisal had already taken cover among a cluster of rocks at the summit. I dove in beside him and started reloading. Bullets were splintering rock above our heads.

"Stay focused on the grove down there! Anyone tries to cross over from those trees to the base of the hill, you kill 'em!"

I peeked back in the direction from which I had just come. More men had appeared over the crest of the hill but they were moving cautiously from cover to cover now. I counted roughly two dozen. We had the high ground and that was about it.

"You see anyone down below, Faisal?"

"No. Not yet."

"All right. I want to hear that goddamned rifle of yours going off. Saleem and his men are down there somewhere."

"I am ready to fire."

"Good."

Just then, I spotted a fighter sprinting along the backside of the hill, trying to flank us. He appeared briefly among the rocks and brush and disappeared again. I grabbed the SAKO and waited for him to reappear. The minute he did, I fired and he dropped face down without moving.

I returned my focus to the north. The fighters had settled into position behind an outcropping of rocks. Roughly two hundred yards of open space now stood between us. With us holding the high ground, a head on assault would have amounted to a suicide mission. Again, they were zealous, but not stupid.

"Look, Faisal," I said while using the scope of the SAKO to search in that direction. "I'm not going to sugar coat this. If these hostiles can circle around us to our south and west, we're screwed. From one or even two directions, we can pick them off like fish in a barrel. From four directions at once? They'll quickly overwhelm us."

Our eyes met.

"For now, just keep your eyes focused down there. And if you see an RPG pointed in our direction, I want to hear you squawking."

"What is squawking?"

"Like it's urgent."

"I will squawk then."

"Good."

We both sat there in the now eerie silence, watching and waiting. Again, I didn't like the feel of it. Something was up.

"I see men at the edge of the trees," Faisal whispered.

I turned the scope in that direction. They were at least a dozen strong. So more men had arrived down there too. I focused on one of them and put a bullet into his head. That led to a lot of yelling and a hasty retreat. I nailed one more in the back before they had completely disappeared.

With those men out of sight, I refocused to the north. The quiet bothered me. Wanting to get a better look at the back of the hill, I poked my head up and several AKs barked out.

"Fuck," I said with bullets ricocheting off the rocks above us.

"What did you see?" Faisal said.

"Just what I feared. Some of them have flanked us to the west."

"Then what do we do?"

"I don't know, Faisal. I'm thinking."

I had refocused the scope to the north, searching the terrain for any sign of the fighters when Faisal yanked on my arm.

"RPG! RPG!"

I whipped around with the SAKO, spotted the man near the edge of the trees and fired. The man had fired the RPG in nearly the same instant and the smack of the bullet into his chest sent his grenade spiraling up into the sky. I heard it explode off to our southwest and down out of sight. That was followed by a number of men yelling excitedly.

"Like I said, Faisal. Some of them have circled around to our west."

I sat there weighing the options. We were flanked on at least three sides now and could expect an assault. Somehow we had to make our way to a vehicle, any vehicle.

"Look Faisal. We've got to go on the offensive. I'm guessing back towards the house. That's probably the direction with the fewest number of hostiles. If we can get to the house and one of the vehicles there, we've got a chance."

I shrugged.

"I'm sorry. It doesn't look good. I'd say our odds of survival are 50/50. Probably less than that."

"So we fight to the end, my friend."

I nodded.

"Just remember. If it comes to that, it's best not to be taken alive."

Faisal nodded and patted me on the shoulder.

The storm looked to be brooding just a few miles away now and coming fast. A snowstorm wouldn't be the worst thing that could happen right then, but no magic bullet.

I had taken a deep breath, still weighing things, when the assault began, and with a vengeance. I peeked out with an endless barrage of bullets cracking off the rocks above my head. I had seen enough to know that the advance was coming from both the north and the west.

"They are coming from the grove!" Faisal said.

"Then shoot the motherfuckers!"

With his AK going off next to my ear, I raised mine up over my head, raked the hillside to the north and west, grabbed another AK when that magazine was empty and continued firing. It was impossible to tell if I had hit anyone but the return fire had stopped for the moment.

"What's going on down there?" I said.

"I have killed two or three more but some have made it to the base of the hill."

"All right. Time to use these grenades."

I handed one to Faisal.

"Pull the pin, count to three and then throw it, okay?"

"But where?"

"Throw yours down there towards the base of the hill. I'll throw mine back the other way."

I grabbed my pin. He grabbed his.

"Ready?"

He nodded.

"Okay, go…"

At the count of three, we both tossed our grenade and hunkered down tighter among the rocks. A few seconds later, the two explosions rocked the afternoon. That was followed by screams and shouting and return gunfire. I sprayed the surrounding terrain again for good measure and settled back.

"You still have that Springfield?"

Faisal patted his waist band.

"Okay. You've got thirteen rounds. If it comes down to that, you hold one round back…"

I shrugged and poked my head around a rock, hoping to see what was coming. That was met with another barrage of gunfire. They had to be within seventy-five yards to our north now and I assumed even closer to our west.

I felt the first snowflake hit my face and looked up with Christmases of old flashing through my head. Friends stopping by for good cheer. A turkey dinner and hot totties by the fire.

Then Emine was in my heart. Darling Emine. Please forgive me if I don't make it back. I would have done anything to free you from your bondage.

"Look," I said, glancing at Faisal. "If we're going to die, let's damned well go out fighting."

"Yes. Let us go out fighting."

"At the very least, I'm going to try and take out Saleem before I'm dead."

"Yes. I will be happy to help you with that."

"Okay. I'll lead the assault down the hill. You cover our rear. We go from position to position. Move. Cover. Move again. Okay?"

He nodded.

"All right. I'm going to send this RPG down there first."

I put it over my shoulder, got down into a cleft in the rocks and watched until I saw someone moving among the trees before firing. As soon as it exploded, I grabbed the two extra AKs.

"Let's go!"

We had barely gotten to our feet when all hell broke loose again, bullets clanking off the rocks everywhere and the sounds of dozens of men charging our position. I ducked back down and sprayed over my head with an AK.

Then my phone rang. I saw the blocked number and answered while still firing.

"Great timing, David."

"Is that you, Blake?" a voice said.

"Yeah? Who the hell is this?"

"Danny."

"Danny? What are you doing, calling me?"

"David said you might need a hand. I'm coming in from the northwest this very minute."

I peeked over the rocks and caught a brief glimpse of his helo before a barrage of bullets sent me back into hiding.

"You see me?" he said.

"Yeah. You see me?"

"I see a bunch of monkeys laying siege to the peak of that hill."

"That's us. My partner and I are cornered up here among those rocks at the summit."

"Got it. Give me a minute and I'll have those hajis scrambling for cover."

"All right, Danny, but look. The man I've been hunting is down on the other side of this hill so as soon as you start lighting things up, we're going to push out in the other direction. I want my hands on that fucker before he's dead."

"Roger that, buddy. I'll clean up topside and await further instructions. You run into any other resistance, just let me know where and give them hell."

"Roger that. We'll be here awaiting first contact."

"Got your back, partner."

I put the phone away and patted Faisal on the arm.

"The cavalry just rode in."

"Who is the cavalry?"

I looked up from loading fresh magazines.

"A friend of David's. I don't know how in hell he got here and I don't care. He's in an assault helo and coming this way."

Just then, we heard the first roar of the blades and the sound of men fleeing in panic. I smiled at Faisal.

"It is written, my friend."

He smiled back.

"All right. As soon as we hear his incoming fire, we start our assault down the hill. I don't want that Saleem getting away."

A few seconds later, I heard a .50 caliber going off, quickly followed by an explosion.

"All right, move out! And remember to cover our rear!"

I slung the SAKO over my shoulder along with the two extra AKs and jumped out of our enclosure. The snow was starting to come down in earnest now. The groves and the house had grown lost in a mist.

I advanced a hundred feet along the hillside and paused with my AK sweeping the groves. Danny was still raking the hillside behind us. It sounded like the action was quickly moving north, back towards the entrance to the valley. Faisal came up behind me.

"Anything?" I said.

"I see no one."

"Okay. I'm moving out again."

I proceeded cautiously the rest of the way down the hill and waited on the valley floor. Faisal pulled up a few seconds later and joined me in a crouch. I was peering back towards the house through the swirling snow. When he started to speak, I held up a hand. It was nearly impossible to hear over the commotion from the other side of the hill. Then the sound of voices echoed through the grove.

"They're trying to get away!" I said and ran off in a gallop. "Stick with me!" I called out over my shoulder.

Halfway through the grove, I saw forms materialize through the swirling snow and got back down in a crouch. Faisal caught up with me and did the same.

"All right, here's what I want you to do. Go down towards the entrance and watch for any vehicles trying to escape. If you see one, rake their tires. I'm going to look for Saleem back at the house."

Faisal started to leave but I grabbed him by the shoulder.

"Not too close. Stay away from the road. We've gotten this far. I don't want to see you getting killed now out of carelessness."

"Khabur Force One."

I chuckled.

"All right. I'll try to neutralize everyone else. Text me if you see anyone leaving and I'll come pin them down from the rear."

I slapped him on the shoulder.

"Go. Give me a couple of minutes and I'll be right on your heels."

I watched him head off through the blinding snow and raced off in the other direction.

Nearing the back of the house, I slowed and moved cautiously towards the far corner, then slid down towards the front along the side wall. Halfway there, I heard a burst of gunfire go off down by the entrance and checked my phone. Nothing from Faisal. This had the smell of trouble about it but I couldn't risk calling him. Not until I had cleared the house.

I continued on to the front of the building and peeked around the corner. The Toyota truck was idling out in front with a man standing alongside it. I carefully pulled the SAKO from over my shoulder, made sure the man wasn't looking my way and put one bullet into his head. He fell forward with a gasp and was silent.

The front door to the house was open and I had to assume someone was in there, but who? And how many? And had they seen the man go down?

I paused, thinking. It couldn't be Saleem. He wouldn't have waited behind. And even if he had, he would have been in the Land Cruiser, and with more men surrounding him.

I checked my phone again. Still not a word from Faisal.

Fearing the worst, I threw all caution to the wind and ran past the front door while firing into the house. There was return fire, but only from one rifle.

Fine. Whoever it was, he wasn't getting away. I galloped down towards the valley entrance while calling Faisal. After several rings, someone answered. Then the screen went to Facetime and I was looking at Saleem. He said something in Arabic and turned the screen the other way. They had Faisal with a gun to his chest in the backseat.

Saleem turned the screen back on himself, pretended to rake his knife across his own throat and smiled.

"Motherfucker," he said and pointed the knife at me.

"Fuck! I'll come find you, Faisal! I'll come find you and kill every one of those motherfuckers!"

The screen went dead.

"Goddamn it!"

I dialed Danny's number while racing back towards the house. He was still raking the other side of the hill with the .50 cal.

"What's up, buddy?" he said.

"My target got away and took my partner hostage."

"Shit. Bad business. What can I do?"

"Well, if you're done back there, drop in over here so we can talk. I've got one more hostile to terminate at the house and then we're clear."

While running in that direction, I saw headlights coming out of the snowstorm.

"Hang on. I've got the bastard in my sights right now."

I set the phone down and waited until the truck was nearly upon me before spraying a short burst of fire. The driver slumped over and the truck veered off the road, crashing into some shrubs. I grabbed the phone and approached the vehicle cautiously. The man was alone and clearly dead so I opened the driver's side door and dragged him out into the snow.

"We're all clear," I told Danny. "See you back at that house."

"Roger. On my way now."

I rifled through the car and found some food and utensils from Faisal's kitchen. The man had also helped himself to several blankets and a coat. Out of anger, I kicked the dead man in the head, climbed in and backed the truck up the road until I was at the house.

There was an extra AK and some ammunition on the shotgun side of the cab. I ran around to the far side of the house and retrieved my own weapons.

While placing everything in the cab, I heard Danny circling in overhead. I stood back and shielded my face as he dropped in.

With the helo on the ground, Danny jumped out and ran over to greet me. Another man jumped out of the back and joined us.

"Popeye," Danny said, introducing us.

We shook hands. Popeye looked the part. Arms as big as hams, a goatee and bandana, an AK across his chest.

"Tough luck about your partner," Danny said.

"Don't tell me that. We've got to track that fucker down before they cut his head off."

Danny looked up at the sky.

"Not in this weather."

"Come on, Danny. Don't bail on me now."

"Hey. It's over. You did everything you could. David arranged for me to drop you off in Mosul before I head back."

"Forget it. I'm not leaving my partner behind."

"Yeah, sure. Understood."

He shrugged.

"If it wasn't for this storm, I wouldn't hesitate but I shouldn't even be here in the first place and I'm sure not going to head back into the teeth of this blizzard. Especially not with all those hills in that direction. Hell, we'll all end up a charred ruin and puff of smoke. As it is, I'm going to have to race south for a spell and circle back around."

"Fair enough, but I've got to move out."

"You know where you're going?"

"I've got a lead."

Danny nodded his chin at the truck.

"It's going to be a hell of a ride with that windshield blown out."

"Yeah. There should be a Land Cruiser just to the other side of that passageway."

"Yeah. I think I saw it."

"Yeah? Those hostiles didn't take it?"

"No. It's still there. You want me to guide you in?"

"Yeah. I roughly know where it's parked but with all this snow, it's going to be a bitch finding it. It's going to be a bitch getting it back out to the road."

"We'll get it. You'll find me hovering over the top."

"Thanks."

"Hey, sorry again, partner. You're sure you don't want to just...we could have you back to civilization in about three hours."

I reached out and shook Danny's hand, then Popeye's.

"Appreciate you boys coming to save my ass but I've got to roll."

I brushed some of the glass off the front seat, climbed into the truck and gunned the accelerator. The snowfall was growing more furious by the minute and I had maybe ten of them before Saleem's tracks got completely buried on the road ahead.

I heard the helo going airborne behind me and moving out over the hills. When I cleared the passageway, I found Danny using his rotor blades to push the snow aside. I followed him in and spotted the Land Cruiser. The snow was up over the tires but otherwise looked intact.

I drove off to the side and climbed out with Danny hovering over my head. It took me a minute to clear the windshield and side door of snow but the keys were where Faisal had left them. I started the engine and flicked the lights on and off several times. Danny rocked the helo back and forth in response, rose a few hundred feet and banked away to the south. I quickly transferred all the weapons from the other vehicle and headed out in the storm.

The visibility was shit and the road even shittier but I had the tire tracks to guide me and raced forward as fast as I could without careening off the road. I had one clue to guide me. What the Iman had told Faisal. On the road between Deir ez-Zor and Al Suwar. Somewhere close to halfway, there was a home off to the left and back up among the hills. How I was supposed to track things down from there, I had no idea. The distance between those two towns was thirty miles. Never mind that I would be driving through ISIS held territory and into the teeth of a snowstorm.

I was just wishing for David to call when my phone rang.

"You fucking madman," he said before I could speak.

"I wouldn't leave your ass behind and I'm not leaving Faisal."

"Yeah, well. Good luck finding him now."

"They still have the Isuzu."

There was silence.

"Goddamn it. I can't keep bailing you out. This hunting trip's going to cost me my job. It's got to end."

"I saw that buck."

"Yeah?"

"Yeah. I find that Isuzu and I find that buck. I find that buck and I find my guide."

There was more silence.

"You have any clues."

"Yeah. I'm heading that way now. East, then north. Probably driving right into the teeth of trouble."

David scoffed.

"When haven't you been?"

"Yeah. Should have taken a desk job like you."

"Desk job, my ass."

"Just track the Isuzu. That will lead me to the buck and I'll take it from there. This hunting trip will be over soon enough, one way or the other."

"Yeah. I'll believe that when I see it."

"I'm one shot away. Just guide me in."

"I'll get back to you when I have some fresh intel."

The phone went dead.

I forged ahead through the blinding storm, a man on a mission, but I had always been a man on a mission, at the end of which, I always expected to find a moment of peace awaiting me, a place where I could finally leave all the madness of this world behind. Except each time I got to that place, I found another mission awaiting me. The truth was, I wouldn't know what to do with myself without a mission. Life without a mission was abhorrent to me, an infinite black hole of nothingness into which your soul got sucked for all eternity.

Well, I definitely had a mission in front of me now.

I felt pain in my side and touched that area. It was tender but did not seem to be infected. Still, I took another one of Faisal's penicillin pills and grabbed a protein bar from my vest to chase it down.

Don't worry, Faisal, I thought as I removed the packaging with my teeth. I'm coming to save you.

"I'm coming to save your ass!" I yelled out loud.

I tried to picture the scene. They'd get back to wherever they were going. Throw Faisal into a room. Talk. Eat. Get their video equipment ready. Talk some more. Then drag Faisal out, make him kneel and start their bullshit spectacle. The infidel this, the infidel that.

I had two, maybe three hours to catch up with them.

I turned up the heater and pressed on through the driving snowstorm.

Then Tom was back. I had been so busy in battle, the images had almost completely escaped me. So fast. So frantically bloody and gruesome. As gruesome as your partner stepping on a land mine and lying there with his legs blown off. The writhing and screaming in pain were the same, just a different end of the body.

I tried to think of Emine and the Alps again. Someplace simple. Someplace far away and pure. A place where the horrors of this world would once and for all go away and leave me in peace.

Seventeen

I stumbled back upon the main road without warning and slammed on the brakes. By the time the Land Cruiser came to a halt, I had careened across to the opposite shoulder. I dropped it in reverse, backed around until I was pointed in the right direction and sat there staring at the map on my phone. According to GPS, there were bridges at both Madan and Halabiyah and I was now roughly halfway between the two. Detouring west to Madan and further away from ISIS control was probably my best bet. Besides, I already had a reputation in Halabiyah but Madan meant going twenty miles out of the way and I had no the time for that. I had to cross the river here. There would not be another chance until much closer to Deir ez-Zor and that would definitely be a suicide mission.

I turned right, to the east, hoping that nobody else was dumb enough to be out in this weather. Even if there were sentries watching the bridge, I wasn't stopping.

Five miles ahead, I flew by another turnoff and slammed on the brakes. With the storm blowing in from my left flank now, it was nearly impossible to see in that direction. Having careened down the road a few hundred feet, I backed up and made the turn.

The road slowly swung from due north to due west, increasing my visibility. The bridge was five miles up from the turnoff. I passed the mosque and then the dirt road to where Faisal and I had encountered that ISIS patrol. Then I was alongside the Euphrates with farmland and scattered homes on either side me. Darkness was setting in.

Sighting the bridge up ahead, I slowed to a crawl. There did not appear to be any sentries. I should have guessed. This was no man's land, no longer ISIS territory, but not yet controlled by the coalition.

Proceeding cautiously, I crossed over to the north side of the river and turned right. The town of Zalabiye straddled the road on that side and passed for cosmopolitan in this remote area. I saw a sign for what looked like an electronics store, with crude images of a cell phone and computer, and then another mosque. No one was out in the storm.

With Zalabiye in my rearview mirror, I expanded the map on my phone and glanced at it while driving. Deir ez-Zor was twenty miles straight ahead but the road to Al Suwar ran right out of the city center, another a suicide mission. I expanded the map further and saw a maze of streets five miles back up the road from ez-Zor. Assuming I made it that far, it appeared that those streets would provide me with a way to bypass the main road and skirt around the city proper.

I turned my attention back to the road ahead. Snow was swirling in my headlights and blinding my vision. The road itself was getting lost in the snowdrifts. I leaned forward and peered into the darkness.

Half an hour later, I had neared the maze of streets that would be my detour when I came upon a line of stalled cars and tail lights, disappearing off into the snowstorm up ahead. Given the snow and darkness, it was impossible to tell just how far the line went, but this was definitely trouble.

I expanded the map further and saw that there was another maze of side streets some distance behind me. Most of them appeared to wind off through farmland, and in the wrong direction, but if the map was correct, one of them would eventually get me back to the main bypass road.

I had started to put the Land Cruiser in reverse when I noticed a man approaching down the line of cars, an AK in his hands while peering into each driver's side window.

Okay. There was no getting around this situation now. I turned off the wipers, quickly screwed the silencer onto the Glock and slipped out the shotgun side door.

The car in front of me was a Toyota sedan. I got down in a crouch behind the trunk and peeked out. The man was three cars up ahead now. I lowered my head further and watched for his feet.

When he came astride the Toyota, his progress stalled. He must have noticed my windshield wipers being off. I watched his footsteps continue forward cautiously. Then he appeared in my vision with the AK pointed at my windshield. I sprang up and delivered one bullet under his chin. The back of his head blew off and flew away in the storm. I took him by one arm and dragged him off to the side of the road before wiping my bloodied hands in the snow. Then I walked back around to the Toyota's driver side door and lowered my head. The middle-aged couple glanced my way, looking terrified. I put a finger to my lips and they both nodded. I nodded back and quickly jumped back into the Land Cruiser.

With the lights off and the windshield wipers back on, I made a U-turn and headed west. A few hundred yards farther down the road, I turned the headlights back on. I had the phone on my knee and the map expanded, searching for that other maze of streets.

When I spotted what I thought was the right road, I turned off, only to find myself at a dead end. In the middle of nowhere, and in the middle of a snowstorm, a dog started barking.

Christ. Time was of the essence. I had to find Faisal before they took his head off. And I had to make the main road to Al Suwar before they found that hostile back there dead, but here I was, driving around in circles. What a shitshow.

I looked again at the maze of streets on the map. Some of them clearly did go nowhere, and most of the others went off wildly in the wrong direction. I went back to the main road, turned right and tried again.

The next turn went on for a quarter mile before coming to a T-intersection. If the map was correct, the main bypass road was now one mile to my right. Buoyed by this prospect, I made the turn and checked my watch. Nearly ten minutes since I had killed that man. They would start missing him soon, if they hadn't already.

I expanded the map again and looked at where the bypass met the road to Al Suwar. It was barely five miles out of downtown ez-Zor at that point and gut instinct told me that I did not want to be anywhere that close to ISIS headquarters.

By chance more than anything, I arrived to the bypass road and felt delivered. It is written, I thought, and turned left, heading north. Two miles farther on, the road veered to the east. I passed the road back to Tall Tamr. The Al Suwar road was a mile ahead.

A half mile shy of that, I spotted a road on my left and took it. It wound off through a small community and came to an end. Oh for fuck's sake. Going by the satellite image, there was an industrial complex of some kind just to the other side of these homes.

I searched in every direction on the map but this was it. Either I got to that industrial complex from here or I'd have to head back towards Deir ez-Zor and take my chances.

Ready to scream, I checked to make sure the Land Cruiser was in 4-wheel drive and headed off through the brush. On a clear night, it might have been a simple excursion. In a snowstorm, it was madness. Even with 4-wheel drive, I went along with the tires spinning and the rear end fishtailing wildly. For all I knew, I was about to drive into a ditch.

In less than the distance of a football field, I felt as if I had just navigated two hundred miles of broken terrain but finally spilled out onto a road. A foul scent hit me straight off. Apparently, I had found my way to a sewage treatment plant.

At least I was back on a good road. The highway to Al Suwar was straight ahead. I stepped on the gas and checked my watch. Twenty minutes since I had terminated that hostile. Nearly an hour and a half since they had abducted Faisal. Madness. Madness. I had no hope of finding Saleem's hideout without a trace on that Isuzu. And that was assuming they still had it, and that I was anywhere near to where they had taken Faisal.

Arriving back out to the main road, I paused. Where the hell was David? Just as I was cursing his name, my phone rang.

"About time," I said, answering it.

"I have a day job, you know."

"Yeah, yeah. Just tell me where the hell I am."

"You're warm."

"I already know I'm warm. I need to be hot. They'll be skinning that buck without me if I don't get there soon."

"All right. A minor problem though. You see that Circle K up the road a bit?"

I pulled back on the map and saw where there was a roundabout of some kind about one click up the road towards Al Suwar.

"Yeah. I see it. What about it?"

"Don't stop there. I hear the foods deadly."

"Fuck!"

I zoomed back in on the industrial area I had just exited.

"What the hell? It just looks fubar every which way I turn. You do realize I'm in a driving snowstorm, right?"

"You're the one who decided to go on this hunting trip."

"Just fucking get me there!"

"All right, cowboy. Calm down and cross the road."

"Cross the road?!"

"You want me to get you there or not?"

"All right. Fuck."

I did as instructed.

"Okay. Now what?"

"Straight ahead."

"I can't see shit but snow."

"You're on a road."

"You could have fooled me."

"You're on a road."

I drove along, going further mad with every second. Faisal's life was probably measured in minutes now and I had just blown nearly half an hour on this bullshit detour.

"Whoa, whoa," David said. "Slow down, slow down...Okay, now turn left."

"Turn left? It's a snow drift."

"It's a road."

"All right, goddamn it. Now what?"

"Straight ahead...Nice country?" he added.

"Fucker."

"All right. You're doing good. Another hundred yards and you're going to veer left at a 45."

"Oh fuck, yeah. A 45."

"Just picture it in your mind."

I did, as best I could.

"Okay," David said. "You should now be looking at a flat expanse of terrain off to your right."

"A road?"

"I don't know. I don't think so. A wash. Farmland. Whatever it is, just gun it and plow through. Then about a mile up ahead, you'll come up on another road."

"Madness," I said.

"Well, it's flat, isn't it?"

"Yeah. I'll give you that much...Okay, here goes."

I punched the accelerator and went flying through the drifts, dodging whatever shrubs I saw poking up through the snow as I did. A few minutes later, I came to a road running perpendicular to my direction. There was a farmhouse across from me.

"A miracle. I'm back to civilization. So now what?"

"Turn left. You'll find the main road a quarter mile up ahead."

"And that Circle K?"

"It's about a half a click back down the road from you now."

Still wanting to scream from all the delays and lost time, I raced up to the main road and careened onto it with barely a look back.

"Okay. Now what?"

"About five clicks up the road, you turn left. And then it looks like another two clicks up into the hills from there."

"Okay. Don't you dare go anywhere."

"Sorry. The day job's calling."

"Goddamn it, David! Don't leave me here hanging!"

"Just chill out. I'm watching. I'll ring back as soon as you're near."

I had started to yell at him again when the phone went dead.

Son of a bitch. I did scream. I had come here, intent on a nice, clean, straight forward mission. Track, locate, execute and get out. Now things were complicated beyond anyone's ability to understand it.

Remembering that flask of Wild Turkey in my vest, I pulled it out and had a good slug. It burned my throat but warmed my guts. I had another swig to calm my nerves and put the flask away.

With a glance at the odometer, I made note of the miles and peered back at the road ahead. I was driving into the teeth of the storm again, with the visibility about a hundred feet ahead, if that.

I had one thing in my favor. No one else was dumb enough to be out in this blizzard. I had the road to myself and was plowing right down the center lane.

I had driven another four clicks and was ready to curse David again when the phone rang.

"I'm still pissed at you for hanging up on me."

"Shut up, slow down and listen. You're almost on top of that road."

"I hate to tell you, but there ain't no roads around here."

"Slow down. Stop stop stop! You're there. Turn left."

"Turn left?! There's a cliff over here!"

"It's not a cliff. I've seen this shit before. The road's just elevated above the surrounding terrain."

Still wary, I eased over to the left side of the road.

"You're sure about this?"

"I'm telling you. You're there. Go."

I eased the left tire farther in that direction and felt my heart drop as the Land Cruiser went briefly airborne before hitting solid ground again. I eased forward a bit more until the right tire also dropped from the lip of the asphalt. The incline was bordering on 45° but I quickly came back to level ground.

"Okay," I said. "I'm still upright. Now what?"

"Straight ahead for two clicks."

"Straight ahead. I wish you could see what I'm seeing."

"It's farmland. You've got four-wheel drive, don't you?"

"Yeah."

"So quit bitching. If you get off the road a bit, you're still on level ground. Just move out. I need to get back to what I was doing before you intruded into my life."

"Well don't you dare hang up on me again."

"I'm hanging with you. Just move out."

I headed off with the wind on my right flank now but still unable to see a damned thing. There were heavy snow drifts everywhere I looked and gusts of it blowing past my windshield.

"So, what are you doing for Christmas?" David said.

"Fucker...You know, Lydia gave me a Dear John call just before I left for this hunting trip."

"Wow. Bummer. Great timing."

"No shit…The truth is, I've always had this feeling that she was scheming behind my back."

"That sounds like fun."

"Yeah. Some people just don't know how to come clean with their baggage…So what the fuck? Where am I going here?"

"You're almost there. You should be starting to see the shoulder of a hill."

"Did I mention that I'm in a goddamned blizzard?"

"Yeah yeah. You'll have it in your sights any second now."

I had driven another hundred feet when the base of a hill rose up in my headlights. I hit the brakes and turned off the lights.

"Okay, got it. Now what?"

"All right. Open up your map app."

"It's already open." I zoomed in on my location. "What am I looking for?"

"Scroll northwest. You see that farm compound? About half a click from where you're sitting?"

"Yeah, I see it. Is that my target?"

"That's where that phone is. I don't know about anything else. Best to park around to the far side of that knoll and walk in. If this is the buck you're looking for, he's not alone."

"All right. Got it. Thanks for guiding me in."

"Sure. You did know it's Christmas Eve, right?"

"Yeah. Thanks for reminding me…Look, I'll mute my phone so check in with me in an hour. I'll either be dead or have command of the situation."

"Just don't lose your head."

"Yeah. Funny."

"All right. Back at you at 0700."

"Roger that."

I ended the call and looked at my watch. A bit past 0600. Christ, it felt like midnight. It felt as if I had been on the road for twelve hours when it was just a bit more than two since I had left the valley. I got out and gazed into the snow flurries.

Without the lights, you couldn't see fifty feet in front of your face.

Screw it, I thought. There's no time to waste. I could get at least another quarter mile closer without being seen.

I climbed back into the Land Cruiser and eased forward. Going by the map, there was a barn or something in the lee of the hill, with the house two hundred yards off to my northeast. Best to clear the barn first. There were bound to be fireworks when I assaulted the house and I didn't need any hostiles crawling up my back. And that assumed I could clear the barn quietly. Otherwise I'd have the main force crawling up my back.

Without really knowing where I was, but sensing I had gotten close enough, I parked, ate the last of my protein bar, checked my phone to make sure it was on mute, put fresh magazines into the Glock and Sig, grabbed the AK on the seat next to me and double checked that magazine. If I couldn't neutralize these hostiles with that much fire power, I was probably in over my head.

Climbing out, I pulled the hood up over my head, cinched it tight and moved forward. The blizzard raged around me.

I had walked a few hundred yards when I froze, thinking I had seen an orange light through the snow flurries. Then I heard voices over the wind. I inched forward and listened again. I had moved forward a few more feet when the side of the barn suddenly loomed out of the storm. Startled, I nearly let off a round. Fortunately there did not appear to be a sentry outside.

I retreated several paces and slipped around to the backside of the building. The orange light I had seen appeared to be a fire flickering away inside. I put my ear to the wall. There were voices and laughter. It sounded like three men, maybe four.

Checking again for sentries, I started slowly down the wall until I was alongside the barn door. Peeking through a crack, I saw the fire and three men sitting around it. Each of them had an AK in his lap. I eased over to the latch side of the door and tried the knob gently. It wasn't locked.

I got down low and peeked inside again. The men were still busy talking. I had started to back away and prepare my weapons when a wild gust of wind blew up and one of the men looked my way. I froze. The other men were now looking my way too. I remained frozen in place, knowing that if I moved, I would give myself away.

The men kept staring. The storm raged on around me.

Then one of them said something and they turned their attention back to the fire with a laugh.

With their conversation resuming, I stepped back one pace, focused all of my thoughts into the center of my being, placed my left hand on the door knob, took a deep breath and flung the door open. In a swift succession of shots from my Glock, I cut short what was a mad scramble to lift their AKs and fire.

While approaching the bodies, I scanned for more hostiles. There was an old tractor nearby, a pen with goats off to my right and a storage room of some kind beyond the pen.

I heard one of the men groan and looked back that way. The other two men were clearly dead. I walked over to the fire and added a bullet to each brain cavity, just to be safe. Even the dead bodies visibly heaved in response.

My thoughts had turned to the next phase of my mission when I noticed a fourth AK lying on the ground and in that instant sensed the shadow over my shoulder. Reflexively, my forearm rose up in defense, blunting the slash of a knife, but in all of that, the Glock had dropped from my hand and the man had gotten his left arm around my neck.

While battling to keep his knife from my throat, I pivoted my hips and jammed my left elbow into his solar plexus. He recoiled from the loss of breath, freeing me to slam my right elbow into his throat. As he stood there with both hands at his collapsed trachea, I took his head and jammed his face into my kneecap. There was a gasp as his nasal bone crushed into his frontal cortex and he went limp in my hands. I let him drop to the ground, picked up the Glock and added a bullet to his brain, then added a few more out of anger.

With a look at my arm, I cursed out loud.

"Motherfucker!"

The bastard had cut me down to the bone.

My senses alert for any other possible hostiles, I grabbed the shemagh from the man's head, cinched it off above my elbow and headed out into the blizzard, running as fast as I could back to the Land Cruiser. My plan was to bring it and my arsenal up to the barn and have everything in one place. Then I would assault the main house. I could only hope they hadn't already taken off Faisal's head.

☐

Eighteen

Standing in the lee of the Land Cruiser, I peeled back my coat and shirt sleeve and had a good look. The sight of the wound made me nauseous.

I grabbed a handful of snow and held it against my flesh. The insanity of my mission raged on in the blizzard. I knew how it had gotten started. I had lost sight of where it was headed

You're just flat out crazy. That's the truth of it, Blake. You don't know what the fuck you're doing anymore.

No, no. Lock that shit down. You're here to rescue Faisal. Nothing else matters now but saving your partner.

With my wound now numb, I climbed back behind the wheel of the Land Cruiser, left the lights off and moved forward in the blinding snow. Sensing I was close to the barn, I parked and approached the rest of the way on foot. Rule number one. Make no assumptions. No telling if someone had come down to check on things while I was gone. I could hardly see ten feet in front of my face and assumed the same could be said of the enemy.

My heart jumped, seeing the side of the barn loom up again unexpectedly. I peeked through the cracks in the door. Everything appeared to be just as I had left it.

Before gathering up all the weapons and ammunition inside, I searched the back of the barn and found a storage room with a sealed door. Opening it, I nearly fell over backwards. The room reeked of something foul. With a sleeve over my nose and mouth, I pulled out my pen flashlight and peered inside. There were dozens of plastic barrels stacked inside.

Holy shit. I quickly reclosed the door before the fumes got anywhere near that fire.

Back outside, I tossed all of the weapons into the back of the Land Cruiser and paused with another look at the map on my phone. There was an out building of some kind not far from the main house. Hard to tell what it was from the satellite shot but by the size and shape, I had my money on it being a shed or chicken coop. Whatever it was, it had to be cleared first.

I walked off into the storm a short distance, realized there was no way anyone could see my approach from fifty yards, let alone three hundred, and hurried back to the Land Cruiser. With the lights still off, I inched forward, making a mental count of the distance as I went.

When it seemed as if I had gotten close enough, I stopped and stared into the blizzard. A minute passed before I geared up and headed out. Every ten feet or so, I stopped to scan the darkness and had gone on like this for a minute or so when I saw lights through the storm. I pulled my phone back out. Based on my best reading of the situation, the lights had to be from the main house, which would place the out building off to my left a hundred yards.

I circled around some distance, hoping to come in from the rear of it, and was beginning to think I had gotten lost when a sudden gust of wind cleared the sky and I saw the building, fifty feet in front of me. There were no signs of lights or any hostiles. I approached from the rear wall, put my ear to a boarded up window and heard a chicken cluck. Good. That many fewer battles to neutralize.

I looked at the map again, gauged how far it was to the main house and headed that way, moving step by step now and bent down low. Failing to see any lights and thinking I had somehow gotten off track again, I circled around to my right. Then, with another wild gust of wind, the house appeared out of the snow, a hundred and fifty feet to my left. I froze. A man stood guard at the front door and seemed to be staring in my direction.

When a heavy gust of snow flurries blew up, I dashed over to the side wall of the building and peeked around the corner. The guard was where I had left him and seemingly unaware of my presence.

I set everything down except for one of the AKs. I still had the Glock in my vest and the Sig in my waist holster. Preferring a weapon in my ankle holster for close contact, I placed the Sig down there instead. It wasn't a perfect fit but offered a second option.

With that done, I started around to the backside of the building and quickly came to a curtained window. A faint light was pouring out, as if from a candle. Having paused to listen, I was about to move on when I heard voices. First one, then two, then a third one. Whatever they were doing, there were three men I had to account for.

I moved on to the next window and listened again. Nothing.

I moved on to the far end of the house and paused alongside a window facing back towards the road. It was also curtained and had a much brighter light pouring out of it. As I stood there listening, I heard three more voices, then a fourth. So there were at least seven men inside, and possibly more.

I continued down to the next corner and peeked around. The man was still standing guard out in the snow, and clearly not happy about it. Very soon now, he would no longer be unhappy about anything.

I retreated back around to my weapons stash and got down in a crouch, thinking. There was really only one way to go about this. I had to take the front room and deal with whatever followed. Best case scenario, they were setting up to record Faisal's beheading and not in an ideal defensive posture. That would leave me with the three men in the back room. If I was able to take control of the front swiftly enough, a flash grenade down the hallway would most likely neutralize the other three men.

All this assumed that Faisal was in the front room. If they had him tied up in the back somewhere, I had an entirely different set of problems on my hands.

There was one other thing to consider. Assuming Saleem was in the front room, my intention was to wound but not kill him, and that was always a dangerous proposition in a firefight. Fool around and you'd find yourself dead.

I grabbed one of the grenades from my pack, placed it in my vest, double checked all my spare magazines and peeked around the corner. The man was still there, battling the cold. I had one shot and didn't dare miss. It was also essential that he fall away from the building, not against the door. Otherwise the element of surprise would be lost. Several times, he bent over, slapping his arms against his body. The next time he leaned forward, I fired twice with the Glock and he collapsed away from the house with a gasp. I raced over, set his weapon against the wall and put my ear to the door. The men inside were discussing something back and forth.

I placed the Glock back in my vest holster, waited for the man to bleed out, stood him up in front of me and arranged the AK so that it looked as if he was the one holding it. With a deep breath, I once again envisioned the coming moment in my head and opened the door.

Everyone in the room looked up, thinking that the man was merely wanting to come in from the cold, allowing me that split second to assess the situation. Faisal was kneeling with his hands tied behind his back. Two men stood facing him at ten feet with a video camera, getting ready to record his beheading. Two more men stood at the outskirts with their AKs at the ready and Saleem stood behind Faisal with a knife in his hand.

And then that split second was gone and all hell broke loose.

I quickly took out the two men holding AKs before shoving the dead man to the floor and shooting Saleem in his legs. While he fell, cursing, I sprayed the men who had been standing behind the camera. They both died on the way to grabbing their AKs. I focused the AK in the direction of the hallway, back to where I had heard the other three men and saw nothing. So maybe the three men I had heard in back were part of the five men out here.

I turned back towards Saleem. He was crawling across the floor towards his own AK. I put another bullet into his legs and he stopped with a curse.

I had turned back towards the hallway with a grenade when a burst of fire rang out from that direction. I instinctively dove for cover and fired back while cursing my own carelessness. Most of the bullets had slapped harmlessly into the plaster walls around me but one of them had clipped my left arm, just below the shoulder.

I rolled over, dragged Saleem's AK out of his reach and pulled the pin from my grenade. Seeing that, Saleem shouted something in Arabic and the men down the hallway began yelling as if they had just met a tiger. I tossed the grenade and lunged towards the farthest wall, dragging Faisal along with me.

The ensuing explosion rocked the building and quickly filled the living room with a cloud of smoke. In the chaos, I got my knife out and cut Faisal loose.

"You're hit," he said.

"Yeah. I'm starting to look like a back-country road sign."

I grabbed one of the shemaghs and tied off my arm with a curse.

"All right, here," I said, handing Faisal my AK. "Watch this son of a bitch and if he tries anything, shoot him in the legs again."

I had started off to clear the back of the house but stopped.

"Good to see you, my friend." I patted him on the shoulder. "I told you I would come."

"Thank you. Thank you again for watching my back, my friend."

I smiled and proceeded cautiously down the hallway. Smoke was still pouring out from that direction.

A few feet farther on, I came to the first door and showed the tip of my AK in the opening. Nothing. I coiled and sprang past the door. Still nothing. As I had discerned from outside, that room was empty.

The next door was a bathroom. With a quick look inside, I moved past it and towards the back bedroom. The grenade had blown out the rear window, allowing the snowstorm to swirl inside.

I saw a pair of legs through the opening. So one man was down. That possibly left two men unaccounted for. I poked the barrel of my rifle through the door and was met with a burst of fire. I got the AK into my left hand and sprayed the room with a long burst of return fire. Everything went silent. I peeked in, got no response and slipped cautiously through the opening. There was another man, now dead, with his blood all over the wall. I assumed nothing and added a bullet to all three brain cavities before gathering up their AKs and heading back out front.

Saleem was up on one elbow and staring as I walked into the room.

"Motherfucker," I said and pretended to smile at him.

I turned to Faisal.

"You okay."

"I'm okay, but what about you?"

I looked at my arm again.

"I'll live. I would have been here sooner but..." I nodded out at the storm. "It's a mess out there."

"There are more men," Faisal said.

"I already terminated four hostiles out in the barn. Were there more than that?"

"Originally, yes."

We stared.

"Two of them were Turks," Faisal added.

"Yeah? And what happened to them?"

"I don't know. These men brought me here and after some minutes, the Turks arrived. My Turkish is not perfect but I'm sure there was talk of someone else coming. Then several of Saleem's men drove away with the Turks."

I shook my head.

"I don't know what that means but I think we're good for now."

I set my AK to one side.

"Let's get him tied up. You keep your AK pointed and if it becomes necessary, shoot him. But only if it's absolutely necessary. I think he's too wounded to try much. If he does, I'll just break a few bones."

I got my Glock out, went around behind Saleem and dragged him to his feet with my left hand. When he started to struggle, I got my left arm around his neck and cut off his air passage. While he struggled to breathe, I dragged him over and shoved him down into a chair.

"All right," I said to Faisal. "Bring all those shemaghs over here."

I waited with my Glock to the back of Saleem's head.

"Okay," I said, taking them from Faisal. "Cover me."

With Faisal's AK pointed at Saleem's chest, I bound his hands behind the back of the chair and then his ankles to the legs of it. His left leg was bleeding badly so I tied it off at the top of his thigh.

With that done, I cautiously checked outside the front door. The storm was still raging.

"Keep your rifle on him," I told Faisal. "I'm going to retrieve the rest of my gear."

I went around to the back of the house and returned, dragging my pack and all the weapons inside with me. Faisal watched me dust off.

"I can't see anyone driving around in this shit tonight."

He kept staring.

"Look. I don't want you sticking around for what comes next."

"No. You watched my back. Now I must watch yours."

"No, Faisal. This mission is over."

"But..."

"No."

I went over and put a hand on his shoulder.

"I wish I was as good a man as you are, but I'm not."

"No, you are a good man. You just have a broken heart."

"Call it whatever you want. I don't want you sticking around now."

"Even if I left, how would I go?"

"Take his Land Cruiser. It's practically new."

Faisal was still hesitant."

"Keep an eye on him and I'll go check the gas."

I went out and returned a minute later.

"It's almost full. You could probably make it back to Khabur with what's in the tank."

I got out my phone and showed Faisal the satellite image of the compound.

"All you have to do is go this way until you see the base of these hills, and then bear left and it will take you down to the road."

Faisal stared at me stubbornly.

"Please don't make me force you, my friend."

I saw his parka on the floor and handed it to him.

"Here," I said and retrieved two full magazines for his AK. "Just head north to Al Suwar. They'll be watching the roads back towards Deir ez-Zor."

"And you?" he said.

"I still have the other Land Cruiser. It's parked a hundred yards off in that blizzard somewhere."

Faisal kept staring. I put my hand on his shoulder.

"Please. It's over. I'll be done here in half an hour and on my way too. And I'll be in touch. As soon as I'm safely back on the ground, I'll have David send you a message. Like I said, you should come to the States. You can have a good life there and start over."

When Faisal failed to move, I put a hand at his back.

"At least let me treat your wounds," he said.

"Yeah, all right."

I got the first aid kit out of my pack and let him clean things up a bit, grimacing as usual at the touch of the antiseptic to raw flesh.

"Did you want me to wrap them?"

"No, I'm fine. I'll find my way back to the coalition forces before the night is through and they'll patch me up again."

I patted him on the shoulder and gave him the soldier's handshake.

"Brothers for life."

"Brothers for life."

"All right. Go on. The sooner you leave, the sooner I can end this thing and get out of here."

Faisal started to speak again but stopped himself and walked out into the storm. I stood at the door with one eye on him and one eye on Saleem.

Behind the wheel of the Land Cruiser, Faisal started in with his usual mirror and seat belt ritual. I had to smile. He noticed me noticing him and shrugged sheepishly.

I waited until he was pulling away and waved. He waved back and disappeared into the blizzard. I closed the door and turned to face Saleem.

"And now it's your turn, motherfucker."

I dragged a chair from the far side of the room and sat across from him. Saleem watched intently as I pulled out my phone, hit play for the video of Tom's beheading and turned the screen his way. With the first recognition of what it was, his eyes darted at me, and then back and forth several times. I sat watching Saleem until it was over, then closed the screen, unzipped one of the sleeve pockets on my jacket and pulled out a photo of Tom and me from a few years back. We had driven down to the beach together one late summer afternoon and asked a passerby to take our picture, the two of us leaning up against the side of Tom's '56 Corvette. It had been a fine day, and the last time I had seen my brother alive.

I pointed at the photo and tapped my own chest.

"My brother," I said.

I tapped my index and middle finger together.

"My brother."

With Saleem still watching me intently, I got out my knife and stone and slowly started sharpening the blade. Every now and then, I glanced up at Saleem.

In the many hours of envisioning this moment, I had never imagined myself shrinking from the task, the need for revenge had been burned so hot in me. But now, with the cold, calculated task of taking off another man's head actually in front of me, I wavered. Never mind the horrific gore, I was about to butcher another human being, just for the pleasure of making him suffer.

I felt the edge of the blade with my thumb, put the stone away and stared at Saleem. God, how I despised the man. His self-righteousness, his zealous ignorance, everything he represented. So sure of his beliefs, until ideology had become more valuable to him than another human life.

And yet, in saying so, I saw a mirror held up to my own impulses. An eye for an eye. You harm to my people and I'll do harm to yours. How could I claim to be any better than he was?

Thankfully Faisal was gone and did not have to witness the impending barbarism. I hated to think of how far down I had already dragged him into my moral abyss.

With a great sigh, I stood up, determined to go through with it. I had come here to take the man's head off and I was going to have my moment. A bullet in his brain just wouldn't do his sins justice.

I had walked around to the back of Saleem when a gust of wind rattled the door, distracting me. I looked that way. Something didn't feel right. I grabbed one of the AKs.

Thinking to peek out through the adjacent window curtain first, I had edged that way warily when the door flew open behind me and knocked me off my feet. Men poured into the room in a cacophony of shouts and gunfire. I was reaching for the Sig in my ankle holster when someone fired off a round into my chest. It felt as if a bull had rammed into me.

While I lay there struggling to breathe, a half dozen men gathered around. One of them kicked the AK away from my hands.

Then those men parted and someone else stood over me. It was Colonel Arslan. He stared down with cold vengeance.

I cursed my own failings. You fool. In your fever for revenge, you had forgotten the first rule of good soldiery; vigilance.

Casually, as if he were retrieving an article of dropped clothing, the colonel reached down for my AK and stared into my eyes for a long moment before slamming the butt of it into my head.

Nineteen

I came to in a dimly lit room. The pain in my chest ached badly.

When I groaned, a chorus of voices quickly erupted. Someone hobbled over and yanked my head back by the hair. I tried to open my eyes but only one of them responded. Everything in the room was smoky, as if in a dream.

After a moment, I realized I was staring at Saleem.

"Motherfucker," he said and slashed at his throat with my knife.

He let go of my head and it fell against my chest. I was aware enough to know that I had been tied to a chair, and had seen enough to know that a camcorder was set up across from me.

What irony. I had come here to take this man's head off. Instead he was going to hand me mine. Well, fuck him. Fuck all of them. I'll never give them the pleasure of seeing me squeal. I won't even put up a struggle. I'll spit at their camera and take it like a man.

I heard them talking and hated the very sound of their voices. Their language was guttural and without poetry to me.

Then something struck me. I hadn't seen Colonel Arslan. With all of my strength, I lifted my head but he wasn't in the room. So, he had left it for these men to finish me off. The heartless prick.

I became aware again of the deep throbbing pain in my chest. Well, soon enough, I wouldn't be feeling anything. But there would be terrible pain first. Thankfully my agony would only last a minute.

I stole a glance at the men around me, praying the hell of their existence would go on forever.

Later, I sensed a new urgency in the room and looked up to find the men gathering around. Two of them stood behind the camcorder, with two more in back, holding AKs. Saleem came around behind me, pulled my head up and began to speak while gesturing with the knife.

So the time had come. Against every effort to the contrary, my heart began to race. The muscles in my neck turned to knots. God help me. Help me to be strong. The pain will soon be over. Everything will soon be over. But still, the horror of what was to come pumped my entire being full of adrenalin. Having your neck sliced open like a tomato. The esophagus. The trachea. The carotid artery. The tendons and ligaments. And finally the bone.

Please, just get it over with. Make it fast. I am only human. I don't want to suffer.

On and on Saleem went, and my heart raced ever faster. Any second now, his voice would stop and the sting of the blade would dig into my flesh. I wanted to disbelieve this moment, but could not. The nightmare would soon begin.

Even with Saleem holding my head up, I was growing weary. Perhaps I would pass out first. That would be better.

Oh god. All of the things I had left undone. The many longings raced through my mind, Emine foremost among them. I had so much wanted to go rescue her. To be her prince and sweep her away to our happy kingdom.

Shit, Tom. When all is said and done, I'm just a fool like you, wondering why the fuck I even came here, a fool hoping for some kind of miracle, a fool wanting to undo what had been done, when there was no going back now, and no changing what was to come.

I felt my head drooping but Saleem yanked it back again, said a final word and brandished his knife at the camera. The knife's edge gleamed in the dim light. I took a deep breath and steeled my will against the first cut.

Here I come, god. Please be there to take me into your holy light.

But the sting of the blade did not come. Instead, I heard concerned voices and opened my good eye. A man was moving towards the front door with his AK pointed. He had reached to open it when a deafening explosion sent both him and the door flying across the room. The shock wave was enough to knock me over in my chair.

With men shouting and gunfire filling the room, I did everything in my power to look small and not get shot again. It seemed as if the bedlam would never end.

Then, suddenly, it was quiet again, save for the sound of the storm blowing in through the door. I opened my eye to find someone in a forest green uniform crouched in front of me. Straight black hair and beautiful eyes. Such beautiful dark eyes.

I was still struggling to focus when a voice said, "Are you okay, Mr. Blake?" It was a woman's voice. A sweet voice. A voice that made me feel overjoyed.

"Ariman."

She reached out and squeezed my right hand.

"How did you get here?" I said.

"Faisal called us."

"Faisal?" I struggled to raise my head and look. "Where is he? Is he all right?"

"Yes, yes, Mr. Blake. Relax. Everything is fine now."

Suddenly, there were more footsteps rushing into the room and voices talking urgently in Kurdish. Then Firat was squatting down alongside Ariman."

"Firat," I said. "What is going on?"

"Someone is coming. We think the Americans."

He patted me gently on the shoulder.

"We will watch to make sure. And if it is?" He shrugged. "We must go but perhaps we will meet again one day, high up in the pine forests of the Zagros Mountains."

He smiled and patted me on the shoulder again.

"Even?"

It took me a moment to realize what he was saying.

"Even," I said, nodding back

Ariman came closer and kissed me on the forehead. Then all six of them fled out into the storm.

I had been lying there with eyes closed for several minutes when I heard vehicles pull to a stop outside. Footsteps came inside and moved towards the back of the house in starts and stops. Moments later, they returned my way.

"All clear, senior!" someone called out from the front door.

I wanted to look but felt too weary to open my eyes. Then I heard another set of footsteps entering the room and sensed someone crouching down beside me.

"Cut loose him," a voice said.

It took a moment for me to place the voice. I opened my one eye and looked up at David. He shook his head in return.

"Look at you. What a fucking mess." He looked around the room. "This whole situation. A fucking mess."

David turned to one of the men standing nearby.

"Secure the perimeter. And get that door back in place."

Moments later, the two of us were alone. David patted me gently.

"The medics are on the way."

I nodded imperceptibly.

"So what exactly happened here?"

"I don't know. I was out."

David scoffed.

"You don't know anything?"

"I know Saleem was going to take my head off. Then the door blew in and I went out."

A man groaned nearby. I looked that way and saw it was Saleem. He was the only one still alive now. I struggled to get up.

"Where's my knife?" I said.

David held me back.

"Are you crazy? Get the hell out of here."

"No. I have to finish this."

"Finish it? I hate to tell you, partner, but this situation is long past finished. You obviously have no idea what a mess you've made for me."

Not having any answers for him, I closed my eye again.

"I have a question for you," David said.

I looked back at him.

"Does that piece of shit over there know why you came here?"

I stared for a long moment before nodding.

"Shit."

David stood up, calmly walked over to Saleem and put two bullets into his chest. Then he was back crouched at my side.

"There are a lot of people who wanted to ask that son of a bitch a lot of questions. People who are going to be all over my ass now because he's dead. And the only reason he's dead is because of your madness."

"I found him. When the rest of you assholes couldn't."

"Yeah. I'll give you that much...Look, let's get this straight, before anyone else comes around here asking questions. I set up this op and you were working for me. This all has to be on the books now, partner. I'm going to send you up to Raqqah, get you patched up and get your ass out of country before anyone starts asking questions. In the meantime, if anyone *does* start questioning you, you just tell them you're not at liberty to discuss your mission."

"That's what I tell everyone I meet."

"Yeah? Like who for instance?"

"Sgt. Benson, for one."

"Yeah, and he and a platoon are going to be pulling up here any minute now so you stick to that story."

"Why? Did you invite them?"

"I didn't have to. I didn't have to invite anyone. With all the wreckage you've left in your wake, you're all over CENTCOM. We'll be lucky if the president doesn't walk in here next."

We stared.

"There's more," I said.

"Yeah? Like what?"

"Colonel Arslan was here. The Turks were in on this."

"Son of a bitch."

"Yeah. There's one more thing you can sweep under the rug."

"Yeah, well. If there's some way to nail that rogue SOB, I will, but you stay out of it. I don't want you saying a word."

"Sure, partner…But there's more."

"Christ. What more trouble could you make for me?"

"Check the barn. I think you'll find your chemical weapons."

"Are you serious?"

I nodded and turned my head to look at Saleem. As with all men, he looked diminished in death. Whatever it was that constituted the spirit, it greatly magnified a man's presence while still alive.

I looked back at David.

"I'm not so sure I could have done it."

"What? Cut his head off."

I nodded. He nodded back.

"Can't say I blame you. That's why they don't cut you any slack for pre-meditated murder. With time to think about this shit, a sane man is supposed to come to his senses."

With David staring, I shook my head.

"No, I haven't, if that's what you're wondering."

"Hell. I knew that about you twenty-five years ago. Back in the Balkans. You get your teeth into something and you won't let go."

While we stared, there was the sound of trucks rumbling up and coming to a stop outside.

"Could use some morphine," I said.

David smirked.

"I think we'll have your head examined first."

David patted me gently on the arm.

"I'll go see about getting the medics in here."

"Hey," I said before he could stand up. "How did you know to come?"

"I figured you were in trouble....I mean, when aren't you?"

"Yeah, up yours too, you desk jockey."

He smirked.

"But seriously. I had called and when you didn't answer, I knew things must have gone fubar on you."

"Yeah, well, setting aside all your bullshit, thanks brother."

"No problem. It isn't the first time we've saved each other's asses. I'm just hoping it's the last."

He stood up and pulled the battered door aside. The storm blew in, along with Sgt. Benson.

"Sergeant," David said and shook his hand. "My man here could use some medical attention."

Benson had a look at me and nodded to the corporal standing next to him.

"Get the medics."

Benson looked back at David.

"Any chance I can debrief the captain?"

"Not before I do."

"Any chance you're going to explain to me what happened here?"

"I can tell you this much. Captain Jeffers tracked down Saleem but got caught in an ambush and we had to run an op to extract him. Unfortunately, in the ensuing firefight, we weren't able to take Saleem alive. The good news is, Captain

Jeffers seems to have found your chemical weapons. Out in the barn, wherever the hell that is."

I pointed as best I could.

"About three hundred yards in that direction."

Two medics came in. One of them was Polanski.

"What are we doing here, Sergeant?"

"Get Captain Jeffers stabilized and up to Raqqah. He's going to need some surgery."

"Yes sir."

David and Benson went outside. The medics dropped their bags and went to work on me.

"Some pain meds, captain?" Polanski asked me.

"Would be much appreciated, soldier."

He smiled and dug out a syringe and a vial.

"This should make you feel a little better."

His partner had pulled up my sleeve and wiped the inside of my elbow clean. I felt the needle go in, watched the droplet of blood as Polanski pulled back on the plunger and felt the dizzying effect of morphine flooding into my brain a moment later.

"As soon as you're comfortable in the transport, sir, we'll get you on an IV. Let's get a stretcher in here," Polanski said to the other medic.

"I don't need a stretcher."

"Sir, I would highly recommend…"

"Fuck it. This is going to hurt no matter how we do it."

My left side was the damaged one so I used my right arm to prop myself up.

"See if you can get me to my feet without yanking on this shoulder too much."

"Will do, sir."

Polanski went behind me and got his hands around my waist.

"Ready, sir?"

"Ready."

The other medic got hold of my belt buckle and helped pull me up.

"Where the hell's your stretcher?" Benson said, coming back inside with David.

"We're fine," I told him.

"Fucking John Wayne," David said.

I gave him a look and nodded to the medics.

"Come on. Let's do this before it turns into a pissing contest."

With my right arm around Polanski and a last look back at Saleem, we walked out into the storm. David and Sgt. Benson joined us a few moments later. Polanski was busy setting up an IV. I was reasonably comfortable on a couple of sleeping bags.

"You'll be in good hands up there," David said. "They have a damned good field hospital in Raqqah."

He patted me on the boot.

"Once they get you patched up and walking around, I'll be down to work on your extraction. For now, I've got to run. More trouble up north."

"Yeah. Say hello to you know who for me."

David gave me a look and left.

"Take Perry and his Humvee crew with you," Benson told Polanski. "We want to make sure Captain Jeffers makes it back to Raqqah alive."

As Polanski went to close the rear door, Benson saluted.

"Appreciate all your efforts, captain."

Wearily, I saluted back. He was a handsome, sandy-haired fellow, but utterly taciturn.

A minute later, I felt the Humvee slowly moving out. My mind was swirling with a thousand thoughts. It was over, but it wasn't. I was headed back the way I had come, but there was no going back to the way it had been. I had been so fixated on taking off Saleem's head, I had never considered how I would feel if I failed in that mission. I guess I had just imagined myself going out in a blaze of glory somehow.

Well, he was dead now, Tom, if it's any comfort to you. Probably not. If there was still a Tom out there somewhere, on another plane of existence, that Tom had probably already forgiven Saleem.

I thought back to the last image of the man: lifeless, blood splattered, deformed and diminished. I had had my revenge and had found revenge wanting. I had no idea what to do next.

Somewhere along the road back from where I had come, I grew too weary for another thought and passed out.

Twenty

When I reawakened, I was lying alone in a dimly room. A drip was attached to an IV in my left arm and a vitals monitor clipped to the index finger of that hand. A machine beeped periodically behind me.

The left side of my chest ached. My right arm ached above and below the elbow. My abdomen on that side ached too. I felt stiff and sore pretty much everywhere. The drip had to be morphine because I was loaded.

By the wrecked apartment building across the street from my window, I assumed I was still in Raqqah. How much time had gone by? It seemed like days but I had no real idea.

A nurse walked into the room just then with a string of miniature Christmas bulbs flashing around her neck. I smiled, as much as a man can smile under the circumstances.

"Good to see you awake, Captain Jeffers. I'm Nurse Wentworth. I'll be keeping an eye on you until you're fit to travel."

She had grabbed the chart at the foot of my bed and went about checking my vitals.

"What day is it?" I said.

She looked at her watch while taking my pulse.

"Christmas Day. You had surgery last night. Lucky you, that bullet in your chest just missed the collarbone. And your lung. Made a pretty nice mess of the general area. Then there were the bullet wounds in your arm and abdomen. Oh, and that nasty cut."

She looked up from her chart.

"Must have been fun."

"I go all in for holidays."

She smiled and hung the chart back at the foot of my bed.

"How are you feeling?" she said.

"I'm not sure I have a word for it…melancholy, maybe?"

"To be expected. I have found over the years that any trauma near the heart leaves patients with a sense of ennui."

She smiled philosophically.

"You'll live…Feeling hungry?"

"A bit, yeah. Now that you mention it."

"What sounds good?"

"Protein of some kind. I don't know what."

"I'll work on that and get back to you."

She had nearly disappeared when I called out. She paused at the door.

"My belongings?"

"That locker over there. What we didn't cut off of you and burn while prepping for surgery. I believe Sgt. Benson has all or most of your weaponry. You'll have to talk to him about that."

She stood there staring.

"That money belt of yours is still there, if you're wondering."

She raised her eyebrows and left. I was glad to hear about the money. I didn't much care about the rest of it. I had a reasonably good idea what David was planning, once I was ready to travel, but I had other ideas.

Nurse Wentworth was back twenty minutes later with a hamburger.

"Straight from Wendy's," she said with a wink. "I had the cook double up the patty."

She got me sitting upright with a tray situated on my lap, then stood back to await the verdict. I had a bite.

"Hmm, good," I said. "Thank you."

"My pleasure. I brought you a Coke, a juice and a milk. Wasn't sure which one you'd prefer."

"The juice sounds good. You can take the others."

"All right. The call button is there beside your bed. Unless I hear from you otherwise, I'll be back in two hours."

I nodded and watched her leave.

I was chewing on another bite when Sgt. Benson darkened the door. As a formality, he tapped lightly before coming in. When he saluted, I felt obliged to salute him back.

"How are we feeling, captain?"

"I've been told I'll live."

"Glad to hear it."

We stared.

"To what do I owe the pleasure, sergeant?"

"I've been instructed to discuss the Saleem al-Ramadi reward money with you."

"Discuss, as in…"

"What would you like us to do with it?"

"I don't know. I hadn't really thought about it. Probably give it to Faisal. Or to a charity."

"You're free to do whatever you wish. We'll just need all the proper documentation in order to transfer the money."

"Suppose we can deal with that another day? I'm a bit weary right now." I gestured with the hamburger. "And hungry."

"Sure. I'll come back when you're feeling better. I'd like to debrief you about Saleem before they ship you back to the States."

"What's to debrief? He's dead and you have our hands on the chemical weapons."

"I'd still like to know whatever intel you were able to glean."

"Not much. He was planning to take my head off and we never got much of a chance to chat beyond that."

Sergeant Benson smiled, as much as Sergeant Benson ever would.

"I'll be back to discuss that money with you in a couple of days."

He started to leave.

Your country thanks you, by the way."

"No thanks necessary, Sergeant."

We again changed the obligatory salutes and he left. I had two more bites from the burger and set it down on the tray. With a final drink of the juice, I closed my eyes and slept, a sleep that seemed to go on for days. Dreams and thoughts and longings flitted through my brain. At times I was aware of being in the room. At times I was gone from this world.

I wasn't sure how long I had been in that state but reawakened to find Faisal sitting there beside me. It was morning. He smiled sadly.

"Faisal. It's so good to see you. It's good to see that you're still alive but you were supposed to go to Khabur."

"I had started that way but realized I could not leave you."

"Yeah, yeah. I know. I watch your back, you watch mine."

"Yes. In fact, I have given it an official name now."

"Yeah? And what's that?"

"The twelfth commandment."

"And what exactly is that?"

"That once you have saved a man's life, and he has saved yours, you are bound together for all of eternity."

"Wow, Faisal. I'm not so sure I want the responsibility."

"It is written," he said.

With a hand to my chest, I waved for him to stop.

"Nothing is written," I said while choking back a laugh.

"Well, I was not about to leave things the way they were, with this fucked up *eleventh commandment* of yours."

I waved at him again.

"Okay. You win…Just don't make me laugh again."

I almost did, just by the look on his face.

Remembering myself, I asked what day it was.

"The 27th. You have slept for two days."

"Wow, yeah. I guess I needed it."

I cautiously moved my shoulders around.

"How do you feel?"

"Better. Not nearly as sore as I was on Christmas."

"And what of your mission?" he said. "Are you happy now that it's done?"

"Happy? Come on, Faisal."

I explained all that had happened after he left.

"It wasn't exactly the way I had planned things, but at least the bastard's dead. Though even that doesn't quite feel the way I had hoped it would feel. The world just seems kind of empty to me now."

"Emptiness is where God awaits us," Faisal said.

"Ah. So we're being philosophical today."

He shrugged.

"Few seek God when life is abundant."

"Yeah, we're definitely being philosophical…but you're probably right about that."

"I am filled with emptiness too, my friend."

"Yeah, I know…So maybe we should team up."

Faisal smiled. I looked down at my hands, thinking.

"You know, Faisal, after what had happened to my brother, there was a part of me that just wanted to give up. This world just seemed so goddamned brutal and senseless. All I could think of was making Saleem suffer."

I looked back up at him.

"You were right. The flame of hatred had completely consumed me…Then I saw Saleem all dead and bloodied and diminished there at the end and almost felt sorry for the poor son of a bitch. God only knows why we've been brought into this world, but certainly not for zealotry and revenge. What a waste of a life."

I looked back at my hands.

"I'm trying to forgive him, Faisal. I'm trying to forgive everything and get the hatred out of my heart."

I looked up at him. He smiled sadly and nodded. Of course he understood. The man knew all too well how I felt.

"Anyway, there's really only going forward in this life. We stop going forward and we may as well lie down and die."

Faisal nodded.

"And so what is moving forward to you now?"

"Well, first thing, I need you to check in that locker for me. See if my knife's still inside."

Faisal rummaged around for a moment among my belongings and returned with it.

"What is it that you have planned now?"

"Don't worry. I'm done with cutting off heads."

He smiled sadly.

"But seriously, bring your chair around here to my right side."

He did.

"Now put your hand here on the back of my arm. Do you feel it?"

Faisal nodded.

"What is it?"

"A tracking chip and I need it out of me. Otherwise David will be able to follow me wherever I go."

"And what do you want me to do?"

"Make a small incision back there and squeeze it out."

Faisal hesitated.

"It's all right. I'm so doped up on morphine, I couldn't feel a punch in the face."

He still hesitated.

"Please. I've decided I want to live. I want to be alive, however crazily, and need your help."

"All right, my friend."

Faisal put his thumb and index finger around the chip, looked into my eyes and made the incision. Quickly, there was blood.

"Oh shit," I said and grabbed a napkin from the food tray.

We worked on getting the blood under control.

"Okay. Now squeeze it out," I said.

Faisal glanced at my face several times while doing so. Then he held the napkin to my skin and showed me the bloody chip.

"What shall I do with it?"

"Oh, wipe it off and put it in the locker. It just has to be here in this room. At least until I'm well down the road somewhere."

"And where are you going?"

"You mean, where are *we* going?"

Faisal stared, looking both curious and concerned.

"Look, I need to get back to Istanbul. I don't know how but you still have the Land Cruiser, right?"

He nodded.

"And I still have the money belt, so we head for the northern coast. You still know that area, right?"

"Of course. Why?"

"I need to find a ship of some kind. A freighter. A fishing vessel. Whatever. Some way to get back into Turkey without being noticed."

"I know a man we can consult," he said.

"Good. For now, the important thing is to get as far away from here as possible, and as fast as possible, before they find me missing."

"But I don't understand. Why are you so concerned?"

"Because if David figures out what I'm planning, he'll try to pull rank and send me back to the States."

"Why?"

"Because he's worried about his own ass."

Faisal turned his head skeptically.

"Look," I said. "Everything that just went down?"

Faisal nodded.

"It got up the chain of command, so David had to say it was part of an op he was running. Meaning we're in bed together now and if I get into any more trouble, it's going to land right back in his lap."

"But why must you return to Istanbul?"

I put a hand on his forearm.

"To rescue someone. I'll tell you along the way...The question is, will you help me?"

He nodded.

"Of course. The twelfth fucking commandment."

I held up a hand.

"Stop."

"But when?" Faisal said when I looked back up at him. "You cannot travel in this condition."

"I'll be all right. Just let me get something to eat and a few more hours of sleep. We'll need to be doing this at night, anyway, when there's less staff around and it's easier to sneak out."

"And then?"

"And then we head north. Do you have a full tank of gas?"

"I can fill up."

"Okay. I need a new jacket. Do you know where to buy one?"

He nodded.

"Something heavy, with lots of pockets."

He nodded.

"Okay. Do you need money?"

"No. I have most of what you gave me before."

"All right. I'll see you back here at eight."

"I will see you at eight."

"Oh, and tell the nurse to come see me."

"I will."

A new nurse appeared a few minutes later. I asked her to remove the drip and sent her off for something to eat. While she was gone, I used the bathroom, then gobbled down the meal she had brought and went off to use the shower. The water was lukewarm but it felt heavenly to wash up.

Back in bed, I quickly fell asleep but awakened before Faisal returned and grabbed my pack. I still had one clean pair of pants, two clean shirts, two clean pairs of socks and three clean pairs of briefs. I dressed except for my boots and climbed back under the covers.

Faisal showed up promptly at eight, wearing my new jacket over his own.

"I did not think it would be wise to come in carrying it."

"Good thinking."

I tried it on.

"Perfect. How's the coast out there? Clear?"

"I did not see anyone except a lady by the door."

"Good."

I laced on my boots and grabbed my pack.

"You still have that Springfield I gave you?"

He nodded.

"And the AK?"

"There are two of them in the back, and ammunition."

"Good. Hopefully we won't need them, but just in case."

I went to the door and peeked out. My heart was racing.

"Okay. You go ahead and make sure the coast is clear."

I watched Faisal go down to the stairwell door. He looked both ways and waved. I hurried on to his position and we hustled down the stairs together. The woman watching the front vestibule did not appear to recognize me and displayed absolutely no concern at seeing us leave.

Out on the street, I saw the young boy we had encountered that first day in Raqqah. He was sitting in the back seat of the Land Cruiser, staring straight ahead.

"What the hell, Faisal? What are we going to do with him?"

"You are doing nothing. I am taking him home with me to Khabur."

"Yeah?"

"Yes. What does it matter to you?"

"Just the danger, that's all."

"What is danger to a boy who has lost everything?"

"Yeah, all right." I patted him on the shoulder. "You're a good man, Faisal."

"I'm just a man who has lost everything too."

"Yeah, I guess the same is true of me…All right. So we start over."

I looked at the boy. He stared back at me with his big, brown sad eyes.

"Look, have him sit in the front seat. It's better if I sit in back with the weapons."

"I don't wish him to see guns."

"That's fine. Just get him upfront and pass everything to me from the rear."

Faisal opened the door and said something in Arabic. The boy obediently got out of the car.

"What's his name, Faisal?"

"Sharif."

"Sharif," I repeated.

Hearing his name, the boy looked up at me.

"Please tell him my name, Faisal, and tell him that I'm glad he's here with us."

Faisal spoke again in Arabic as I held out my hand. The boy shook it while still staring at me. I looked back at Faisal.

"Okay, we'd better get moving. Before they find out we've eloped."

"What is eloped?"

"When a man runs off with your daughter."

"Ah, I see. Well, this has always been a strange marriage."

I grimaced, holding back another laugh. Faisal got the boy situated up in front and came around to open the rear hatch. I climbed in back with my pack.

"Just one of the AKs and the Springfield," I said, reaching over the seat. "And an extra magazine for the AK."

With that done, Faisal went around and climbed into the front seat. I watched him put on his seat belt and check all the mirrors before pulling into the street. I had a thought and opened my pack. The sea sprite was still there. I held its feminine form in my hand as the wrecked city passed by us.

So, we were on our way. I felt my heart skip a beat. What lay ahead? Adventure? Excitement? Love? The unknown?

God, it felt so good to be alive.

About The Author

The product of an Irish/Italian family, Mr. Corcoran was transplanted from the clapboard New England of his youth to the cookie cutter, stucco subdivisions that increasingly littered the old ranches and disappearing orange groves south of Los Angeles in the 1960s. Ever rebellious, and true to the folk music/coffee house idealism that helped shape his early worldview, he chose to resist the Vietnam War, was a man without a country for several years and can count incarceration in a Mexican prison as one of his many colorful experiences from that era.

Having pursued a love of reading and writing in various forms all his life, Mr. Corcoran finally took that passion seriously around the turn of the millennium and has dedicated the remainder of his days to authorship. In completing the circle of destiny, he has returned to the New England of his youth and presently resides along the Rhode Island shore.